12/14 P9-DML-281

FICTION

TRI

$17.99

The Accidental Highwayman

BENIAMINVS TRIPP
FECIT MMXIV

[*Kit Bristol and Friend*]

THE

Accidental Highwayman

Being the Tale of KIT BRISTOL,
His Horse MIDNIGHT, *a Mysterious* PRINCESS,
and Sundry MAGICAL PERSONS *Besides*

BEN TRIPP

TOR®

A TOM DOHERTY ASSOCIATES BOOK
New York

THE ACCIDENTAL HIGHWAYMAN

Copyright © 2014 by Ben Tripp

Illustrations by Ben Tripp

Book design by Heather Saunders

A Tor® Teen Book
Published by Tom Doherty Associates, LLC
175 Fifth Avenue
New York, NY 10010

www.tor-forge.com

Tor® is a registered trademark of Tom Doherty Associates, LLC.

The Library of Congress Cataloging-in-Publication Data
is available upon request.

ISBN 978-0-7653-3549-4 (hardcover)
ISBN 978-1-4668-2263-4 (e-book)

Tor Teen books may be purchased for educational, business, or promotional use. For information on bulk purchases, please contact Macmillan Corporate and Premium Sales Department at 1-800-221-7945, extension 5442, or write specialmarkets@macmillan.com.

First Edition: October 2014

Printed in the United States of America

0   9   8   7   6   5   4   3   2   1

For my most excellent friends Zeke & Nora

CONTENTS

CONTENTS

EDITOR'S NOTE

THE ORIGINAL text of this volume is part of a trove of documents discovered in an old sea chest belonging to Levi Bixby, one of my ancestors. The chest had not been opened in 100 years, as the key was lost. It became a family tradition to try any orphaned key in the lock, provided it was of the skeleton type. Whoever found the correct key would own the contents of the chest. Only last year, I found such a key in a box of old silver lobster picks; it proved to be the very key that opened the mysterious chest.

The earliest document found inside is unrelated to this story and dates from 1690. The most recent, also unrelated, is a letter from Surinam, dated 1847. Whether the original author of the manuscript before you was a relative or friend of the family is unknown. Beside the packets of memoirs, there were some curious objects in the chest that appear to corroborate certain passages in the tale.

As a writer, I couldn't let this story languish in obscurity, but neither could I bear to let it reach the public without interference; forgive me for exercising a little editorial judgment here and there, in addition to modernizing the spelling and language to make it easier to read. Many of the illustrations are based upon little doodles furnished in the margins of the original pages.

Any anachronisms or historical errors that have slipped into the text are entirely the result of my own meddling, and I apologize to any scholars who discover them. But this story is not intended as a scholarly work, nor to challenge history as it is known. Rather, I hope readers find this an illuminating counterpoint to what is understood about events of the mid-eighteenth century, and that it helps explain a few obscure points in the established record.

—*Ben Tripp*

PREFACE

by Kit Bristol

Gentle Reader,

This story contains nearly as many dark deeds, treacherous villains, and acts of violence as one might expect to find in a typical morning newspaper. In addition, there is a significant emphasis on heathen magic and demoniacal doings. I cannot recommend that anyone read it.

But it is also a true story. It is a story about bravery, loyalty, and love. Within these pages you will find friendship and laughter alongside the bitter doings of low characters. And, like all redeeming tales, it comes with a moral. But unlike most such narratives, the moral of this story is at the beginning, not at the end.

I shall make no further apology for the strange account you are about to read. Instead, here is the moral of the tale, which should act as a beacon in the darkness to guide you back home, no matter what happens next.

The heart is wiser than the head.

Here's what happens next.

Chapter 1

A PROCLAMATION AT MARKET

I DROVE THE little cart into town on a fine June morning. It was a bright day, and the country round about was green and fresh—what I could see of it past the backside of Old Nell, the dappled mare. I had a neatly inked list of things to buy at market, just enough coppers to buy them with, and that was the extent of my cares.

Market days were one of the great delights of my life back then. I liked the company of the crowd. There's nothing like mingling with a great many people to make solitude seem more pleasant. It was lonely at the Rattle Manse, where I was the only servant. My master, James Rattle, had no one else beneath his roof. It was but the two of us in the big, drafty house, excepting a bulldog named Demon, three horses, and some pigs. Even the pigs spent most of their time elsewhere, rooting for acorns in the dark woods thereabouts.

There was vanity involved, too—I might as well admit it. As a small boy I would have been proud to own a pair of shoes, so it felt very grand to go into town with brass buckles on my feet, commissioned to spend another man's money. Forgive my pride: Respectability is like wine. It goes straight to the head of one who hasn't had it before.

And besides, market days were entertaining. The entire market was like a big theater, every stall a stage, with the actors bellowing out their parts: "Two for a penny!" "A dozen for the price of ten!"

There were also people whose entire trade was entertainment for its own sake. Some were actors, and put on plays; others specialized in puppet shows, or displays of juggling, sword swallowing, gymnastic feats, and magic. In these performances I took special pleasure because I had, until recently, counted myself among the entertainers.

Before I took up service at the Rattle Manse, I had toured for several years with Trombonio's Traveling Wonder Show as "The Infant Daredevil," tramping the British Isles from one end to the other with a company of acrobats, clowns, and novelty acts, as well as Frieda the Tattooed Camel and an elderly baboon named Fred. My own role was that of trick horse-rider. I would spur my mount to a gallop and then dance about on its back, dangle from the stirrups, perform hand-springs, and generally risk death. The act became second nature and I seldom met with accidents, but when I did fall off, the crowds liked it all the better.

It was this trick-riding that had caught the eye of Master Rattle. He had attended a performance by the Wonder Show, and later that night, played cards with Mr. Fortescue Trombonio (birth name Gilbert Tubbins). Neither of them having much money, Master Rattle staked his fine sword, and Mr. Trombonio my documents of indenture. So it was, with a flourish of kings, I entered my present service.

The troupe had since been disbanded, and a number of its cast members transported to America for recidivism*, but I often ran into old acquaintances on market days, and it was pleasant to hear the news of life on the road. Although I was deeply grateful for my

---

* Recidivism: returning to crime. During that period, the law was haphazardly (if brutally) enforced, and honest pay quite low, so criminal enterprise was more attractive than now. Criminal transportation involved shipping convicts overseas for use as cheap labor.

rescue from Mr. Trombonio, the monotony of my new life chafed me. I was bored.

Before allowing myself liberty to see the entertainers, however, I went around the stalls and bought up my list. I haggled and complained and judged the merchandise in the usual way. Then, having fed Old Nell some new oats, I went off in search of any past friends from the road.

They were mostly pitched around the edges of the marketplace, so they wouldn't have to compete with the lusty cries of the merchants. There was a Hindoo snake charmer I knew, and a magician whose specialty was causing live pigeons to fly out of meat pies. Then, to my delight, I discovered one of my fellow troupers from the Trombonio days. She now toured with a team of juggling clowns as Lily, the high-rope dancer. I remembered the clowns, Trombonio's Traveling Wonder Show having spent some weeks on the road with them between St. Bees and Pontefract when I was seven or eight years old.

"It's a pleasure to see you out and about," I said, once Lily's squeals of greeting had subsided. "There were rumors you'd been sent up for robbing a cheese shop."

"Oh, you know how it is. Someone catches you halfway through a window and they 'meejitly think the worst. But look at you! You're a grown man now. How old must you be?"

"Ten and six," said I, a little proudly, as if it were an achievement such as learning Latin.

"Sixteen years!" Lily exclaimed, tossing her yellow curls and pinching my cheek. "Old enough to marry!" She had often made fun of me in this way when I was small, and boxed my ears, too, though when her romantic entanglements inevitably failed after a fortnight or so, she would weep on my neck and kiss my brow and tell me men were cruel and I was her only friend. Now she held me at arm's length and looked me over.

"I remember when you was but a stripling lad, only as high as your own knee. Fresh-bought from the workhouse by Old Trombonio, God rest his soul. You were a tiny thing, and always hungry, but nimble as a monkey. Look at you now! If I wasn't engaged to that Pierrot over there with the white skin-cap on, I'd take an interest in you myself—such a handsome fellow with a fine suit of clothes and a purse at your belt! Whence," she added, "came you by the money?"

This last she whispered sideways, as if it were a secret.

"I'm servant in a good house," I replied, proudly. "The only servant."

"The only servant? Taking care of a fine family?" Lily didn't seem to believe me.

"Just the master and myself," I explained.

"No scullery girls to warm your heart, then? You haven't got a sweetheart, in a manner of speaking?"

I blushed furiously and denied any such thing.

But she didn't much care about my personal life, for the subject of the household swiftly returned. "Your master must be away most of the time, to keep such a small staff. A fine big house, and you all alone in it?"

I couldn't quite understand the line of questioning, but Lily's purpose soon became clear. She continued to alternate between teasing me and pressing for details about Master Rattle and the general disposition of the house, the quality of its furniture, and how much valuable metal it contained. I kept answering her from vanity, when I might better have been silent from prudence.

"He wouldn't miss a few odds and ends, I dare say," Lily muttered, and at last I plainly saw her intent. I should have guessed from the start—in my years with traveling performers I'd come to know their desperate poverty, and how often some of them took opportunity to supplement their incomes by way of a back door or an open window.

I hastily made amends. "My master is a gentleman," I said. "But he hasn't anything of worth, being the third son of a lord; just the

Manse, which is halfway to tumbling down, and a lot of old stuff that's been in it for centuries, not worth the price of a cart to take it away in, I expect. Besides, what he has—he gambles away."

"Ooh, he's a bit of a rake, is he?" Lily asked, and batted her pale eyelashes fit to start a breeze.

"I don't know a thing about his life outside the Manse, I confess," said I, truthfully. "He keeps little enough money." The calculating look was still in Lily's eye, so I added, "One thing he keeps very well, though, is a bulldog named Demon."

"Ah," said Lily, and looked about her as if the animal might leap out at her in the next instant. "Vicious, is he? Jaws like a trap?"

"He can snap a bone with one bite," I said.

This was perfectly true. I did not lie about the dog, who was Master Rattle's constant companion, but rather omitted a few details: he was a *French* bulldog, a tiny beast bred not to fight bulls but to snore lustily, and he *could* snap a bone with one bite, but only a ham bone. In fact, he spent all of his waking moments, which amounted to about an hour each day, gnawing on bones.

The mention of Demon put an end to my old acquaintance's speculations, and after that we had a pleasant chat about doings upon the traveling circuit. Just as Lily was becoming tearful, relating a tragic romance she had recently endured, there came a commotion at the far end of the market square, which drew steadily nearer.

It was a squad of red-coated soldiers with white pipe-clayed crossbelts and gleaming bayonets. They marched through the crowd led by an officer mounted upon a fine brown horse. The town crier followed, carrying his big brass bell. The soldiers halted before the town notice board. The crier mounted the step at the foot of the board, rang his bell, and unfolded a piece of parchment. I took my leave of Lily and pressed through the crowd for a better look. I was grateful for an excuse to avoid further questions about my master, and also to escape being wept upon and kissed, especially by an older woman. Lily was at least twenty-four.

[*Demon the Bulldog*]

"Oyez, oyez!" the crier shouted, in the traditional way. "Oyez." The sellers stopped shouting long enough to see if his proclamation would affect their business.

"Be it known," the crier began, reading from the parchment. "A proclamation by His Majesty King George the Second*: Whereas bandits and highwaymen are flourishing upon our roads, and prey upon rich carriages, royal emissaries, mail coaches, and travelers well-to-do, inflicting their brutal and dastardly crimes upon the innocent, be it known that we have set upon the heads of all who pursue this vile profession a bounty of forty guineas, five shillings, thruppence ha'penny."

A gasp went up in the crowd, followed by a buzz of conversation. That was a great deal of money. One shilling would buy a pound of good soap, although nobody in that fragrant crowd, I thought, would be interested in a pound of soap. Three pennies was enough to have a tooth pulled. A ha'penny would buy a day-old bun. I did the calculation in my head and determined that with such a sum, I could get very clean, visit a dentist, and still retain enough money for two years' paid holiday and a stale bun.

The crier rang his bell again to quell the commotion, and the captain shouted threats from the vantage of his horse until the crowd quieted down.

As soon as there was any chance he would be heard, the crier continued. "Oyez, oyez, oyez! A list of villains is attached herewith, including Giant Jim and his gang, the Spanish Desperado, Dick Sculley, Sailor Tom, the Laughing Priest, Whistling Jack, and Milliner Mulligan, among others. Once convicted, they shall be hanged by the necks at Tyburn Tree. All such bandits in living or

---

* King George II of Great Britain and Ireland (1683–1760) was born in Germany, son of the Hanoverian dynasty that divided its loyalties between the German and English courts. He was a bureaucrat by nature, detested the arts and sentimentality, and was the last British monarch to lead his army into battle. His oldest son, Frederick, died untimely, leaving his grandson George III in succession to the throne.

dead condition shall be presented to the magistrate of the court for inspection, et cetera et cetera. There's a good deal more to this 'ere proclamation, but that's the gist of the matter. Particulars shall be posted on this notice board. Given at our Court at St. James, this day in the year of our Lord et cetera and so on, God save the King!"

And with that, the soldiers recommenced their march behind the officer's splendid horse, and the crier made his way directly to a beer seller, his throat being sorely parched by the crying. The crowd closed back up and the mongers began shouting again.

I had one more errand before returning to the Manse, and took my time about it. The King's proclamation had put me in an introspective mood. I'll relay my thoughts, and how they returned to the matter of the highwaymen; bear with me a while.

My own childhood had been more like that of the highwayman than the major domo, and it was a great surprise to me to find that, after an interval of respectable stability, I pined for excitement again. My life was secure and comfortable now, yet days at the Manse felt like an endless rainy afternoon, and me stuck indoors. The mood was not mine alone: My master had become increasingly like a caged tiger in the last few weeks. He would lounge abed until afternoon many days, then spring up in a fit of energy and meet me in the kitchen yard with rapier and sabers. In these contests he fought with thrice the conviction I did, with the consequence that I became as skilled at defense as he was at offense.

He also spent hours pacing irritably from one end of the Manse to the other, smoking his churchwarden pipe and looking out of the windows as if expecting someone to visit. But no one ever did. He read books about coach-making and studied maps; he took me out hunting and shot no game, but rode his great black horse over every terrain like a madman with the devil at his back, myself trailing along behind on a gray hunter with similar skill but more care, determined not to break my neck.

Sometimes he would stop at a particular crossroads or other isolated spot and study the lay of the land with infinite care, I knew not why. I had begun to understand that my master, as much as I, felt trapped—myself by idleness, and him by some unknown business that worried him.

But here my musings ended, for my steps had taken me to the Widow's Arms.

Chapter 2

THE DAY'S SECOND INTERROGATION

I HAD BEEN instructed by Master Rattle to bring back a jug of beer in addition to whatever else I thought fit. He was not much interested in food, except as it accompanied drink; that and cards were my master's main vices. He was often out all night. I had saved getting the beer for last, because it would spoil if it sat in the cart all afternoon. So it was, with the sun at my back and long shadows stretching out before me, that I stopped in at the tavern.

The Widow's Arms was a low, dark place on the road outside town, always cool within and smelling of damp. There were a number of people at the tables there, it being market day, and the air was blue with pipe smoke. Molly Figgs tended bar, scouring pewter mugs with a rag as brown as bacon. She was a formidable woman with a red cap on her head, not the widow named on the signboard but her daughter-in-law. She knew me well, my master requiring an above-average quantity of beer.

"Brought your jug, I see, Mr. Bristol," she boomed. Bristol, being the town in which I was purchased, was my surname. "Same as always?"

"If you please, ma'am," I said, and placed my coins on the bar. I thought of ordering a dish of tea for myself, but one look at the washing-rag and I decided against it.

Molly arranged the jug beneath a beer-tap in the end of a cask, then aimed a leering wink at me. "Your master's a rare 'un," she said. "There's talk of him from one end o' town to the next, you know."

I did know. I felt my face turning red. It was a proud thing to work for a gentleman, but not so proud if the gentleman was prone to strange behavior.

"It's only gossip," said I, staunchly. "Master Rattle is restless from inaction, that's all."

"Curse of the titled class, boredom," Molly said, and squinted as if she could squeeze me to death with her eyelids. I was searching for a suitable response when there was a great clatter of boots and hooves in the foreyard, and a few moments later the door flew open and banged against the wall.

The officer late of the fine brown horse strode in, spurs ajingle, and tucked his hat under his arm like a bagpipe. He surveyed the room, examining each face turned toward him. To judge by his scowling demeanor, he found some fault in every one. He might have been correct, but it was unkind to make his opinion so obvious.

Still, thirst must be answered. So he clove through the occupants of the place as a ship cleaves the waves, with a pair of soldiers at his back forming a red wake, and dropped anchor right beside me.

"Whisky," he barked in a drill-field voice. The soldiers standing behind him gazed lovingly on the tuns of beer that stood behind Molly. While she fetched the bottle, the captain leaned on his elbow and turned to sweep the room with his eyes again, lingering on the roughest characters. I barely rated a blink's worth of scrutiny.

"I am Captain Sterne," bellowed he, "of the Earl of Bath's Regiment, now designated the Tenth. Look on me well. If any crime is perpetrated upon the roads from here to the Irish Sea, or t'other way to Penzance, or thence to the chalky Cliffs of Dover, I shall pursue the perpetrant to the very gates of hell. But every coin has a backside, and so have I."

At this, several of the customers chuckled, and Captain Sterne fixed them with a glare so ferocious it could have knocked a bird out of the air.

"On the *obverse* of this coin: If any of you have knowledge of a crime done, or of plans to commit one in the future, I am provided with means of instant reward by courtesy of our practical-minded Majesty. There is nothing so soothing to the conscience as gold. When I'm not fixing the noose about your necks, I'll balm your tongues with sovereigns. Am I understood?"

There was a smattering of "yerss" and "aye" from those present, sufficient so that the captain felt he'd done his part.

"The age of land-piracy is come to an end," he said. "And I'm the end of it."

So saying, he threw the dram of whisky down the back of his throat like a shovel of coals onto a smelting fire, coughed once, and clapped a gold sovereign on the bar. "God save the King," said he, and spun on his heel so that he was nose to nose with his men. They parted to let him pass, then followed him out of the place, just as thirsty as when they had walked in.

Every eye in the house turned from the door as soon as it was shut, and fell upon the coin that gleamed atop the bar. After she'd gathered her wits back together, Molly Figgs' red hand leapt out and snatched it up. It vanished into a pocket among her skirts. Then she swept the room with her own eyeballs, no less ferocious than the captain.

"That's what I gets for keeping an 'onest hestablishment," said she, defiantly. "And don't think I'll fail to turn 'ee in one and all if you ain't 'onest yerselfs!"

So saying, she commenced polishing the bar with such determination that part of it nearly became clean. The jug was overflowing, and I pointed this out to her. She corked it up and slid it across to me, but didn't let go. Her brains had been at work, it seemed.

"There's talk," Molly said, "that your master rides out of an evening and don't come back till morning."

"Most gentlemen do that sort of thing, I'm told," I said. "Until they have wife and children, of course. Then they don't come back all week."

"There's some what seen him on that great black horse, riding across the moors by moonlight. Wild as an Apache, they say. Clad all in black," she went on, now leaning over the jug to squint at me more closely.

"I doubt very much that's my master," said I, growing irritated. This sort of talk was dangerous. If they thought my master was galloping around in the dark, it wasn't a far stretch to asking why an *honest* man would do so. People were seeing highwaymen behind every tree these days—they could mistake him for a brigand. And Captain Sterne might not care who he captured, as long as he captured *someone*.

I was about to argue the point, but stopped myself, remembering my earlier interview with Lily the acrobat. If I protested too much, Molly might well take it that I was hiding something. I was an open sort of person by nature—little credit for that, as it caused me no end of difficulties—but my years on the road had taught me a great deal about how dishonest minds work. They tend to attach the worst motives to everything.

"My master's a man of rare habits, I confess," said I. "But there is no harm in him. We go hunting thrice a week, but he hasn't any interest in bagging game, as far as I can tell. He once shot a sparrow out of the air by way of a demonstration of marksmanship, and accidentally trampled a marmot while jumping Midnight over a stile, but that's been the whole of his bag in the two years I've known him. Master Rattle loves to ride, that's all. And Midnight's the finest horse in England. Anyone would want to ride him day *and* night."

Molly nodded, as if this confirmed her worst suspicions. She began to release the jug, lifting one finger at a time in order to prolong the conversation. "He likes his guns, though, even if he don't shoot rabbits," she said, and winked so violently her cap tipped sideways.

A couple of ruffians at a nearby table had begun listening to the conversation. Captain Sterne's eye had lingered upon them earlier. One had a pink scar that ran from his cleft ear to his nose, like a saber cut.

Their pipes had gone out, and they were staring at me in a most curious manner. I watched them from the tail of my eye, and was again reminded of my conversation with Lily. It might be as well to warn people that the Rattle estate was reasonably well defended.

"He's a brilliant shot with pistols," I boasted, raising my voice a little. "And he's a wizard with a sword. Master's taught me a great deal so that I might spar with him, but there's none so quick as he. However, I can play my part."

"Practicing pistols and swords . . . it makes a body wonder what on Earth he needs such talents for," Molly said.

She didn't elaborate on what she was thinking, and when I finally realized what she was implying, I decided not to say another word, lest I make matters worse. Unless I was much mistaken, she suspected my master was—incredibly enough—a highwayman. And it hadn't occurred to me until that moment that I could furnish no proof otherwise.

Master Rattle *did* ride out at all hours of the night, with no word to explain where he'd gone. He was the surest shot and the nimblest sword I knew, and his magnificent horse could scarcely have been swifter if he'd been equipped with wings. What a dreadful thought! But it was nonsense, of course. Highwaymen didn't have manservants, and here I was.

With that thought to sustain me, I departed the Widow's Arms. The eyes of the two ruffians followed me to the door.

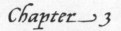

RATTLE RIDES OUT

THE SUN was down and the sky a red bowl over the darkening countryside when I drove the cart through the crooked iron gates of the Rattle Manse, and the stars had come out by the time I had put Old Nell away in the stable. Midnight, my master's fine black hunter horse, was not there, nor his tack. I brought my purchases into the house by way of the kitchen, and there found a note pinned to the long deal table with a paring knife.

> *Dear Mr. Bristol,*
> *I shall be out all night, and possibly longer. Do not wait up, I pray.*
>
> *Yrs*
> *J. Rattle*

This was a fairly typical communication from Master Rattle, who (despite his station in life) seemed to find it amusing that he had any household staff at all. He'd grown up with many servants in the much finer seat of his family. His father was an influential and wealthy lord, and his elder brothers were celebrated, too: one was an admiral in the navy, the other an importer of tea. James Rattle was himself, as he'd once said to me, nothing more than a spare boy in case one of the other two died prematurely. As a result he'd been given one of the hereditary estates and a trifling income. Although he joked about it, I think he acutely felt his father's indifference to him. I cannot speak of my own father's indifference, for no one knew who he was. Neither of us could remember our mothers, who had perished young in the fashion of the times.

The Manse was a big place, to be fair—far too big to maintain, and set in the middle of extensive grounds. Yet among the estates thereabouts, it was the least. The roof was falling in, it was overrun by mice (which Demon the bulldog steadfastly ignored), and the cellar flooded for a month every spring.

🝮   🝮   🝮

Having been employed by him for two years, I thought I understood my master fairly well (which, as you shall learn, shows I understood little enough). He had two reasons for not employing more servants: one was money, always in short supply—gambling consumed his entire annual stipend in a month or two—and the other was privacy. Most servants employed to mind such a wreckage as the Manse would do nothing but carry tales into town all day. Master Rattle detested wagging tongues.

I made for myself a supper of ham and butter between two slabs of bread, a clever way of taking meals invented by John Montagu, 4th Earl of Sandwich. Then I set some sausage and the jug of beer  on the table for my employer—the kitchen door was nearest the stables, and among Master Rattle's eccentricities was his use of the kitchen door as if it were the main entrance to the house. His father, he once remarked, had never set foot in his own kitchen in sixty years.

This accomplished, I took myself off to bed.

❦   ❦   ❦

It was the deepest part of the night, with the moon almost down behind the trees, when I was awakened by the distant sound of breaking crockery. I was quartered in a backstairs room above the kitchen, and the noise seemed to come from directly below. My first thought was burglars. Demon the bulldog had been sleeping on the rug at the foot of my bed. The short fawn fur on his back stood up and he began to screech in the way of barking peculiar to the breed. I bade him be silent.

The two of us went along the passage and crept downstairs, me in my stocking feet. I felt my way along without a candle, not wishing to advertise my presence, and stole to the inner kitchen door. Demon let me lead the way, not being a bold creature. When I looked into the kitchen, my caution was forgotten and I rushed in.

My master was sprawled upon the table, face down, the jug of beer shattered on the floor. By the moonlight coming through the small windows, I saw a dark stain spilling across the boards. It didn't look like beer.

Once I'd ascertained my master was senseless, I lit a candle from the embers in the hearth. Master Rattle was bleeding profusely from a wound in his body somewhere, his face white as paper ash. That was the first thing I saw.

The second thing was that my master was clad entirely in black from head to foot, except for the bright scarlet turndowns on his boot-tops. There was a black mask across his eyes. I smelled horse sweat and gunpowder.

I went to my master's side and my foot collided with something under the table. It was a gold-hilted sword, unsheathed, the blade smeared with blood. I struggled to turn him face upward. The unfortunate gentleman was delirious, his eyes fluttering.

"Mr. Bristol," he croaked. "My apologies."

"I'll fetch the doctor, sir," I said, pressing dishcloths over the wound in his chest. I confess I was more frightened than I had ever been before.

Master Rattle redoubled my alarm by fiercely gripping me upon the arm, as if all his strength was concentrated in that one hand. "No doctor!" he snarled. "Promise me that. Not a soul knows of this but you and I."

"But Master," I said. "You—"

"The devil take me!" he interrupted, and fell into a faint.

🕊 🕊 🕊

I did what I could to stop the flow of blood. I'd had a little experience with such things, acrobatic work being an endless source of injuries. But I'd never seen a bullet wound. It was a terrible sight, and I felt sick in body and soul as I bound it up. Regardless of my master's entreaty, I fully intended to call the doctor at the first possible opportunity. The poor fellow wasn't in his right mind, after all.

At length I could do no more. I wanted to get my master up to his bed, but moving him could have been fatal. Instead, I fetched some bedding from the cupboard and tucked it around the patient right there on the kitchen table, with a pillow under his head. Master Rattle appeared to be sleeping, not unconscious, and a little color had returned to his face. I fervently hoped the worst of the danger had passed. I put Demon up on the table for company, and the little dog sniffed the bandages and licked at my master's face.

I would have rushed out straightaway, but lacking shoes, I hurried up to my bedchamber, the candle-flame stretched almost to the point of extinguishment. Upon catching sight of myself in the small looking glass over the washbasin, I paused to rinse the blood from my hands. It wouldn't do to ride about in the dark looking as if I'd murdered a man. Just as I was buckling my shoes, there came a great pounding at the front door of the Manse.

In a panic now, I rushed down the stairs, through the library, drawing room, and great hall to the grand foyer. The candle went out entirely. Demon had set to barking again, and sounded like a cat with pneumonia. Just before I reached the front door, a chilling thought occurred to me. Someone had done terrible violence to my master. Who else but the assassin would be at the entrance at this hour of the night, come to finish the job? I slowed my steps. The hammering on the door was redoubled, and now I could hear someone calling, "Come out, Jack, d___ your eyes!"

"One minute," I called, trying to sound calm. I relit the candle, which cost me four lucifer matches to accomplish, so much was I trembling. The phossy* stink of them was awful. I could hear the men—there was more than one voice—arguing outside in muted tones. I began to wish there was a pistol about me. There had been one in my master's belt, come to think of it.

If only I presented a more imposing figure! With clumsy fingers I retied the ribbon that held the hair at my neck, straightened my weskit†, and took a long breath. Then I threw back my head and squared my shoulders in imitation of Master Rattle, strode to the door, and opened it—none too wide.

Three men stood on the broad granite steps. The mark of habitual villainy was written plainly upon their faces, visible even by candlelight. One wore an immense two-cornered hat with an ostrich plume in it; this ornament made the stranger look half again as tall as he was. The man beside him wore a sailor's short jacket and Monmouth cap, and had an iron hook in place of his left hand. The third man was the unpleasant character with the scarred face who had observed me at the Widow's Arms; one of his sleeves was torn and spattered with blood.

"What is the meaning of this?" I demanded, before the men had opportunity to speak. I kept a hand on the door, ready to fling it shut if they rushed me.

---

* Matches of that period were made with phosphorous. The smoke from them was poisonous in sufficient quantities.

† Weskit: waistcoat or vest.

"We would have speech with your master," the man in the enormous hat replied. His voice was as unpleasant as his demeanor.

"The master is unavailable," I said, as haughtily as I could manage. "Good night to you, sirs." I moved to close the door, but to my dismay, the second man thrust his hook into the gap.

"Belay that, young squire," he growled. "We come to see old Jack, and we means to see him."

"There's no Jack here."

"Yer master, swab. By whatever name!"

"If you must," said I, trying to imagine what a proper servant would do in this situation. "Please wait here while I rouse him from bed. I doubt he'll like it very much."

I prayed the man would remove his hook from the door, and my relief was tremendous when the sharp point slipped back outside. I closed the door firmly, locked it, and walked unhurriedly back into the depths of the Manse. As soon as I was out of view of the front windows, I ran for the kitchen.

"Master," I cried, and wrung my employer's hand.

To my inexpressible relief, his blue eyelids fluttered open.

"You didn't call the doctor, I trust," he whispered.

"No, sir," I said. "But three ruffians have come to the door inquiring after you. They're outside now."

"Has one of them a hook?"

"Yes, and another a tremendous big hat with a feather in it, and the third a saber cut to his cheek."

"Worse luck," Master Rattle sighed. He took a deep breath and his next words came out all in a tumble. "I haven't the strength to defend us, lad, but I assure you we are in mortal peril. It was Milliner Mulligan shot me; that's him in the hat. But he doesn't know if the ball struck me or not. Everything was confusion. The hook is Sailor Tom, and the third a mate of his: I added a scar to his collection tonight. Escape by the kitchen door, I pray you. Flee."

"I'll not leave you defenseless, sir."

"I know it. But I wish you would. Do not take my part in any of this. If you must remain here, you're going to have to get rid of them somehow. I can't think of a way. My mind is in a fog. There's a loaded pistol in the console by the door. If they attack you, kill one of them if you can; it may discourage the others."

With that, Master Rattle gasped and fell back once again, senseless. Demon sniffed at his nostrils, as if to tell whether life remained. My mouth was as dry as a ship's biscuit, and my heart thumped in my chest with as much fury as the hook I could now hear applied to the front door. I'd no idea what to do, and no time to do it. So I returned through the house, scouring my brains for a means to turn the visitors away.

It took all the courage I had, but with the pistol from the console concealed behind my back, I opened the front door once more. "I am surprised to find the master is not at home," said I. "May I take a message?"

It seemed like the worst possible excuse to avoid allowing these three ruffians into the house, but nothing else had come to mind. They muttered between themselves for a few moments, and then Milliner Mulligan nodded his head, making the hat sway like the masts of a schooner.

"I'm not surprised to hear that," he said with grim satisfaction. "We shall return on the morrow."

With that, the men descended the steps and hurried away from the house. I closed the door behind them, tucked the pistol in the back of my belt, then raced around the ground floor of the Manse, checking that all the doors and windows were locked (those that would even shut properly). It was a futile exercise and I knew it.

I returned to the kitchen and found my master awake, staring sadly at his dog. Demon stared back, his wide-set brown eyes fixed upon our master. "They've gone, sir," I said. "But I expect they shall return soon enough."

"They'll come back with reinforcements," Master Rattle said. "If I could lift my hand I'd take up my pistol, but I'm done in. Save yourself, Mr. Bristol. Take Midnight and ride away from here before they return. But—ere you go, furnish me with some brandywine."

I took up my master's icy hand. "I'll not leave you, sir," I said. "You gave me my first proper home and treated me better than anyone ever has, and got hardly any work out of me in return. I owe you a debt of gratitude and I mean to repay it by defending your life."

"Sentimental fool!" Master Rattle said. "I forbid you to take my side in any of this. Did I not say so?" A thread of blood trickled from the corner of his mouth, and I dabbed it away with a corner of linen. Then he muttered some nonsensical words, as if in a dream.

"If you would defend me, then go fetch the magistrate," he said, after the wave of delirium had passed. "Treat me as an enemy of the law, and do nothing that would aid my cause. I beg you. I'm finished, and there's no rope long enough to reach me where I'm going. But first bring me that wine. And fetch paper and quill, and I'll write out my will. Quickly, before I lose my senses again."

To my shame, I found my face was wet with tears. This was no time for childish grief. I had to save Master Rattle and needed clear eyes to do it. To conceal my sorrow, I fetched wine, paper, pen and ink, and some sand to blot the ink dry. My master propped himself up on one elbow and drank directly from the wine bottle, coughed painfully (which brought fresh blood to his lips), and lay back, his head lolling.

"Don't be long, Mr. Bristol," he said, in a voice almost too faint to hear. "Midnight is quick, but so are my enemies. I must rest awhile." With that, he closed his eyes.

At the thought of the handsome black horse, inspiration came to me. The moon was down and it was the darkest hour of the night. With a little luck—if his enemies were on the road, and if they suspected he was unhurt—I might yet save the Manse, and therefore my master, from further attack.

"I'll need your riding-costume, sir," said I.

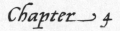

Chapter 4

THE IMPOSTER

IMOVED TO enact my plan as swiftly and surely as I could. Midnight did not tolerate strangers, but of all the people in the world, I'm proud to say the horse was second-fondest of me, who brought him apples and fed him mash. He was still wearing the saddle, his reins dragging along the ground. His flanks were wet and chill with sweat. Never before had Master Rattle failed to put the animal away properly, no matter how late it was, or for that matter how drunk he was.

But Midnight was startled when I approached him. He could smell the blood, and his big dark eyes rolled with confusion at the sight of me dressed in his master's clothes. The black broadcloth costume fit me not too badly (although the long coat was prodigiously heavy), the scarlet-lined riding-boots were only a trifle too large, and with the mask across my eyes and the cocked hat* upon my head it would have taken an owl to spy the difference. I wore my own shirt and weskit, as they weren't soaked with blood. Only

---

* Cocked hat: a hat with the brim turned up to form two or three sides. Also bicorne and tricorne, respectively.

Midnight could tell that I was not his accustomed rider in the clothes. Horses are not so easily fooled as men.

I was surprised to see Midnight had a white, diamond-shaped blaze on his nose, until I patted it to reassure him, and discovered the marking was made with chalk.

On foot I led Midnight out of the stable yard and down the lane behind the Manse, careful to make as little noise as possible. At a suitable distance from the house, I leapt into the saddle and we galloped straight onto the broad road that the trio of villains must have taken to leave the property. It had been less than an hour since I closed the door behind them. With any luck they were still on the road, whether coming or going.

Despite my fear, I was thrilled to ride Midnight. He was a graceful animal, powerful as a bull, seeming to flow down the road like the wing of some huge raven. Again I confess childish vanity: We must have made a fine-looking pair, me in my inky-black redingote* with the long skirts flying, a gold-hilted sword at my belt, and the mighty horse with his neck stretched out and his nostrils flaring, mane whirling like black flames.

We had gone less than a mile when I heard a coarse voice shouting up ahead on the road. Several man-shapes emerged onto the path from the concealment of some trees, and I distinctly heard Sailor Tom cry, "Whistlin' Jack's upon us, men, repel boarders!" There was a clash of steel, the yellow flash of a musket, and I spurred Midnight off the road as the shot whined past my head. The horse sprang over a tall hedge as if it were a whisk-broom and pelted off across a field on the other side. Behind us came shouts of desperate fury and men crashing through the thicket.

I didn't dare shout anything lest I give away the trick—my voice was nothing like my master's—but I could still make noise. I drew the pistol from my belt and fired it wildly behind me. A volley of

---

* Redingote: riding coat. A jacket with long, voluminous tails, cut for horsemen.

curses followed the report of the weapon, and then Midnight was galloping full tilt through a wood, and it was all I could to do avoid being swept out of the saddle by low branches. I kept my course directly away from the Manse, so that none would think "Whistling Jack" intended to return.

Twenty minutes later, I was back at the Manse by a roundabout route, with Midnight tied to a tree behind the carriage house in case the marauders had decided to pursue their original purpose. I crept onward to the kitchen door, then pulled open the small scullery window beside it. I'd unlatched it for just this occasion, the door being locked. I didn't dare open the door in case my master's enemies were already in the house—they would certainly hear the clank of the old, stiff lock.

I climbed through the window, and there the stealth ended. The window frame tipped my hat over my eyes, and then I tangled my legs in the sword. Thus encumbered, I fell headlong over the stone sink, smashed a stack of china plates, broke a couple of bottles, and upset a tin washtub that clanged like the bells of St. Ives Cathedral. Demon started making his shrieking sounds, somewhat like a hyena with its head caught in a jar. So much for caution. I limped into the kitchen.

My master was dead, it appeared, his underclothes stained with blood. Demon stood between his feet, small but determined, his short, tawny fur bristling and his face rumpled with agitation. The Master was entirely still, his eyes fixed heavenward, his face as white as sugar. But when I entered the room, those glassy eyes rolled in my direction.

"You'd make a fine cat burglar," Master Rattle whispered. "But why are you dressed in my costume?"

"Sir, I think I lured them away," said I, still breathless from my adventure. "It worked: They thought I was you. I heard them call your name, and they shot at me, sir. But Midnight took me off like a feather on a hurricane, and we left them handily behind."

"You're a fool," Master Rattle said, his voice as faint as falling snow. "It was a good idea of yours—they won't dare return tonight if they think me uninjured. After that it doesn't matter. But I told you not to take my part in any of this, and now you have. You've sealed your fate."

"You're not done yet, sir," said I, trying to sound encouraging. But my voice broke a little with grief. The shadow of death was unmistakably upon him.

"I think by now you know my secret," Master Rattle continued, ignoring the encouraging words. "I'm Whistling Jack the highwayman. That's why I'm out all night on occasion. My income doesn't support a gambling habit and a drinking habit at the same time, so I've more than made up the deficit by robbing members of my own social class. I once stopped a coach belonging to my very own uncle, in fact."

"I never knew, sir," I said, as if my ignorance were some sort of error. My worst fears had come true. That scold Molly Figgs had been correct in her wicked conjectures, and I had served a criminal for two years and thought myself a gentleman's gentleman. But at the same time, I knew him to be a good fellow, and kind, and a friend when he might more easily have been a tyrant. He *was* a gentleman. How he made his income didn't change any of that. I was pulled both ways, and all the while my head whirled with sorrow and fear.

Demon was licking his master's hand now, and the sight of that little creature's devotion stung fresh tears to my eyes.

"You never suspected, that's why," Master Rattle said. "You're far too generous for your own good. But there's no time. Already my sight fails me. Mr. Bristol—Kit, if I may—you'll find my last will and testament beside my hand. Take it. Turn Nell and the gray loose; they'll find homes soon enough."

"I'll change out of these clothes, sir," said I, "and fetch the king's men once—if—you're gone. There's an end of it. I'm guilty of nothing, so I'll remain. There's no need to flee into the night."

"No, Kit," my master said, and found the strength to grip my wrist. He sat up a little, so urgent was his concern. His eyes blazed. "There's a fellow about named Captain Sterne who will hang any man found with me. But he's the least of your worries. Through your efforts on my behalf tonight, you are now bound to the very task I so feared—the thing that made me such poor company these last few months."

He drew a long breath. It sounded like hard work. "You must bring Demon and Midnight to the deepest part of Kingsmire Forest, and there you'll find an old witch. She'll reveal your folly to you. Give to her my beloved bull-pup for safekeeping. Midnight is yours."

Then my master turned his head to look upon the dog, and said, "Demon . . . farewell."

"An old *witch*?" I blurted. "Oh sir, this is all too much for me. Let's get you a surgeon, and—"

But James Rattle, alias Whistling Jack, was dead.

At that moment there came a great noise at the front door of splintering wood and breaking glass. I snatched up the fold of paper at my dead master's hand, shoved it into the breast of the redingote, and rushed out the kitchen door. At the threshold I whistled sharply, and Demon, with a last, beseeching look at our master's mortal remains, bounded after me.

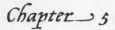

Chapter 5

ESCAPE TO KINGSMIRE

DAWN WAS coming and the sky begun to grow light when I judged us safe from immediate pursuit.

The flight from the Manse had been terrifying. I'd no sooner stuffed the little dog into a saddlebag and urged Midnight back onto the road when redcoats—the king's soldiers—came tumbling out of the kitchen door behind me. It hadn't been the bandits, after all. There were more soldiers running on foot around the corner of the house. Had I not been expecting Milliner Mulligan and his accomplices, I wouldn't have fled in the first place. But now that I'd been seen racing away from the house, it was no good claiming innocence. They wouldn't listen. In calling Demon, I'd even whistled in imitation of my master—the very sound they'd expect from a brigand named Whistling Jack. In any case, I was dressed as the highwayman and riding his horse—they might even think I had murdered Master Rattle!

I thought myself well away from them when I heard a clatter of hooves, and to my dismay saw Captain Sterne in close pursuit. Midnight was tired, but that is when he showed his true strength. His stride was sure, even in the darkness—and he reached into his heart with every pace and found more speed. The brown charged after us, propelled by Sterne's curses.

"I'll have you, Jack!" he cried. "You robbed my fiancée's coach a month ago!"

That sounded rather bad. Having no response, I tucked low against Midnight's neck and we sailed through the night, gaining ground with every stride. But the captain had one more thing to tell me. When I heard it I knew we were deadly enemies and he would never give up the pursuit:

"And she fell," he screamed at my fleeing back, "in love with *you*!"

At the very outermost edge of the estate there was a crossroad. Could I but reach it, I might escape the captain by several routes which Midnight knew so well he could outrun an arrow upon them. Midnight galloped, the captain's horse fell ever behind, and then through the dark hedges I saw the glimmer of pale gravel where the several roads met.

Just as I bore down upon the crossing, a knot of men sprang into our path from behind a broken cart, starlight glinting off the weapons in their hands. Those voices again—it was Sailor Tom, Milliner Mulligan, and the rest of their crew.

Demon, whose furrowed head was poking out of the saddlebag, let loose his uncanny cry. Midnight reared up and threw his hooves about, and a moment later the captain had covered much of the distance between us.

"I'll spare you the gallows," he roared. "You'll die here, tonight!"

I tried to head Midnight around despite the encircling ruffians—we might be able to get past Sterne's whirling sword, if we went off the road. But there wasn't room to maneuver.

It seemed I was a dead man. I thought to draw my sword as Sterne spurred his mount directly at me, but got the handle caught in the redingote, and it hardly showed an inch of blade.

Then there was a blinding hoop of green fire in the air, as if a blazing firework had been swung around us on a cord. My eyes

[*Fleeing Through the Night*]

were fair dazzled, but it went worse for my attackers—they behaved as if someone had flung gunpowder in their eyes. The captain himself was nearly unhorsed. Sparks flew in all directions.

"I'll have your liver," the captain cried, "though the devil himself sets me afire!"

It appeared that was precisely what had occurred, so in terror I goaded Midnight up the verge above the road and clapped heels to his sides. We were well over the top when the green fire suddenly went out.

We rushed across fields of grass and cabbages, flowers and barley. The morning sun would soon meet the sky. I could hear pandemonium behind me: the soldiers pursuing on foot had caught up to their captain, and the bandits were putting up a fight. Ahead of me was a dark band that rose up into broken stone hills: Kingsmire Forest.*

"Just a little further, Midnight," I implored the horse. Whatever the ring of green light was, it had saved our skins. I had no time to ponder the meaning of it, nor to dwell upon the cause of the phenomenon—I was now Whistling Jack, highwayman, whether I liked it or not, and I had a mortal foe in Captain Sterne. He was nowhere to be seen when I looked over my shoulder. Between the blinding light, colliding with a nest of genuine bandits, and the ensuing *fracasso*, he was probably too busy to worry about me for the time being. Still I urged Midnight to keep up a brisk pace, only slowing when we reached the deepest darkness that lurked beneath the trees. As dawn broke, we were already far into the woods, and the rays of the sun penetrated the gloomy mist in slender threads, like fine gold chain.

I walked Midnight for some time after daybreak, and when we came to a hill of massive broken stones with a white waterfall spilling

---

* There is no record of a forest named Kingsmire, but it may have been a local name for part of the New Forest, which at that time covered a broad band of southern central England.

down among its slabs, I bade us stop for a rest. We all drank deeply from the icy pool at the foot of the spate. Then Demon dutifully marked every stone for yards around.

I collapsed wearily against the bole of a massive tree, aching from head to toe. Midnight nibbled moss off the rocks. I expected the horse didn't feel much better. I felt like a fool in daylight with the highwayman's costume on, but I had nothing else to wear. Even without the long coat it was obvious whom I resembled, and without hat or coat I'd be arrested for stealing the horse: Men in shirtsleeves didn't ride. My entire situation was impossible: I was frightened, angry, heartsick, and shocked, all at the same time.

At length, hearing no evidence of pursuit, I decided to take stock of my equipment. Midnight bore, besides the usual riding tack, a beef-roll bag at the front of his saddle, and the two slim saddlebags behind. Without the dog, the saddlebags were empty. Inside the beef-roll was a coil of strong silken cord, a tiny pistol that would fit in the palm of my hand, a penknife, an apple, and a length of sausage.

I immediately gave the apple to Midnight and devoured most of the sausage myself. Tears came to my eyes when I recalled buying the meat just last week, because it was Master Rattle's favorite accompaniment to sherry—and sometimes that was the only way I could get him to eat. He'd liked the stuff enough to take it with him on the highway. This touched my heart.

I fed the remaining sausage to the bulldog. The pup swallowed it whole with his jack-o'lantern mouth, and then directed his paddle-like ears at me, hoping for more. I realized we had eaten our last, unless I could accustom myself to begging or stealing. Then I remembered: Of course, I wasn't wearing my own empty coat. There might be a little money in this one. I rummaged in the pockets of the redingote and swiftly turned out my master's will, a tin of snuff, doeskin gloves, a brace of matched pistols, and a delicate paper rose. The rose mystified me.

Then I discovered why the coat weighed so much. Within a secret pocket was a heavy packet of gold sovereigns, more than two years' worth of income to me. I wondered if it had been stolen the previous night.

I opened my master's last will and testament, thinking it might contain some clue to his final dilemma. But it looked like no will I'd ever heard of: There was not a single word written upon the sheet. Instead, a rough map of the region had been drawn there, with half a dozen little sketches to illustrate points of interest upon it. There was an owl in a tree, and a bull with a crown, and various other subjects. It looked as much like the scribbles of a child playing at pirate maps as anything else. My poor master must have lost his wits and taken to doodling. I was disappointed, although I knew not why. I expected no benefit from the will—and indeed could not lay any claim to it if there was any, now that I was a fugitive.

I could scarcely think what to do next, recalling my master's final words—how should I ever forget a single detail of that disastrous night? He had said I was to meet a witch. The mere idea of this stood the hairs on my neck straight up. The witch was probably a figment of his mind, but in any case the farther into the trees I went, the safer it was. So I continued in that direction, leading Midnight.

It was a dark, atmospheric place, reeking of damp, the air spongy with fog. Hoarse birds argued in the treetops and nothing at all stirred below. Demon walked for a while, but got to panting—his face was quite folded in on itself—so I placed him back in the saddlebag.

My thoughts were as gloomy as the woods all around.

Miles seemed to crawl beneath us, and the forest became ever more silent and airless. We found the half-overgrown vestiges of a road, and followed it. Then we passed through the remains of an ancient village, little roofless stone houses green with moss, chimneys rotted away like bad teeth. Trees grew up through some of the houses. My flesh prickled. Midnight was anxious with his steps, like a dance master with his shoes on the wrong feet. If I had some instinct of being watched before, now it seemed certain: At the corner of my sight I saw a flicker of motion now and again, and there came stealthy sounds from behind the broken walls of the abandoned houses. It might have been men, or wolves, or my imagination, but I was terribly afraid.

We drew alongside the last wreckage of the village. Demon poked his head out of the saddlebag behind me and began growling. Something was amiss. Then, as we passed by the final ruin, it was as if Midnight's foot had tripped some hidden snare. There came a vibration in the ground beneath us, and a moment later I heard a deep, hoarse voice ring out. I would have thought it issued from a bear, except bears don't cry:

"By the Duchess, take him!"

After the events of the previous night I had thought nothing would ever frighten me again. This was incorrect: I was stricken with terror once more. Midnight capered and whinnied, and Demon screeched as fiercely as he could. We heard the clatter of arms, and a moment later terrible apparitions emerged from the shadows all about. Had they been bandits, I would have taken fright enough, but they were worse than the most dreadful cutthroat.

The things that surrounded us were stout and fiercely ugly, with squat, batlike heads mounted directly on their shoulders. Their ears were enormous, like worm-eaten cabbage leaves. Yellow eyes goggled out of green faces. These fiends were clad in armor of leather and iron links, a thousand years out of date. They raised jagged, toothy spears in a gleaming ring. Midnight flailed his hooves at them and I clung to the rearing animal's neck, wild with fear.

When I was a small boy I didn't hear the old wives' tales and legends with which nursemaids and mothers beguile their children. But I'd seen many a fantastical play performed when I was with the circus. Mummers' plays* and allegories were always popular with the public, teeming as they were with grotesquely costumed devils and angels and mythological beings. Part of my mind was convinced I had stumbled into an exceptionally realistic performance of one of these plays. But I could *smell* these monsters. Their teeth were not made of painted wood, nor their eyes of papier-mâché. Though every particle of my brain denied it, they were real.

Then an even more terrible brute stepped through the spears. It wore a filthy kilt girt up with an iron buckle. Otherwise it was clad only in matted black hair—everywhere except atop its knobby, boarlike skull. A pair of brown tusks rose up from its jaw.

This monster belched a further command. *"Tercio in'ards!"*

I thought this was the command to disembowel us, but the pikesmen stepped back into a square, forming a sort of cage. Their hairy leader drew from his rawhide belt a tremendous black war-hammer. It was all I could do to keep Midnight from throwing himself in panic onto the spears that surrounded us, and Demon was struggling to leap free of the saddlebag and join the defense.

I drew my sword—a useless gesture against such a massive opponent—and then something uncanny happened. The weird greenish atmosphere around us grew yellow. The golden sword hilt was radiating light as if it were burning hot, but the metal felt no different in my hand. I hadn't a moment to wonder at this—there was action to be taken right away.

The squat creatures were stumbling back from the golden blaze, so I spurred Midnight around to charge through their ranks. Even as I did so, several spears came up, resisting the light. It seemed my great horse must impale himself—when there came a brilliant emerald-green flash, composed of a million tiny fragments

---

* Mummers' plays are a very old dramatic form featuring dialogue spoken in rhyming couplets. They are often performed around Christmas by roving players. A central element in these plays is the death and resurrection of a primary character.

of fire, like powdered suns. In an instant, the monsters were all thrown back into the woods, even the largest one. The shaggy thing was hurled against a tree, and the heavy branches shook like beaten carpets.

Midnight didn't break his stride—he charged straight over the writhing creatures. But the haft of a spear flew up and struck me in the head, and whatever happened next, I missed it.

Chapter 6

THE WRONG HIGHWAYMAN'S TASK

I AWOKE WITH a start. My head was dangling downward so that all I saw was upside down. I was hanging off the saddle across Midnight's back. It could only have been a few moments later—I still held my sword, and Demon was in the saddlebag—but we seemed to have traveled miles. The trees here were entirely different, and the ruined village was gone, along with its ghastly inhabitants. Midnight had apparently saved us all— but how, I could not imagine. We were in a high, cool place, with rocky hills behind and the forest below.

There was a beehive-shaped stone hut built in the lee of the nearest rocks. I dragged myself upright, and felt a tremendous bolt of pain in my head. Like a fool I tried to shake off the daze, and it felt as if my brain were loose inside my skull.

"Garn wi' ye!" crowed a high, cracked voice. "Yer ain't Jack!"

My eyes flew open, and I saw double. But then the two tiny, hunched figures before me resolved into one, and I was looking at a bundle of rags with a head like a dried gourd poking out of it. She had one age-fogged eye and a sort of milky blue stone in the other socket.

"Pardon me?" I said, which seemed the most ridiculous possible thing to say.

"What done ye wi' Jack?" the little creature piped.

"I'm sorry, who are you?" I quavered.

"Yer on 'ees 'orse, and them's 'ees clothes. But tha ain't 'ee."

"Are you speaking of my master, James Rattle?"

"Whistlin' Jack to me and all," the creature said. "But wait— you his servant-boy be?"

"Yes. I'm Kit."

"And where be yer master?"

"I'm afraid he's dead," I said.

"Dead, says 'ee," the witch muttered. "And you here in his stead."

"I came because he told me to seek you out," I said. "It was his last request. I am to give you his dog."

"Aaarn," the witch said. "'Ee were a scalawag and precious unreliable, so thought I. But the task lay heavy on 'is shouldern. It turned 'im wild these past months—and now this."

"What task?" I asked, surprised to hear my master had had any kind of job to do. Idleness had been his chief occupation, as far as I knew.

The witch ignored my question. "'Ow died 'ee?" she asked, squinting at me with her cloudy eye.

"Shot by bandits," said I. "They pursued me, for I was disguised as my master—as you can see—and I drew them away. But Master Rattle died while I rode out. There were soldiers, as well, and a rather determined captain who wants my head, and I escaped in a green flash and later on ran into these repulsive monsters with pikes and things, and there was another green flash, and now I'm here. Does any of that make sense to you? It doesn't to me."

My head whirled—not just from the blow, but from the memories of horrors that swarmed up before me. I felt ill.

"Goblings, the short 'uns. The large 'n were a troll. They would have cut 'ee ter ribbons nor I cast upon them."

"So the green fire was yours? You took a terrible risk," I said.

The whole idea was so bizarre I could only look at it from a practical standpoint, or my very mind would fall apart.

"Magda's exiled, is I," said the witch. "Nor in the First Realm nor in the Middle Kingdom dwells I, but betwixt the twain. They can't tetch me, but I can tetch them when they're betwixt like me. So they was when they come for you, boyo. Nor I tetched 'em. But now—they'll be a seekin' of ye."

"Goblings," said I, baffled. "Is that the same as goblins?"

"Dorn't be a fool," the old witch snorted. "Goblins are *imarginary* creturs. Goblings is arthentic, as 'ee seen fer thyself."

Goblins were imaginary, goblings authentic. Also trolls. Somehow this hadn't clarified matters. My bafflement was complete, and besides, the saddle felt as if it were floating in the sky. I wasn't entirely well in the head and our conversation wasn't improving this condition.

I dismounted on unsteady legs from my brave horse, and leaned against him until my mind cleared. Everything that had happened after that first flash of green fire must be imarginary, I thought. But if I was sprawled at the crossroads with Captain Sterne's sword through my breastbone and this was all a dying vision, so be it. Best to remain tranquil and carry on.

Remembering I had uncompleted business, I fumbled the saddlebag open and drew out the bewildered little dog.

"Here's Demon," I said, and put the animal on the ground. "A bequest from my master."

To my surprise, he trotted straight over to the witch, smelled her frayed hems, and then sat down beside her, regarding me placidly. They seemed to know each other.

"I sorrow fer yer loss," the witch said, tickling Demon's jowls. "Now boyo: Yer master, Whistling Jack or Master Rattle as might be, 'ee had a compact with I, and I with 'ee. There were a piece of business need doing this very next night, and when I saw 'ee with my scrying stone"—here she tapped the stone eye—"I thinks, 'It's Jack,' thinks I, 'atangle with goblins!' This were a surprise to me, becarn Jack knew better nor to ride straight through a gobling checkpost. So I rescued 'ee. But you ain't Jack. So now it's 'ee must complete Jack's business."

"Me?" I gasped. "I can't do anything for you! I mean no offense, but I am not familiar with goblings and witchcraft, ma'am."

The witch seemed to grow larger before my eyes. Her wizened face twisted with wrath, and the stone in her eye socket glowed with a bloodless light. She rose up like a crow spreading its wings, and roared, "Ye'll do what's told by the Eldritch Law! Fifth verse o' the second chapter: 'What's left to be done will be finished by the next hand.' Thou art the next hand."

"I'm bound by magical law?" None of this could be real. I must have been dreaming in a ditch somewhere, or perhaps I'd gone mad from drinking too much tea the previous day.

"It's no dream!" spat the witch as if reading my mind, which she might very well have been doing. All at once she was just a small, ragged old woman again, the looming apparition gone.

She began hobbling back and forth along the stone ridge, and talked to herself awhile.

"A stroke of luck, says I. This young 'un be a better man.

"Oh, but 'ee got no experience! 'Ee don't know how to do the task.

"Aye, but more there be to 'im than what ye sees.

"It's a terrible risk, it is! What if he fail?

"Then die he will, and she along with 'ee, and there's a black end to the business.

"If die she does, then doom we face.

"If she don't get away we be doomed regardless.

"I likes it not at all, says I.

"Nor I, but 'ee's a better man nor his marster."

I stood by while she argued with herself, collecting my wits. My master had begged me not to take his side, back at the Manse. Now I understood why. He'd been trying to spare me from electing myself unwittingly to this mysterious task. How had *he* come by it? Had he met this withered crone on one of his moonlit rides, or was she some distant auntie he'd failed to mention?

I knew he was sorely troubled by the witch's commission, although he was as capable as any man. So it was a difficult task. He'd warned me not to intervene. But I could have done no different than I did. I was there by obligation.

As an Englishman, I firmly believed that before I was servant to anyone else, I was master of myself. Let the old woman tell me what she had in store, and if it were something I could hope to accomplish, such as purchasing wrinkle ointment or getting a cat out of a tree, I would do it. If it were an impossible job, I would refuse. That was fair. If only I could be bored again!

At last she seemed to have decided how to proceed. She limped up to me and stuck a gnarled finger in my chest as high as she could reach. "Ye'll do, boyo. There's a fine coach upon the road, a coach decked all in silver. Encharnted, it is. Silver's the witching metal. Gold's man-metal: it repels the Folk Between, the Faeries. Tha' be why them goblings were afeared when you drew out your sword wi' its golden basket. Gold don't afear me, as I'm betwixt the twain. But they likes it not. So it is. The coach is all in silver, and drawn by silver 'orses wi' cloven hooves, and upon it two terrible coachmen, and within it a young woman." She ran out of breath and gasped like a trout.

I couldn't imagine where this was headed.

The witch got her wind back and continued: "Yer master's tarsk were to rescue the lady from within that there coach. Now it be *thy* task, boyo."

"It certainly isn't," I spluttered, refusing the job. "I'm not involved with your scheme, and I'm not bound by your Eldritch Law. I don't even believe in Faeries. You hired a highwayman experienced in this sort of work. I'm merely a servant who can ride, but not much else. I'd get myself killed at the very least, and probably this woman, as well."

I felt I was being reasonable, under the circumstances. But the witch spat on the ground with such violence that one of her few teeth shot out.

"Larst me wishin' tooth!" she hissed. "Told 'ee, I did," she added to herself. "'Ee ain't got the courage nor skill."

"I suppose you're right," I admitted.

The witch had another of her internal arguments, none of which I could understand. Then, "Narn!" she cried, which apparently meant "no."

"Ain't a questern of whether ye wants the job or nor—turn thy back on it and ye'll be dead as yer marster in less than a wax o' the moon, I promise 'ee tha'. Many a mortal man be found dead on the roadside becarn he made pledge wi' a Faerie and din't keep 'ees promise! And many o' them died for the vow of another. This be magic. Turn yer back on it and tha steps into thy grave."

At any other time in my life, I would have ridden away without another word, because the woman was clearly mad, even if she did know about goblings and trolls. But I had seen such wonders that day, and witnessed such phantasms all about me, that I believed her threat was genuine. Besides, it was clear that denials would only prolong this unpleasant interview.

Then a thought occurred to me which put everything in a fresh perspective. Of *course* Magda was mad, as mad as an ormolu maker. And because of the blow to my head, or Captain Sterne's sword, or some bad sausage, I was also mad, or had been until now. But I'd regained my senses sufficiently to realize there was no harm in agreeing to take up my master's business with the old witch. There couldn't *possibly* be a silver coach with a young woman in need of rescue within. It was silly.

So I raised my hand and said, "I solemnly swear to do what you ask."

She peered at me with her one eye, and somehow although it was as dim as a dead fish's, I had a feeling she was reading my very thoughts like a penny broadside. But she didn't remark on it. The promise, it seemed, was sufficient.

"Find 'ee the coach on the moonlit road," said she, "and stop it 'ow 'ee will. Take not a farthing of treasure, no matter how much nor the accursed postilion offer to give 'ee, but set the lady free. Succeed, and yer reward shall be what I agreed wi' yer master. Fail, and the next moon shines uparn yer tombstone."

"I ask no reward," said I, nobly.

"Yer'll take it and likes it," she said.

Although I still didn't believe the task could be genuine, some part of me was worried. I thought of my master's behavior the past few weeks: The very thought of it had set him to pacing and fretting, beset by worries. What if there *was* a coach, drawn by cloven-footed horses? If it was a difficult job for Whistling Jack, the dauntless highwayman, the exploit would likely prove impossible for me.

Still, I must make the attempt, for I had given my word. I could wait a few hours behind a tree somewhere, and if the coach didn't come, I was free to go. If it did somehow turn up, bad luck for me.

"Where's this moonlit road?" I asked.

"Beneath thy feet," said the witch.

There was no apparent motion or passage of time, yet in the next moment Midnight and I were standing in the middle of a deeply rutted dirt road, speckled with moonlight that splashed down through the trees. It had been daylight, and now it was night. Magda was gone, the hillside was gone, and before us was the far edge of the forest, with open country beyond. I heard a distant, echoing yodel—a farewell cry from Demon—and then there was silence.

Something was clasped in my hand. I opened it, and found upon my palm Magda's spat-out tooth. With a cry I flung it away. Then I mounted unsteadily, my mind stunned with shock, and Midnight took me down the road. He seemed to know where to go, which was useful, because I scarcely knew whether I even rode at all.

Chapter 7

THE OWL AT THE CROSSROAD

MY THOUGHTS grew morbid upon the road. Any bush I passed might conceal that Captain Sterne, or those bandits, or these gibbering goblings. Or Magda herself might be lurking up a tree waiting to smite me with green fire. For the first time, I knew fear of the dark. Every shadow was a crouching monster, every branch a grasping claw, every twig a bayonet. I had scarcely the courage to ride down the lane—how could I gather the mettle to rob an enchanted coach of its passenger?

I had more or less convinced myself to abandon the old witch's task, and instead to flee the country as soon as I could find a change of clothes that didn't mark me for a highwayman. Midnight's chalk blaze I'd rubbed off earlier; it was surprising how much this little detail changed the appearance of the entire animal. I, however, still matched the description of a wanted man, even with the mask in my pocket instead of across my eyes.

I let the horse walk slowly—he was more weary than I. We emerged from the forest into moonlight that seemed bright enough to read by after the darkness under the trees. The road was empty at that hour, and no sign of human habitation stood nearby. Ahead I spied a place where we could rest awhile.

It was a derelict churchyard down a crooked lane, within sight of a crossroad marked by an enormous, gnarled oak tree. The church itself bore a short, square tower at one end, the top broken off as if struck by a giant hand, and the whole almost swallowed up with brambles. It might have seemed picturesque if I'd been in a better humor, and if it hadn't been the witching hour.

I found the old oaken door standing open, nearly rotted away. Midnight went inside readily enough, and within was rude shelter. Half of the roof remained to blot out the stars. We were entirely alone, unless one counted the hundreds of tombs jumbled together in the overgrown yard beside the church. In the darkness they reminded me of the slope-shouldered goblings.

My intention had been to rest, but now I could not sleep. Magda's curious warning rang in my ears. I'd live a month, if the curse lasted from moon to moon. But such things were all nonsense! She had been trying to frighten me. There could be no lady, no silver coach! I stood in the doorway of the church and looked out upon the crossroad. That is when a large owl alighted silently in the oak, and a cold hand of fear clapped itself around my heart—for *I recognized the scene.*

My master's will contained a drawing of an owl in just such a tree! Despite my superstitious fears, or perhaps because of them, I advanced toward it. The great bird sat on an upper branch and regarded me with enormous, gleaming eyes. I was seized by the urge to throw rocks at it—the creature looked so smug. Its troubles were limited to the supply of field mice, while I was beset by disaster on all sides.

But as I was contemplating the owl, there came a noise from the nearest hedge: Men were walking along the ditch, speaking in low voices to each other. I cursed myself for a fool, standing out there in the open as I was. The men would emerge onto the road before I could escape back to the concealment of the church. They would surely see me by the moonlight. I heard the distinct scrape of a sword being drawn from its sheath. It might be bandits or soldiers; whichever, it was nobody good for me.

Heart leaping, I clambered up into the branches of the tree, the only place of concealment near to me. I climbed until my coat-tails didn't hang down where anyone could see them, and crouched upon a thick limb, as still and silent as I could.

"Did you hear that?" a voice said, perilous near. "In the tree."

The owl gave me a quizzical look, hooted softly, and then spread its wings and rowed away into the night sky.

"'Tis but a rat catcher!" said a second voice.

Two men emerged from the shadow of the hedge. They made a most extraordinary pair. One of them might possibly have been five feet tall, if he stood on an ant-hill; the other was a giant. He would not have fit through the door of the old church. But the man's head was hardly larger than his own fist. Even by moonlight he didn't look very clever. He need not be clever to operate a club, however, and he carried a tremendous wooden staff that I doubt I could have lifted off the ground.

The shorter man wore hip-height boots—all boots were hip-height to him—a brace of pistols, and a very long coat that nearly brushed the ground, giving him the look of a child dressed up in his father's clothes. But he was the indisputable leader of the pair.

"D___ that owl," he said, and added a few more maledictions. Then he turned his attention to the road. "The carriage of what we have got wind is to come down the forest road, there. We shall wait in amongst them bushes. You come out in front of the horses and I'll come out behind the footman, but wait until the signal."

"What is the signal?" the giant asked in a booming cistern of a voice.

"The same signal as always, you clot."

"Oh," said the giant. There was a pause, during which crickets fiddled and a light breeze soughed across the fields. Then the giant continued. "The same as what?"

The short man scrubbed his face with both hands, grinding back a palpable fury. "The problem with you," he said, "is that you're too small. Your brain is too small and you are too delicate for this kind of work. One must be of rippling brain and massive in size as I am, in order to rule the highway. There's a reason they call me Giant Jim, and there's a reason you're only my gang."

Now I understood it. Giant Jim was among the thieves specifically named in the royal proclamation. By now, both of them stood directly beneath me; the large man was *so* large the point of his hat nearly brushed my boot-heels.

"What if," said the large man, after he'd spent some more time thinking, "you hide up in amongst this tree?"

My blood ran cold—when he pointed into the tree his enormous hand nearly toppled me from my branch. Luckily, Giant Jim did not look up. Instead he kicked the real giant's shin.

"How dare you! Mutiny, I call it! This little sapling couldn't bear my tremendous weight. No, we conceals ourselves in those bushes, and springs out in the order described upon the signal aforenamed."

"The same signal as always."

"Yes."

"Which is what?"

Giant Jim threw his cocked hat upon the ground—a brief trajectory—and danced upon it, hurling vile curses at his companion. Once the frenzy abated, he snarled, "I shout 'get them' and you get them."

It seemed as good a signal as any to me; but then, I wasn't really a highwayman.

The two bandits went to their positions down the road, a great relief to me. I could still smell the stink of the giant, which had filled the space inside the tree. Had I been detected, that mighty club would surely have killed me with a single blow. But now I was well and truly stuck. I could not descend from the tree without being observed, and although I might be able to outrun their legs, I couldn't outrun a pistol-ball. So I carefully changed my position (my legs had fallen asleep), drew out the mask and tied it about my face to make me harder to spy in the tree, and prepared myself to wait it out. I hoped Midnight would remain quietly inside the church, the broken spire of which was not very distant.

Now, mad things had been happening, so it was not a great surprise when I began to think I could hear voices in the tree with me. They were very small voices, as if two men were speaking from far away; but unless my ears deceived me, they were coming from somewhere inside the canopy of the tree, a few feet above me. I couldn't quite make out what the voices were saying, but it sounded like an argument. It might have been a trick of the night air. Or insanity.

Then a new sound came, of horse's hooves and the creaking and rattling of a fine coach, and I forgot the voices. A terrible fear overcame me—here I was up in a tree, dressed as a highwayman, with pistols and sword and a commission to rob a coach and kidnap its passenger. What if this was the very coach? Or worse, a magistrate on his way home from a late game of cards?

The terror was still with me when I saw a team of six horses emerge from the forest, and there behind it was the coach on the moonlit road. There could be no mistake: This was the one of which Magda had spoken, the very coach I was required by some magical treaty to do my worst upon. Its green sidelights swayed, revealing glimpses of pale metal trimmings and the outline of a tall, thin postilion driving at the front. The moonlight fell upon ornate carvings on wheels and cabin. The horses were silvery. I saw a heavy bull-whip in the hand of the postilion; he scourged the horses without mercy. Within a minute, the vehicle had come to the place where the two bandits were hidden. I thought I might faint.

There was a cry of "Get them!" and Giant Jim leapt from his hiding place, pistols drawn. "I said 'get them,'" he repeated. A moment later, the actual giant lumbered out of the bushes and stood squarely in front of the speeding carriage. He was nearly cut down, so close did they come. The horses reared and clawed, and I saw that they did indeed have cloven hooves, as those of goats. It also appeared they had sharp teeth, like wolves' fangs, and they didn't so much whinny as bark. The giant waved his club at them and they backed away from him, almost crushing Giant Jim.

"Get down with you," Giant Jim commanded, and waved his pistols at the footman and driver as they climbed down from the coach.

"You'll suffer for this," the postilion said. He didn't sound the least bit afraid, but rather like a man delayed by a broken martingale buckle.

"Shut your gob, you miniature mannckin!" Giant Jim said. The postilion was at least two feet taller than him. I suspected the bandit was laboring under some kind of delusion.

"We should cooperate with these gentleman, Mr. Bufo," said the postilion.

"Yes, Mr. Scratch," the footman replied. He was a heavy, barrel-shaped fellow with a startlingly flat head beneath his too-small periwig. They took up positions at the doors on each side of the coach.

I wondered if they were guarding its passenger from the bandits, or guarding against the passenger's escape. I knew nothing of the circumstances of my own mission, of course, except that a kidnapping was required. I didn't even know if the lady *wanted* to be kidnapped, or if she knew of the plan. But to be this close to the coach I was supposed to rob—my pulses throbbed enough to make me see spots. So far, everything Magda had said, no matter how peculiar, had come true.

If these other bandits got the result I was supposed to achieve, would I be released from my duty? And if they got their hands on the lady, what evil might befall her? I began to understand why the old witch had not been enthusiastic about employing my master. Highwaymen were not to be trusted.

Giant Jim swaggered up to Mr. Bufo. "You down there," he said, looking up. "Take out the luggage."

The footman bowed, his wig clinging to the top of his head like a flatfish to a rock. Then he opened the coach door and handed out a carved wooden chest upon which silver mountings gleamed. I saw on the door of the coach a curious device, of serpents intertwined with insect's wings, all wrought upon a silver crest.

"What's in the box?" Giant Jim demanded.

"A fortune in silver and jewels," Mr. Scratch replied.

"Silver and jewels," Mr. Bufo added. His voice was a croaking thing, wet and low.

"Open it or I'll crush you beneath my enormous boot," Giant Jim said.

All this time, my mind had been racing. When the footman opened the coach door, I strained my eyes to see inside the compartment, to no avail. How could I rescue the lady within? If she was in danger from the peculiar servants, she was in more danger from these criminals. But at this moment, with Mr. Bufo's hand upon the lock of the chest, a new voice was added to the scene.

"*Levantar los manos!*" it cried, and when nothing happened, "Raise your hands."

A man dressed in a bullfighter's costume revealed himself. He had been hiding behind a fence across the way. He was a rather threadbare-looking fellow, very thin, with black mustaches that hung past his chin. In his hands was a blunderbuss or espingole, a gun capable of firing several balls at one shot. He kept the entire party covered as he advanced.

"Place down *las armas* upon the ground," he said. "*Pronto.*"

"You wants us to raise our hands and lower our arms? It's impossible," Giant Jim said.

"Your weep-ons of danger," the stranger clarified. Giant Jim and his accomplice dropped theirs, and the postilion laid down his whip.

"I yam Don Pinto, the Spanish Desperado," the man said, grandly. "At your servants. You will to me give the chest of money, and I will away with it go."

"We were here first," Giant Jim complained.

The bandits started to argue among themselves. There seemed to be an understanding that gentlemen of the road in Britain didn't interrupt each other's conquests. The Spaniard disagreed, saying there was no such custom in his country.

Mr. Scratch interrupted after a few exchanges, practically hopping with impatience. "We have a schedule to keep," he hissed. "There lies the extent of our wealth; take it if you dare, and allow us to be gone, sirs, or I shall not be responsible for the consequences."

This speech stopped the bandits in mid-argument. "It is mine," the Desperado said, and bade Mr. Bufo open the casket. Up came the lid.

Within was a dazzling heap of bright silver coins and ornaments, the latter richly adorned with jewels that struck the eye: red, green, purple, and blue stones that seemed to treble the moonlight upon them, dancing with color. I cared nothing for that stuff, pretty as it was, but it so impressed the bandits that they quite forgot their quarrel, encircling the treasure. The moment their eyes were off him, Mr. Scratch raised a hunting horn to his lips and blew a single note, loud enough to stir the leaves of my tree.

In a trice the Desperado brought his blunderbuss around, but the very next moment a strange cloud descended upon him, and he and the other bandits were screaming and flailing the air as if they'd stepped in a wasps' nest. I saw flickering green lights encircling their heads, and then they were running for their lives pell-mell through the dark landscape.

The servants wasted not another second, but threw the chest back inside the cabin and leapt to their positions on front and back of the coach. Mr. Scratch slashed at the weird horses with his whip, and they were rolling directly beneath my perch in the tree a few moments later.

I hadn't the faintest idea what had befallen the bandits, who continued to flee screaming across ditch and field, but what befell me next was clear enough. A wee voice directly beside my ear said, "Now's your chance," and I was so affrighted I fell off my branch and landed on the roof of the accursed coach.

Chapter 8

RESCUE, AFTER A FASHION

LILY WOULD not have approved of my acrobatic skill. I fell through the branches in a great shower of leaves and landed facedown on the very cabin of the coach, knocking the wind out of my lungs, the hat off my head, and my teeth together. I hadn't an instant to collect myself before a powerful fist closed around my ankle and Mr. Bufo was dragging me toward him.

His eyes were set almost on the sides of his low skull, and when he opened his mouth his whole head seemed to hinge wide like a snuffbox. He looked more like one of Magda's goblings than a man.

"Another one," he croaked.

"Kill him," said Mr. Scratch, not even looking back. For my part, I had not been idle; I was gripping the silver top-rail around the roof of the coach with one hand, and with the other trying to pry the footman's fingers loose. Even in my alarm I could not help noticing the man had only three thick fingers and a thumb, and they were as fast around my leg as leg-irons. Then he shook me loose and threw me over his shoulder as if I were a handkerchief.

He hadn't reckoned on the general anxiety I felt for my own

welfare, however. Rather than tumble to the road as intended, I threw out my hands and caught Mr. Bufo's silver-bullion collar in the midst of my flight. His wig flew into my face. My boot-toes scraped along the road as I hung from the man's neck, and his limbs were so thick and overmuscled, he could not reach back to disengage me while maintaining his hold on one of the handles at the back of the cabin.

The coach rumbled to a halt, and I released my grip, alighting on the road. I fumbled one of my pistols out, cocked it, and raised it in time for Mr. Bufo to wrest it from my grasp.

"Have at you," I cried, and drew my sword. The handle flamed yellow again, and I fancied the footman showed a little hesitation, at last. But then a dark blur whistled out of the darkness above the coach, and the sword was torn from my fingers. It sang through the air and was lost. My hand stung as if burned. Mr. Scratch mounted the roof of the coach, recoiling his bullwhip for a second stroke. Now I saw what had happened, but it was too late to devise another defense.

Sometimes, in the midst of turmoil and crisis, we catch a glimpse of the reward for struggling on, and it renews our determination with hope. So it was, with the murderous whip seething through the air, that I was rewarded by a vision. The door on my side of the coach peeped open and a slim figure emerged. It was a lady, dressed in some dark stuff. Our eyes met. She seemed to give off her own light, a portrait in a stained-glass window.

Time slowed until the world was drowned in honey; every second was an eternity. At first I saw only her eyes, green as gemstones, fringed with black lashes in a pale olive face. Her dark hair sparkled. Then it was as if I had tumbled *into* her eyes, and I was surrounded by scenes of strange pageantry, heard glorious songs in languages beyond comprehension, and marveled at purple oceans arching through a star-cast sky, tossed by scented winds upon which rode strange winged creatures. I saw a castle clad in silver that hung in empty darkness with its curving ramparts thrust upward and downward alike, floating like a cloud. And somehow I knew these things had been witnessed by the lady herself. Once again I saw her glimmering face. She half smiled, threw a cloak about her, and fairly vanished before my eyes.

At that moment, with time still passing sluggishly, I had occasion to reflect: This, surely, was the woman I had been entreated to rescue. With her flight from the coach, my debt to master and witch was paid. Events gathered speed around me, and I was enough renewed to fling myself out of the way of the whip-stroke into the dark beside the road. There, with time running again at its usual pace, I collided with a tombstone in the overgrown churchyard.

I had hurled myself in the opposite direction to that which the lady had taken. Mr. Bufo was already trundling after me, and I had little fight in me to make good my escape. But then, for the third time, a ring of sparkling green flame appeared around me. The footman was dazzled sightless for a few precious seconds, and Mr. Scratch fell altogether off the roof of the coach. There was a drumming of hooves, and Midnight came galloping into the circle of light. I threw myself bodily into the saddle as he surged past.

Whether the servants pursued me farther, or whether they discovered their passenger had fled, I did not learn at that time; instead, I rode as fast as Midnight could take me, hysterical with fear, until neither myself nor the horse could go another step.

We were in an area miles distant from the scenes of horror I'd witnessed before, with small shadowed hills and stony brooks chuckling between them, when at last we stopped. The moon was down and the prosperous town in the dell below us showed only a few dim lights. I guided the poor shivering horse along a track that ran away from the road, and when we found a tumbledown barn, we made our beds in it. I set Midnight's sweat-soaked tack to dry, rubbed his flanks down with straw, and then we both lay in a pile of rotten hay, too spent to move even if an entire regiment were marching our way.

I was well on the road to sleep when I heard whispering.

It was the tiny voices again. As you can imagine, I was instantly awake. But I did not stir so much as a finger, instead lying there in the darkness with my eyes closed, listening. The voices were moving in a straight line above me, as if the speakers were walking along a rafter. They spake in such small tones I could hear but the occasional word.

At length, they seemed to be directly above my head, and I heard one of them say, "Then I'll do it," and there was a papery clatter. I opened my eyes and looked up into the inky darkness, my fingers closing around the grip of my remaining pistol.

There was another clatter, and the entire barn lit up with a bright green glow like sunlight through spring grass.

There, at the very source of the light, was a tiny man. Or rather, an insect shaped like a man, for he fluttered on quick transparent wings. I must have cried out, because no sooner had the light come up than it went out again.

"Who goes there?" I shouted in a high-pitched voice.

"Don't shoot, Whistling Jack," the small voice said. It was the same one that had spoken into my ear up in the old oak tree.

"Show your light again," said I.

The tiny insect-man lit up again, this time near the roof, revealing great holes in the thatch. "You won't shoot?"

"I won't shoot," said I, because truly I could not hit so small a target. "Come down here."

It had been such a day that I was not intimidated by the sight of a miniature flying man. Why would there *not* be a miniature flying man? There had been everything else.

The little fellow flitted downward, following a wobbling trajectory like a large beetle. He was about as tall as my hand. He alighted on a wooden hayrack fixed to the wall; his light cast long shadows like prison bars through the staves of the rack. It was then I realized the light was coming from his bottom, which lit up like a firefly's. His britches seemed to possess a flap for that very purpose.

"I'm that nervous," he said. "Such a thrill to meet you."

"Me?" said I, bewildered.

"Whistling Jack the Highwayman? Word's already gotten about: You rescued HRH Princess Morgana and fought off half a dozen highwaymen for the privilege."

"That's not what happened," I protested. "You know that—you were there." And then, as I realized what he'd said: "Wait. *Princess?*"

"The Faerie King's daughter," said the tiny man, now seating himself comfortably on the top bar of the hayrack, bare feet crossed. "Didn't you know?"

"I don't know anything," said I, with feeling.

The wee creature still looked nervous, his doll-size eyes darting about. "I shouldn't be telling you all this. I shouldn't be telling you anything at all, for the matter of that. Never done such a thing in all my puff. It's in the Eldritch Law, eighth verse of the tenth chapter, 'Be not seen nor heard nor ever known by mortal man.'"

"Nor cast your comprimaunts before them," said a second voice. This one had a broad country accent. The speaker did not reveal himself.

"I did cast my comprimaunts before him, didn't I," the little man said with regret. "Anyway, I'm Willum, leader of the rebel Faerie army, and him up there in the shadows is Gruntle."

"And who's Gruntle?" I asked.

"He's the rebel Faerie army."

"I see," said I, seeing nothing but a tiny man with light streaming out of his backside. "What, pray, is a comprimaunt?"

Willum became concerned, his light flickering uncertainly. "Didn't Magda tell you all this?"

"She may have told my master," said I, "but she told me nothing at all. I'm merely a servant, you see, in Master Rattle's house. And he is, or was, for he has met his maker, also the highwayman called Whistling Jack—as I discovered but yesterday."

Willum shook his wings with alarm. "But your costume—your horse!"

"They belong to my master."

"So you have taken up the highwayman's mantle in his place! Brilliant!" The little man clapped his hands together.

I shook my head. "It was not my choice. As soon as I find some different clothes, I shall bury this highwayman's stuff beneath a stone and live a quiet life somewhere far away." It felt very strange to be talking to this small person with an illuminated posterior, overheard by his secretive friend in the hayloft, but I was—to my horror—rapidly becoming accustomed to it.

"You can't be finished," Willum said, and his light grew dim. "This is the beginning of the revolution, I tell you. You're the secret to our success."

I stood up and brushed damp straw off myself. Midnight bent his neck around to watch what was happening. He didn't seem at all put out by the tiny apparition.

"I'm Kit," said I. "Christopher Bristol, indentured servant to Master James Rattle, and before that indentured to Fortescue Trombonio, impresario. Why I'm dressed like this and how I came to be tangled in this business with the Princess I can hardly explain, for I hardly understand it. That's my entire story. Now, what is yours?"

Chapter 9

A ROYAL WEDDING FORETOLD

I T'S LIKE this," said Willum. "Gruntle and myself are feyín*, which is a type of Faerie. All magical creatures are Faeries. We are now in the First Realm, that being the human world. But we are from the Middle Kingdom, which regulates the natural part of the First Realm. On the other side there's the Realm Beyond, which is where the Elden are, and we have no more to do with that dark world than manlings have to do with ours."

"But I have to do with your world!" I exclaimed. "I was surrounded by goblings and so forth, and met that witch, and now you."

"No, that all happened here in your world. We only pop in and out for periods of time. Except Magda. She dwells here. It's her what coordinated the rescue mission. She'd like to get back, you see, and she's most unhappy with the king. Elgeron, he is. King of Faerie. We planned the whole thing by bee."

---

* *Feyín* is an approximate rendering of the original *feþyn*, in which the thorn character (þ) represents a voiceless palatal fricative about halfway between "sh" and "th," sounded close to the base of the teeth. Borrowed from the Faeries themselves, it may originally have been the source for the Old English *fæcce*, pronounced "fethch" or "fetch"; by Shakespeare's time the species distinction was lost, and all magical folk were described by mortals as *fey* or *Faerie*, much as in modern speech.

I dwelled upon these words for a while, my thoughts illuminated by bottom-light.

"Allow me to summarize," said I. "Please correct me on any point. Faeries include you lot with the glowing bums along with other, different creatures. Goblings and trolls and whatnot. That old witch hired my master to rescue the Princess, but he died, so I had to rescue the Princess instead to fulfill his bargain, which I did."

"Exactly," said Willum, and brightened up quite literally.

"Why did I have to rescue the Princess?"

"Well, she's Princess Morgana ne Dé Danann Trolkvinde Arian yn Gadael ou Elgeron-Smith, she is. Lady of the Realm, Keeper of the Silver Leaves, Duchess of Springtime, daughter and only heir of King Elgeron. And her father arranged a marriage for her. She's supposed to get hitched to some hapless Hanoverian halfwit from the human herd to cement a political alliance."

"Are you telling me," I said, "that George William Frederick, grandson of King George II*, is to marry a Faerie princess?"

"It's absurd, isn't it?"

Absurd was hardly a strong enough word. "Why, though?" I asked. "Why would a human royal marry such a—"

"Such a what," Willum said, springing to his feet, ready to take offense. He put up raisin-sized fists.

"—Such a dream of beauty?" I concluded. And I meant it. She was a vision plucked from a reverie on a warm moonlit night. "After all," I added, "human kings and princes and so forth are the most worldly men alive. There's not a drop of magic in 'em, I should think."

---

* King George III (1738–1820), grandson of King George II, was English-born. He was a shy, conscientious man by most accounts, and his nearly sixty-year reign saw the rise and fall of the first British Empire. Although it is claimed he suffered from insanity caused by the congenital disease porphyria, in fact he was suffering from the effects of a Faerie curse, which is another story.

"Ah," Willum said, mollified. "And I see you're a fellow of quick insight. You have touched the very root of the source of the wellspring of our rebellion. Our King would see us turn our comprimaunts—that's our magical abilities—over to human endeavors, like manufacturing and agriculture."

"And war-making," Gruntle added, from a hiding place somewhat closer than before. "Manlings love war. I just like the unionforms."

"I see," I lied. "And you and Magda the witch plan to put a stop to all that, by rescuing the Princess."

"That's just the *first* step," Willum said. "But we need your help. You might not think of yourself as a highwayman, but you've got talent."

I ignored this, and asked, "Was it you that made the rings of green fire around me?"

"It was 'im," Gruntle said, and stepped into the light from a small gap between two boards.

Gruntle was clad in homespun and a shapeless cap; his wings stuck out to the sides, like those of a dragonfly. "'E broke eighth verse of chapter thingummy, did 'e. Cast witchfire all about you on no fewer than more than one occasion. And now I've broke the law as well by revealin' meself, and we'll both have our wings plucked for it."

"If it wasn't for my quick thinking back there he'd be dead, or worse," Willum said. "Some army you turned out to be, cowering in the bushes."

"Pleased to meet you at last," I said to Gruntle. He shyly tipped his hat.

"Princess Morgana didn't like our plan," Willum said, resuming his narrative. "She thought your master was the lowest kind of scoundrel, may his soul find the moon. But nobody else could do the job so well. Then someone—her father the King, I'll be bound—hired rival bandits to see your master never went through with it. That's when the Princess told us to watch out for him. She might not like rogues, but she's got a conscience. Apparently too late, for we watched out for you, instead. It's a rum go."

I wholeheartedly agreed. "In any case, your Princess is free. The task is done, and I'm finished with it. Thank you for saving my life."

Willum smote his open palm. "You're just what the Princess needs! An honest criminal, if I may be so bold. We must get her out of England before our King finds her and marries her off!"

"Nonsense," said I, and meant it. "Lots of people marry someone they don't much like. Whose business is that but their own? They're only a woman and a man after all, regardless of their royal blood!" Then I added, because I was getting worked up, "Besides, she's no Faerie. She hasn't got wings. She's not very tall, but she's as human as I am."

Willum looked around him as if he was about to say something quite tasteless. Then he whispered, loudly, "You're half right. Her mother was a human woman, you see, hence the 'Smith.' King Elgeron himself took a mortal wife, and she died in childbirth. But he got the Princess out of the bargain. Halfsies* can't fly nor cast many comprimaunts, but they sometimes have the deeper magic that comes from the Realm Beyond."

"That will do," said I. "Not another word."

"You're right, I've been telling shameful tales about our beloved Princess," Willum said, and removed his tiny cocked hat, the better to hang his head.

I decided not to explain it wasn't propriety bade me stop him: it was confusion. He was telling me gossip about a world that somehow lapped over my own, and secret engagements between royal persons, and besides he had wings. I felt certain I would be found in the morning, stark mad, bleating like a sheep. It was time to conclude this bizarre interview.

---

* "Halfsie" is a colloquial Faerie term for one of mixed human and magical blood. "Elf" means the same thing but is considered an appalling slur.

"It's been lovely talking with you," I said. "But it is time for me to sleep, and after daybreak I must go into the town and determine how far from this place I can go on the money I have. My role in your revolution has ended. Thank you very much for explaining things to me, and safe travels to the Princess. Best of luck with the revolution. Never speak to me again."

With that, I lay down in the straw once more, and put my hat over my eyes. The last thing I saw from beneath the brim was the pair of Faeries sitting side by side on the hayrack, looking absolutely dejected. Willum's light went out.

ℑ   ℑ   ℑ

I hadn't meant to sleep; at first I was only pretending, to keep them from bothering me any more. But at some point genuine sleep took me, and I did not awake until Midnight nuzzled me out of a chaotic dream of flying kings. He was standing in a beam of morning sunlight that streaked in through a hole in the barn wall. I stood up, stiff as a leg of mutton. My stomach growled at the thought of mutton. It was time to disguise myself somehow and see what news there was, and plan my escape.

Ordinary, nonmagical luck was with me. Propped in a dry corner of the barn I discovered a pair of scarecrows on poles, dressed in ragged old clothes. Although the garments were worn and shapeless, brown with dirt, I was able to assemble shirt, weskit, and trousers between the two. The trousers were of the sailor type, and fell over the red turndowns of my boots. Following a thick application of mud, the lower parts of the boots did not appear out of place on a peasant's feet.

I concealed all of Whistling Jack's gear beneath the hay, tied Midnight to a railing so that he would not wander off, and emerged from the barn looking for all the world like an impoverished tatterdemalion* living rough in the countryside. Which is precisely what I was, except for the poverty—I had fifty gold pieces concealed in my shirt. Thus prepared, I walked into the town I'd seen the previous night.

There were a few people on the road, most of them going to work in the fields or at a nearby felt-fullery. It was a blessed relief to see no soldiers about. I found a bakery in the street, and purchased a day-old loaf for a penny. My pennies were worth more than gold, in this particular situation: It would be very difficult for one who looked as poor as me to pass a gold coin without raising suspicion. That was why I bought the loaf day-old, as well—a pauper wouldn't buy new bread. I knew a good deal about poverty, having spent only two years out of it.

There was a peculiar incident when I got the penny from my pocket: What should I find beside it, but the old witch's tooth? It was a horrible yellow fang; there could be no mistaking it. How it got there I did not know, but as I left the bakery I threw the foul bone over the roof of the shop.

I ate the entire loaf of bread at one go, cramming fistfuls of it into my mouth and then dashing water down my throat from the river that ran past the town. Profoundly refreshed, I ventured deeper into the street and found a post-tavern named the Bull & Crown. There they would have newspapers and all the unprinted rumors, because post-taverns were where the mail coaches stopped, and so they served as informal hubs of information along their routes. And the name of the place—was this what the sketch by Master Rattle had meant? It might have been fate that drew me here, if I went in for that sort of thing.

It was busy inside the bar, because beer was the foundation of most breakfasts. I crowded to the board and thought of having a beer myself, but decided against it. People would talk about the

_____
* Tatterdemalion: raggedy fellow.

young beggar who could afford a half-pint. Instead I feigned to in-
quire after the price of a fare to London, claiming I was on an errand from a gentleman. It was perfectly common to use starvelings
for odd tasks such as carrying messages. The landlord retailed a
list of fares and the time of departure for the various coaches, and
I pretended to remember them. But all the while I had my ears
bent to the talk in the rest of the tavern. It was most edifying, although unhappy memories crowded my thoughts.

"Found shot through the heart," one man said. "Discovered
him in the kitchen, murdered by Whistling Jack. Not ten leagues
from here."

"So I heard," his companion said, smoking a Turk's head pipe.
"Word is they've captured a dozen desperate men already. They
nearly got Whistling Jack as well. They seen his black horse with
the white nose, and him battlin' his way through soldiers and rivals
alike. Fought like a devil and rode like the wind, they say."

I turned my attention to a couple of women with fish-baskets
who stood on my other side. "They say he lost his mind, they do,"
one clucked. "Giant Jim, it was, mad as an hatter. Captured him
wandering about in a field, and he went gentle despite his great
strength. He spoke only of the little elf-arrows, says Captain Sterne.
'Off to Tyburn with the banditti, regardless of their mental state,'
says he."

Captain Sterne! So he was still abroad in the land. It gave me a
thrill of alarum to think of that relentless fellow upon my trail.
There was good news, though: In none of the talk was any mention made of a bloodthirsty servant doing James Rattle in. Kit
Bristol and Whistling Jack were not associated, except by circumstance. I thanked the landlord and ducked outside again, elated
just to be alive. It was then, as I squinted in the bright morning and
began to think about my future, that a very ugly woman crossed
my path on the way to the town marketplace, and my fortunes
took another turn.

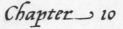

Chapter 10

LONG-SUFFERING RADISHES AND NEW CLOTHES

DRESSED AS a beggar and none too clean after all my adventures, I scarcely had reason to keep my head up. Nor did I want anyone to fix my features in their mind, in case an inquiry into Master Rattle's missing servant were made. So I tucked my chin into my chest and stepped into the street, eyes cast down. It was for this reason that I did not see the portly woman crossing before me until it was too late, and I collided with her. She let out a small cry and tumbled to the street, spilling large radishes from a basket. For my part, I fell across her, and the two of us struggled upon the ground. It must have been a comical sight, for a couple of red-faced gentlemen and a member of the clergy laughed heartily as they stepped over us.

I got as far as my knees, a string of regrettable words prepared for utterance just behind my teeth. I had no patience left. "Why did you not look—" I began, but the words perished on my lips when the woman's hood fell back and I beheld her face.

A good woman is no less good for suffering some deformity, and I'll credit myself for not judging people on that score—I've known many a handsome face behind which lurked an unattractive soul. There is no shame in ugliness, except what beauty lends it. But when I say that this woman was ugly, I mean she could have knocked the eyes out of a potato. I doubt the troll could have gazed upon her without fright. I am not proud to say I gasped aloud.

Her nose was that of a pig—a genuine snout, with large, flexible nostrils pointing straight forward, set the same distance apart as her tiny pink eyes. The swollen flesh of her face hung in folds, weeping sweat. The sweat ran down the creases in her cheeks and coursed around the warts that decorated her jowls. Brown-edged teeth protruded from between her lips like a fire-grate. I had never seen such a dreadful collection of features all gathered in one place for a common purpose.

"Good heavens," cried I, and clapped a hand across my mouth. She threw the hood back over her face, then scrabbled in the dirt to pick up her radishes. I did nothing to help, but leapt to my feet, shocked at the sight of her. The woman struggled upright—she was enormously beamish and could hardly walk—and hobbled away down the street with her head tucked between her shoulders.

Conscience often arrives too late, but never comes in vain.

As I stood there beside the tavern door trying to dust off my already filthy scarecrow clothes, I was overcome with shame. If that was my reaction to a brief glimpse of her, what must it be like to live every day with a countenance such as she had? Had I not known a man with three legs when I was a traveling entertainer? And a bearded woman? And a boy my own age with skin like a crocodill's? They hadn't seemed repugnant to me once I got to know them, whatever my first reaction might have been. So I cringed there by the inn door, ashamed, until the unfortunate woman was out of sight among the people in the street. Then, with vague thoughts to make amends somehow, I followed in the direction she had gone, but did not see her anywhere.

So that was an end of it. I'd been a slubberdegullion* and there was no repairing it.

---

* Slubberdegullion: all-around wretch, completely without virtues.

It was in my mind to return to Midnight and continue my journey, perhaps to Ireland or France, whither to begin a new life. I had my liberty, a fine horse, and a purse of gold. What else was needed, after all? Clothes, of course. I wouldn't get very far—or at least, not without great travail—dressed as a vagabond. But how could I purchase a new suit without revealing I had money above my station? The answer came to me when I passed a Lombard banker's premises—a pawnshop. It was set a little way down a narrow alley, as if embarrassed of its business. Nobody, however ragged, would be turned away from such a place.

A few minutes later, I emerged in a fair enough secondhand suit of brown worsted, not too shiny at elbow and knee, with the scarlet of my boot turndowns tucked inside the shafts to conceal them. There weren't any shoes fit to walk in among the broker's stock. I stepped into the main street and retraced my steps back up through the town, and nobody spared me so much as a glance.

My complacent mood was rudely shattered, however. For what should I see on the road ahead but a file of soldiers, led by Captain Sterne on his fine brown horse? I nearly bolted, but recalled in time that he had not seen my face, and without my *own* horse I looked nothing like a highwayman. So I did what everyone else was doing, and got up against the shopfronts to make room as the procession went by.

The redcoat soldiers were somewhat the worse for weather. They'd been living rough and fighting desperate men, and their crossbelts were not so white as they had been. Sterne sported a blackened eye, which only made him look the fiercer. He fixed his bloodshot gaze upon everyone he passed, much as he had done in the Widow's Arms. When his eye fell upon me, I contrived to be scratching my brows so that my features were concealed. But he wasn't interested in my face—he was examining my boots. From between my fingers I watched him pass, and did not breathe again until his attention was directed elsewhere in the crowd.

In the vanguard behind the soldiers came the desperate men

themselves: On the back of an ox-wain, or open-sided wagon, stood a cage of iron bars, after the fashion of a lion pen. Inside the cage were Giant Jim and his gang, the Spanish Desperado, Milliner Mulligan, the sailor with the hook, and several others I didn't know.

They were all marked with wounds and bound with chains, or they would otherwise have been strangling one another. As it was, they scowled and spat and recited the most appalling litany of curses I had ever heard. Although several of them happened to cast their eyes in my direction, none recognized me at all. I watched the heavy cart lurch out of sight and then continued my journey.

Well beyond the town, there was a stone bridge. It wasn't far from the track down which Midnight was hidden in the barn. I was still some distance away when I saw several soldiers upon the bridge, presumably posted as a watch. Bridges were an excellent place to lay for wanted persons; everyone must cross or swim, and few could swim. Anxiety flooded me once again. Although I had ample proof that I was entirely unknown, the thought of passing among the soldiers made my pulses race and my body run with cold sweat. One may avoid conviction, but one can never escape guilt. Still, I had to retrieve Midnight, and my path lay across the bridge.

As I drew closer, I saw that most of the soldiers were lounging against the parapet of the span while one of their number tormented a person halfway across. They laughed insolently and slung cruel jeers back and forth, tossing a small object their plump victim kept leaping to intercept. My heart gave a bounce when I saw the object was a radish, and that there were more scattered about. The object of their derision was none other than the dreadfully ill-favored woman from the town.

There had been many a test of my mettle the last two days, but none tried me as sorely as that which followed. I will be absolutely honest: Had not I already humiliated the poor woman, and owed her a debt of conscience, I would have turned away and forded the river elsewhere. *I* could swim, and I wanted no part of those soldiers whatsoever. Cruelty was so commonplace in those days, nobody could have faulted me for ignoring it. But ignore it I did not.

Almost without my permission, my feet lengthened their stride, and in a few moments I was at the bridge.

"Unhand that radish," I cried, and all eyes were bent upon me.

My heart turned to ice. The soldiers were much larger than me, and with their tall miter hats and bright bayonets they looked the very picture of danger. I was reminded of the goblings, who gave me similar menacing looks. There might even have been a troll under the bridge, as in the children's tales.

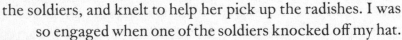

The radish fell forgotten to the stones, so I had accomplished that much. The woman in the hood began gathering up her vegetables again, in just the way she had done when I knocked her down, except now she seemed weak and bewildered, as if under the influence of strong drink. Now I felt a great obligation to assist her. So I crossed midway over the bridge, ignoring the soldiers, and knelt to help her pick up the radishes. I was so engaged when one of the soldiers knocked off my hat.

"Pick it up," said he, and placed his boot upon its brim, pinning it to the ground.

"Lift your foot, then," I replied, growing angry despite the peril of my situation.

The other soldiers laughed, and I saw the one who now trod upon my hat was the same who had taken the chief part in bedeviling the ill-favored woman. I rose to my full height, which reduced the vertical distance between his eyes and mine to about a foot and a half, and said, "First I saw a cartload of bandits, and now I see a dozen knaves. The roads aren't fit for decent folk."

Something I have learned since then is if you must insult someone, it's better to shape taunts into questions that invite a rejoinder. Most aggression is relieved by speech; if you leave your antagonist with nothing to say, he shall have to find some other outlet to release his hostility. Mine found an outlet in my nose.

The soldier, deprived of an opportunity for wit, biffed me upon the conk with a fist like a milking stool. I stumbled backward, cupping the injured appendage between my hands, and the back of my knees struck the parapet of the bridge. I toppled over the side. Any befuddlement the blow had caused was cleared from my head by the icy water into which I plunged. Blowing and sputtering, I flailed to the surface and was born downstream until the bridge was out of sight.

I crawled to the riverbank, completely covered in ignominy, and upon the shore was soon covered in goose excrement. Thus bedighted, with water spilling out of my boot-tops, I sloshed up the bank and made my way back toward the bridge. By now I had no pride left to repair, nor any intention of pursuing the quarrel, but simply wanted to retrieve my hat.

Luck, however, had returned from whatever errand it had been upon. I was approaching the bridge when I spied Captain Sterne upon his horse, bellowing at the soldiers. They now stood in as pretty a row as potted geraniums. The woman in the hood was gone, along with her radishes.

I didn't dare approach the bridge while the captain was upon it, for even with their unusual tops concealed, my boots were far too fine for the rest of my costume—as he might have observed in town. So I waited behind a holly bush, wringing my coattails, until he had run out of abuse and spurred his mount away. Only then did I return. Every soldier's eye was upon me, darting knives and lightning, but they dared not trouble me further.

I found my hat upon the ground, placed it upon my head, and tipped it to the soldiers. "Be kind to radishes," I said, and went upon my way.

Chapter 11

THE PRICE OF A BUTTON

WHEN THE excitement wore off, all I was left with was nerves. My legs felt like jelly as I wended up the path to the decrepit barn. "Midnight," said I, stepping through the door, "we are leaving this confounded place."

But there was another surprise in store for me. Standing beside Midnight was the radish-woman, with her hood thrown back to reveal her ill-assorted face.

"I don't know what to make of thee," she said, in a cool, musical voice that seemed incompatible with the rest of her.

"Dash my wig!" I cried.

"Thou hast no wig, sir," said she.

Were I blind, her voice would have enchanted me; as it was, her looks made me fear for my sight. But now I was determined to master my reactions, so I looked her in the eye without flinching. After all, I wasn't in much better array after my excursion in the river. Then practical matters took the fore in my mind, as they usually did, given enough time.

"How came you here?" I asked.

"I heard thine horse," she said, easily enough. I didn't believe it for a moment, but let it pass. Instead I scraped up the courage to offer a serving of humility.

"I owe you an apology," said I.

"For what?" the woman said, and looked as surprised as her inflexible features would allow—mostly a matter of her nostrils opening wide.

"Ah," I said. "Of course you don't know me. Since first we met, I've swapped my clothes and exchanged dust for guano. Earlier this morn, it was I who collided with you outside the Bull & Crown, and fairly knocked you to the ground. I was dressed in sackcloth then, and terribly uncivil." I swept off my hat and bowed low, so that waterweed fell from my pockets.

"I would not have known thee," she said, and her lips bent in as coy a smile as her teeth would permit. The meaning was clear: She knew very well who I was. Still, I was determined to play my part.

"Pray accept my apology," I said, "and take my actions on the bridge as proof of my sincerity. Or, if you don't believe me, take my plunge in the river as divine justice."

The woman seemed to be deep in thought. I occupied myself with battering the dust off my hat.

At length she said, "Thou art nothing like thy master, from what I have been told." I fairly leapt out of his boots, but held my tongue, and she continued, "I took thee for a scoundrel and a coward last night, and then I took thee for a shallow-hearted boy this morning. But now I take thee for a gentleman."

Well, you can imagine how this speech took *me*: I was at once filled with consternation that she knew who my master was, ashamed that her opinion of me had sunk so low, and delighted it had greatly improved. But how came she to know all this? I hadn't long to wonder. Her dreadful features took on a look of resolution.

She swung her cloak from her shoulders, and as the dark garment whirled about her and fell away, the snouted woman was gone. The lady from the silver coach stood in her place.

Had a thunderbolt struck me, I could not have been more

amazed. I lost my legs, and sat heavily upon the floor, dropping my hat. The poor garment had spent nearly as much time that day upon the ground as upon my head.

"Your Royal Highness Morgana Elgeron-Smith," said I.

She curtsied very gracefully. Now I saw that her entire appearance had changed, not just her face. She was about my own age, and wore a gown of green silk that was almost black; it shimmered like water, and everywhere was embroidered with fine silver thread. Her hair was ink black, caught up in a silver net decorated with silver leaves. Her olive skin and green eyes were as I'd glimpsed them the previous night, accented by strong black brows.

She was beautiful—I had never beheld such beauty—but in precisely the opposite way that convention dictated. It was such an uncanny beauty that I felt something like fear at the sight of her: Every time I looked into her eyes it seemed I might drown in their sea-green depths.

"Thou hast had enough duckings for one day," said she.

It was as if she had read my thoughts. Her voice alone had not transformed; it bore a slight accent, as of someone returned from a decade overseas, and she used the antique form of speech.

"I was due for a rinse," said I, foolishly, still stained with guano. She smiled her half smile, which somehow made her look sad.

"But come," she said, and her smile fell away. "There's no time. I've sought thee since daybreak, though when we met I doubted you too much to pursue my business. I promised thine master a reward for rescuing me from that hateful coach, and thou hast fulfilled his obligation. So the prize is yours, along with my thanks."

She raised a slender hand, and although an instant before it had been empty, now there was a wine-colored velvet purse resting in it. Then it was I saw the two rebel feyín, Willum and Gruntle, standing on Midnight's back. Whether they'd been there for the entire interview or had only just arrived, I could not guess.

"Sorry we couldn't help you on the bridge, Squire," said Willum. "But you told us not to interfere with you any more."

"You might at least have come to *her* aid," said I, indignantly.

"The flowing water makes us weak. We have no magic on rivers," Willum said, as if this were the most obvious thing in the world.

"But what of puddles and things? What about rain?"

"*Flowing* water, dunce," Willum clarified. "In waterways."

"I also forbade their interference," the princess said. "It would be of little use to disguise myself if my servants revealed themselves, would it not?"

"Begging your pardon, ma'am," Gruntle ventured, in a timid voice. "You said we wasn't servants no longer."

"Gruntle, you blister-pated newt, show some respect," Willum hissed, nudging his companion.

But the princess turned to the wee flying men and inclined her head, revealing a slender neck along which curled a few stray locks. "Gruntle is correct. Forgive me," she said. "It is the habit of a long lifetime."

"She gave us our freedom, she did," Gruntle said, addressing me. "And then she tole us it was never hers to give, but ours all the time. We're in amongst deep waters, Master Bristol."

By this time I was on my feet again, if a trifle unsteadily. The princess held out the purse and bid me take it.

"I cannot," I said. "That's my poor master's price, not mine."

"Thou need'st not be sentimental," she said. "This is a purse of plenty. Merely reach into it and draw out whatever sum you require, as long as thou shalt live."

I laughed aloud. "At the rate I'm going, your Royal Highness, I won't live long enough to get the price of a button from it. No, you keep your purse of plenty, and the best of luck with it."

"I cannot compel thee?" she asked once more, fixing me with a peculiar, urgent kind of look. Her eyes were the color of spring leaves, greener than the greenest eyes I'd seen before, and flecked with darkness like small sorrows.

"No," said I.

I wasn't trying to be chivalrous, you understand. Money was the farthest thing from my mind, that was all. And it seemed a filthy thing to take a price settled upon by a dead man. In fact, I felt there was something contemptible in the very offer of it.

But as soon as I'd refused the purse this last time, the princess closed her hand as if crumpling a piece of paper, then opened it, and the little bag was gone. Willum and Gruntle clapped like spectators at a match of *jeu de paume*.*

"In your stories about us," she said, "our people are always full of tricks and tests. That much is true, and I'm no different: The price of magic is trust. Hadst thou taken the purse, we would have vanished, and you'd be alone with a fortune in thy pocket. That's what has always happened before; you full-bred humans are a greedy lot. Now I confess I know not what to do."

I didn't know what to do, either. "I was thinking about fleeing to France," I said.

"Ireland is a free Faerie state; can I but reach its shores, my king has no claim upon me, but I am exiled," she said, and looked very unhappy.

"You've run away from your father," I replied, trying to sound encouraging. "If he's anything like he sounds, what with the goblings and so forth, I'd put as much distance between us as I could. If I were you, that is. Or me, for that matter. Which I am." I was babbling. She had that effect.

The princess shook her head, and the feyín did likewise, drooping their wings. "Even Ireland may yet fall to his legions. There's no safety in all the First Realm whilst my father is upon the throne, and it's worse in the Middle Kingdom."

"What about the other one? The Elden Kingdom?"

"The Realm Beyond? There is no safety for *anyone* there."

---

* *Jeu de paume*: precursor to tennis, played mostly on indoor courts. The game has the oldest actively contested trophy in the world—since 1740, when Kit would have been a small boy.

They feyín shivered at the very thought, rattling their wings.

I felt a tremendous need to get a grasp on the larger picture in my mind. We all had urgent reasons to be on our ways, but until I understood what I'd gotten into, I could scarcely string two coherent thoughts together. I'd need my wits if I were to avoid Captain Sterne and begin a new life elsewhere.

"Pray believe I doubt not your father's greatness," said I, "but there is an aspect to this situation which I cannot understand. Here stands Britain: Her greatest city is London, with close to three-quarters of a million inhabitants; I'm from her second-largest city, Bristol, whence my name. Her citizens have plunged to the bottom of the sea in a diving bell, harnessed the power of steam to mighty engines, captured electricity in a jar, and revolutionized weaving; we produce more woolen cloth, better iron, and finer beer than any other nation in the world."

Here I drew breath; the others were regarding me with either bemusement or amusement, I could not tell which. So I continued, "The British Empire stretches from the American colonies to Bengal, and she rules the seas of the world with two hundred naval ships, over eighty of which are ships of the line,
bearing some five thousand cannon and forty thousand crew aboard. Her forces at arms extend to another hundred thousand men—several dozen of whom are in pursuit of myself—and I cannot imagine why such an empire would require the services of a crowd of wee magical folk who specialize in making their bottoms blink like semaphores."

after Thos. Butterworth

There was a moment of silence while the others waited to see if I had finished my inventory. They didn't appear particularly impressed. I was about to mention our improved blast-furnace technology when Princess Morgana raised her hand in a gentle bid for pause.

"Here, too, stands Britain," said she. "The average span of life is one score and ten years, and half of her citizens are beneath the age of twenty. Inclosure acts are consolidating land holdings into the hands of the gentry, driving her peasants into the cities, where poverty is rampant and wages low, a crisis that will only get worse as industrialization replaces local agrarian culture. The empire's overseas holdings are largely beholden to such entities as the British East India Company, whereby the strength of a nation is bent to the advantage of an incorporation; in the meantime, thine empire has just endured the Jacobite Rebellion and war with Spain; she is presently at war with France and the native peoples in the American colonies, as well as with France *and* India in Hyderabad, and her grip on the Caribbean relies upon human slavery. In addition, everyone smelleth of horses and tobacco smoke, and thine king was born in Germany."

With effort I drew my eyebrows down out of my hairline. "You seem to have an extensive grasp of world affairs," I croaked.

The princess brushed my remark aside with her hand. "I know not the first thing about daily life in the manling world, but ask me any question about politics. One doth not sit at my father's court for half a century without learning a thing or two."

Half a century? She could not have been more than eighteen years old.

"So in fact it would be rather a great advantage to have your magic at our nation's disposal," I concluded.

"'Tis so," said she, "and my kingly father bethinks his advantage lieth in cannon-shot and coke-fueled engines. So must I marry the human king's grandson and hasten the union of our worlds, or flee."

A gloomy silence fell upon the barn. Dust swirled in shafts of sunlight much as my own thoughts churned between light and dark. It seemed to me that the Faerie rebellion wasn't off to a very good start.

"Right," I said. "Well. If nobody else has a plan, I have a suggestion."

I went to the straw where I'd concealed Whistling Jack's equipment, and from the dusty redingote retrieved my master's will. I spread the document on a cask-head and the others gathered around it, the feyín perched atop the cask itself.

"Before he perished," said I, "my master sketched this map. I don't understand it entirely, but this doesn't seem to be a map of places so much as a map of *time*. Here's an owl in a tree; there I met your coach. Here's a bull with a crown; there I met you. Each of these little drawings happens somewhere along this line. So if we follow it, it seems to me we might meet with what's next to be done. Which appears to be a frog."

"'E's clever," Gruntle remarked.

"How came your master by this?" Princess Morgana said. "Only a scrying stone could tell him of what was to come."

"Magda has one of those," I cried. "Dreadful thing in her eye socket."

"She didn't tell me this. I haven't seen her in many years," the princess said. "She was my nursemaid when I was a child. It's been two score years at least; we have sent many a bee back and forth, but never met since her exile. If Magda has a scrying stone, she's been to the Realm Beyond, and knew what she was about when she told your master of these things."

"But then surely she knew my master must die," I said, horrified.

"Manlings die like mayflies, scarce knowing the sun," said the princess. "A quote from the *Book of Songs*."

I began to understand something: These people didn't adhere to the human schedule. If, as she had remarked earlier, it had been fifty years since she was an infant, and she looked about ten-and-seven now, then she was all but immortal, as far as I was concerned. There was something chilly and ruthless about her way of saying these things; I wondered if that was the true measure of her after all.

"That's comforting," I mumbled. "Anyhow, back to the map: the next sketch shows—" And then I realized I didn't know what the next sketch was. "What is that?"

The others leaned close. The princess was so near I could smell her: It was a strange scent, like the air after a rain, or snow melting on a warm day. Pleasant, but not altogether human. I observed the tips of her ears came to distinct points that swept back away from her face.

"'Tis the gobling crest," she said.

Gruntle made frightened noises, and Willum explained, "The King has three legions, called 'Above, Upon, and Below.' That's their relationship to the earth, you understand. Our cousins the pixies patrol the air, the goblings guard the surface, and the trolls are underground. In great emergencies the goblings take all three."

"So you can't tunnel your way out of the country," I said, hoping to amuse them.

"We tried that," Gruntle said. "My nuncle got et by a mole."

Chapter 12

A PARTING OF WAYS

M IDNIGHT HADN'T been properly groomed since the beginning of our adventures, so I spent a while rubbing him down with straw, cleaning his hooves, and attending to his tack. Then I transferred the contents of my master's pockets to my own, including the heavy stock of gold, and buried his criminal costume beneath the straw. I kept only the hat and boots, for the hat was of a common type, and the boots were too good to give up. Later I would discover they were too good to keep.

While I worked, Princess Morgana occupied herself at the far end of the barn, whispering through a crack in the wall; it seemed there was someone on the other side, or else she was speaking to a person within, concealed from my sight. An uncommon number of bees flew in and out of the place; I thought there must be a hive in the eaves. I heard small voices, but only in fragments, as one might hear choirboys trying valiantly to be quiet before a hymn.

My mind was all in a kippage.* We each had pressing problems,

---

* Kippage: confusion, turmoil. Also a ship's company.

but literally worlds apart: I was in danger of apprehension by a vindictive officer who saw enemies in every face and suspicion in my boots. The princess was in danger of apprehension by magical henchmen and marriage to the prince regent. Her so-called rebel forces had rescued me from destruction more than once; I had rescued her almost as often. Had I taken the magical purse, we would never have met again. Because I had refused it, we were still thrown together. But there wasn't any mutual business left between us. I resolved to do the decent thing and wish her farewell, then be on my way. Wherever that was.

Midnight, much refreshed, attempted to eat the ribbon in my hair, and I thought it well to get him out-of-doors for some exercise, as he was prone to mischief when bored. So I inquired politely if Princess Morgana was prepared to take to the road.

"Go when thou wilt," said she.

"Allow me to escort you away from this turbulent town," I suggested. "There is a crossing a short march to the west, and there we may part. As friends, I hope."

"France lies in the other direction," she said. "Thou needst not turn away from your path on my account, for I will disguise myself in some manner as thou hast seen, and thus travel anonymously. My feyín companions will remain invisible."

"Pray forgive me for questioning your readiness for such a journey, ma'am. My concern is that a royal person of your high station might not be accustomed to traveling alone. If we walk but a league or two together, I might acquaint you with the essentials."

"I have oft traveled in the manling world," said she, haughty as a bishop.

"In a fine coach, with those uncanny servants at your side?"

"As befits my station," she spake, and the air seemed to grow cooler inside the barn. I am certain that it did. Although I could have gazed upon her for the rest of my days, I had no desire to suffer her scorn for another minute. She made me feel common.

"Then," said I, "I shall press the matter no further. I'm sure you know well enough of inns and wayhouses, of coach-hires and vag-abonds and rank-riders, of sore feet and broken shoes and many a league between breakfast and dinner. Best of luck."

I thought that concluded our business, but the princess seemed as if she might burst. There was a species of fury rising up in her features that distorted them by degrees until it appeared she was transforming herself by magic. I pretended not to notice, but cinched up Midnight's saddle and set the bridle upon his head, then turned his nose toward the door.

"Do not *dare* to call me sheltered from the storms of life," said the princess.

I shrugged. "The rain falls on everyone, but it's paupers get wettest, they say. If you cannot fly across the country, you must ride; if you cannot ride, you must walk; and if you walk, you walk among men. If you are confident you'll require no guide, I'm confident Midnight will carry me far away, and there's an end to it."

She stared at me a long while, her eyes flickering. I could not say if she was defiant, dismissive, determined, or disappointed. All of these emotions seemed to take a turn playing upon her features, and none gained the upper hand. At last she composed herself and nodded once.

"Fare thee well, 'prentice to a highwayman," said the princess.

I walked Midnight from the barn and threw myself into the saddle, then made some show of adjusting a stirrup leather, to give the princess time to reconsider. But no word of compromise issued from within, so I got Midnight reared up into a pesade with his forelegs waving prettily, tipped my hat, and off we went. I thought I detected the whispering of small voices in the shrubbery there-abouts as we made our way back to the high road.

One might question my valor that I left such a rare creature as the princess to the whims of fortune, but I'd heard such resolve in her voice when we argued the point—and felt the very fluid of the air grow cold that I knew any further argument was fruitless. There was more to her than obstinacy, however. She had great hidden strengths. And she had *magic*. I only fancied I might be of service to her because I'd spent my life underestimating the female sex, as was the fashion of that time. So instead, I rode on.

I confess I was profoundly disappointed, although it was an absurd thing to feel: I'd no place in this mysterious princess's life, nor she in mine. It was a mad coincidence that brought us together at all. Yet—yet. Still I seethed with disappointment. It was the first time in my life I ever regretted what had *not* come to pass, disaster though it might have been.

I reached the road and looked left and right, deliberating which way to go. To the east was the Channel, where I could find a boat to take Midnight and I abroad. To the west was Ireland, across the sea. Went I the one way, and I could leave my human pursuers behind. Went I the other, and I would be safe from goblings and the like. I had neglected to ask if there were goblings in France.

Whichever route I chose, there was a deal of ground to cover. Last I had seen him, Captain Sterne was riding west, so I resolved to go east, and turned Midnight toward the town. Once we were through it, he could run for many a mile before we came to another settled place. My disguise was proved with every passerby: None spared me a second glance, though Midnight drew the admiring eye of any who knew good horseflesh.

What happened next would not have transpired, had I not been so preoccupied with the events of the last two days. My head was crowded with strange things: goblings, trolls, ancient witches, exquisite princesses, and tiny winged men with lanterns in their trousers. I thought of royal weddings. I considered the implications of enlightened science working hand in glove with magical powers, and a war among invisible people waged across England, of which hardly a soul would know—or perhaps they would. Perhaps this magical rebellion would split the island of Albion right up the middle and sink it into the sea. I knew nothing, and I wasn't likely to learn anything more.

So engrossed was I that I rode through the town without much caution. There weren't any soldiers afoot, and none but them would have any reason to suspect me. If my horse was of better quality than I, it meant nothing; the lowest stable boy may ride the finest champion. I reached the far end of the town without altogether knowing what we passed on the way. Then I was popped out of my study the way a cork pops out of a bottle, for I heard a familiar voice.

"I've decided, lads," I heard Captain Sterne remark. "You on this side, take the prisoners in their cage to London. The rest of you, I'll commandeer horses and we shall ride out until we find him."

The voice came through the gates of a courtyard to my right. It was a large inn, the yard surrounded by a tall brick wall, and Sterne and his men were on the other side of the wall. I could see the back of Sterne's head over the top, but only the plumes on the soldiers' hats. So the captain was sitting on his horse, and the men were standing to attention. Although none of them could see me, I ducked down low in the saddle.

"To this countryside, Whistling Jack has been a nightmare," Sterne went on. "Now I am his nightmare."

Had I not heard his voice, I would have ridden straight past the gate, and he would have seen me. Would not Captain Sterne find it peculiar that I had been first dressed as a peasant, next clad in a brown suit, and on the third occasion astride a magnificent horse, always in the same boots? Then his men would further identify me as the chap that fell off the bridge. And *then* the captain would discover the turndowns tucked into my boots. Between those, the pistol, and the gold, I'd surely hang.

Just before we reached the gate, I reined Midnight around, still bent low in the saddle, and clucked in his ear to urge him back the way we came.

"First, we shall ride toward—" Sterne's words ran out abruptly. I urged Midnight to stand still.

"Did you hear that?" Captain Sterne said. I could tell by his voice that he was now facing the wall between us. "Those footfalls and the creak of the leathers? It's the very beast we seek. I never forget a horse, lads. Not sight nor sound of it."

I heard the clip-clop of hooves approaching the gateway. If only I had paid attention as I rode through town! Before me was a maze of streets bisected by the crowded main thoroughfare, lined with little cottages. I could gallop straight up that and hope we didn't collide with anyone, or pelt off among the lanes and hope we didn't circle around back into Sterne's embrace. There must be some other way. I looked at the houses, the gardens. I hadn't any idea what to do.

"You there!" came the voice of Captain Sterne behind me. "On the black. Come here."

I pretended not to hear him, or rather I didn't listen, but rode on, moving away from him at a dreadfully slow walk. On either side were dwellings of thatch, all roof and hardly any walls.

"On the black horse," Sterne cried. "Halt!"

I heard the song of his sword rising from its sheath, and knocked my heels against Midnight's sides. The horse had been waiting eagerly for my command, and sprang forward. But I didn't guide him up the thoroughfare. Instead I drove him straight at the nearest cottage. Sterne's mount clattered after us in a trice, and I heard the hobnailed boots of the soldiers coming up behind. But I didn't look back, because Sterne himself might not remember my face. He might only remember my horse. I urged Midnight to jump an instant before he would have collided with the stone wall of the cottage.

He might not have followed my command, except the thatch of the roof looked as much like a steep hill as anything else, I suppose. He must have thought we could climb up it. So he sprang with all his strength. We soared up over the wall, crashed into the roof, and the thatch—being little more than reeds laid on a frame of staves—collapsed entirely. We went straight through it like a cannonball through a sail.

I caught a fleeting glimpse of a homely interior and a very startled woman bending over a pot on the hearth, and then Midnight alighted and sprang again, driving us through the roof on the other side. I felt terrible about the cottage. It was Sterne's fault, really. But I couldn't stop to offer amends. Instead we tore through the back garden in a spray of carrots, vaulted a little stream, and galloped away over the fields, still doing a fair imitation of a cannonball.

We were a couple of furlongs away from the town when a fusillade of gunfire rang out. I heard a musket-ball purr lazily past my head, and the distant crash of crockery. Chancing a look over my shoulder, I saw soldiers in the back garden, and glimpsed through the hole in the roof of the house that Captain Sterne had got his horse indoors, but it had shied away from bashing through the other side as Midnight had done. Now he was shouting and waving his sword and knocking over the furniture.

"You're the finest horse in Christendom," said I to Midnight. My plans had changed. I decided to ride west, after all.

Chapter 13

UP ANOTHER TREE

A S HAD become our habit, Midnight and I fled across the countryside, through hill and dale. I found myself hoping old Magda would launch us somewhere beyond the reach of the king's law, such as Africa or Belgium, using her powerful magic. But that bit of my life had concluded. I was off magic for good. So we covered the distance in the usual manner.

After an hour of riding, we reached a path that ran along the hilltops overlooking the high road, and roughly parallel to it. It commanded a good view for miles. There were slow carts and swift riders, peasants bent beneath mighty burdens of sticks and straw, milkmaids balancing buckets across their shoulders on slender yokes. I saw no redcoats. We could slow down at last. If pursuers came, we would spy them long before they spied us.

Although I should have learned my lesson well, my thoughts again began to wander. This time I was thinking of a pale olive face, and green flashing eyes with worlds behind them. A mind so wise in some ways, yet simple in others. I remembered her pointed ear tips and the net of silver leaves that bound up her dark hair. My ears were filled with the lilting accent of her voice. Midnight kept looking over his shoulder at me. I hadn't a clue what state I was in, but horses always know.

We stopped to rest beneath a tree on a hilltop, with warm sunshine and birdsong all about. Midnight nibbled the tender grass and I contemplated my near-fatal boots. After a while, my thoughts turned again to the princess, but in a more practical way. She was traveling afoot, unless she'd conjured up a horse. If she chose a direct route along the road, unlike my wandering path through the landscape, it would require her two hours to go the distance I had reached in one.

I did some calculations and determined that she might well pass below us in the next half of an hour, if she hadn't stopped along the way. After three or four impatient minutes, I did some more calculations and decided we might safely descend to the main road, as long as we remained concealed behind a hedge. No sooner had we done so than I further calculated it had been half an hour and the princess still hadn't come along. Midnight grazed on the tender grass, concealed by the hedge, and I peered through the leaves to watch the traffic, seeking a girl with a green velvet dress—or warts and the nose of a swine.

None came past.

My worries increased with every minute that went by without her. At last I calculated still more and decided there was no harm in revealing myself to one of the travelers who was coming from the direction of the town.

I stood beside a stile next the road and accosted the very first fellow who chanced to come along, a drover with several dozen geese marching before him, all tied together with string.

"Prithee," said I, "have you traveled long on this road?"

"Oo aar," said the goose-drover.

"Then perhaps you've seen a young lady on the way, all in green velvet?"

"Aar, aar," quoth the goose-drover.

My heart leapt. "So you've seen her? Did she fare well? I was expecting her along this road, some time ago."

The goose-drover appeared to be thinking, or at least his brow furrowed, his complexion reddened, and he stroked his chin with his forefinger like a scholar with a flea in his beard.

At last, as my nerves were about to come unstrung with the suspense of waiting, he pointed up the road behind him and said, "Nar, but 't grockle rumney garley 'er come cropper moile ha'moile back."

Well! I hadn't the remotest idea what he was talking about, but it did not sound good. My anxiety had blossomed into something like a frenzy. So I whistled up Midnight, whose arrival frighted the geese, and to a chorus of honks and Somerset curses I rode back down the road at such a clip that my great steed's shoes rang like Cullan's hammer*.

If Captain Sterne and his men were on the same road, let them pursue me. I could not bear to spend the rest of my life with my back to danger. Besides, the goblings had it in for me as well, and they could pop up anywhere. Nowhere was safe. Midnight sailed down the road and I searched every face we passed, hoping to see some evidence of the princess in disguise. The old woman with the starched cap? The bulbous fellow with a book under his arm? The girl in blue bows, rattling along in a dog-cart? None of them afforded me a glance.

So great was my haste that I might have ridden straight past Princess Morgana and back to the market town and the tender attentions of Captain Sterne, had not I heard a faint cry of distress from beyond the hedgerow upon my left. Midnight reined up and I sprang from the saddle, then threw myself through a gap in the hedge and into the field on the other side. There I saw a sight that

---

* Cullan, legendary Irish blacksmith; had a hammer that sounded like Midnight's shoes.

would have set me to laughing until I fell down, except circumstances would not permit it; for as ridiculous as it was, it was equally perilous. Particularly for a man standing on his own legs.

There before me was a bull, a great red beast with curling horns, fiery eyes, and brisket so deep his chest nearly touched the ground. More a man than I, was this bull. He had not spied me yet. The object of his attention was a stout tree some little way into the field, not very tall but sturdy about the middle. Lowermost in the tree was a motley, thick-necked ruffian, whose arms and legs were locked about a branch in such a way that his nethermost parts hung down just out of horn-prick of the bull. There was an ironbound cudgel hanging from his belt by a strap; the bull knocked this instrument with every toss of his head, as a bell knocks its clapper.

Directly above the ruffian was Princess Morgana, looking less regal than when I had left her. She was perched on another, more slender branch, and sat most ladylike upon it, sidesaddle. Both of them, princess and ne'er-do-well, were shouting at each other and crying for help from passersby, of which there were but few, and none inclined to distress the bull. It was only my haste which had brought me into his field, or I, too, might well have hesitated.

As I looked on, a wee voice spoke from the hedge beside me. "O marster Kit! You come back, like!"

It was Gruntle, concealed among the leaves. I threw myself back into the gap in the foliage and peeked around at the bull. So far, none of the party had spied me: not princess, nor ruffian, nor beast. The bull sensed someone about, but looked over his shoulder and saw no one.

"That there princess," Gruntle whispered in my ear—I still had not seen him, so cunningly was he disguised—"she told us afore we went out that she'd have our heads and wings and whatnots nor we showed ourselves to living mortal. So I can't do nuffing to save her!"

"Nonsense. Give that bull a comprimaunt right in the hindquarters," I suggested.

"The Princess forboden it!" Gruntle wailed. "It's Willum breaks the law. 'E's a renegade through and through. I'm but a numble conformist." The bull had renewed his attack upon the tree.

"By her own word she's not your ruler any longer," said I, reasonably enough. "You're free and equal Faeries. Forget your book of laws and knock the old wooly-pate down with a magical jerry-cummumble*."

"Princess or not, 'er word is law to me," said Gruntle.

"So there's nothing for it but that I should be tossed by the bull?"

"If'n you please," the Faerie said.

There wasn't time to argue further, for I saw that the princess's branch, light as she was, had begun to sag with the weight of her. And the ungentle fellow on the branch below was drooping, too, soon to find himself punctured most cruelly by the raging beast. So, with my customary cunning and forethought, I stepped out into the open and called to the bull: "Here's a fresh goad for you, old Bucephalus."

The creature swung about, astounded, I think, that anyone further would have the temerity to invade his field. He fixed his hard eyes upon me, lowered his head, scored the earth with a mighty hoof, and charged.

I ran. That was the extent of my plan, and I made the best of it, racing through muck and nettle alike, as fleet as a deer. Sadly, the bull was fleeter, and had soon closed much of the distance between myself and his great curving horns. There before me was an expanse of rough turf, the hedge increasingly distant, and no succor otherwise unless I could double my speed and reach the fence at the far end of the field before the bull made a wimple of my guts.

Then the ground descended to a pond, lined with reeds and churnish with mud. I turned my steps toward it, urged my legs to one final exertion—I could feel the bull's hot breath on my neck—

---

* Jerrycummumble: toss, tumble.

and flung myself into the water. With a *smack* I struck the pond, there was a chorus of outrage from the local frogs, and the bull splashed into the mire at the water's edge, his forelegs sunk deep in the slop. So great was his fury that he continued after me, deeper into the water, and soon all four of his limbs were secured in the sucking mud.

For my part, I paddled across the slime and emerged on the far side, streaming with brown sludge as fragrant as a fishmonger's shoe, bedizened with watercress, my dignity drowned. I observed my bellowing foe for a few moments to determine that he was suffi-ciently stuck, then hurried as much as I could  in my moistened condition back across the field.

The ruffian with the cudgel had already decamped from the tree and scampered away. Princess Morgana was picking her way down from branch to branch with a delicacy that ill became the circumstances. The bull was soon clear of the pond and trotting in our direction, huffing and snorting.

"Jump down!" I cried. She did so, falling as lightly as a feather into my arms. I now believe some enchantment arrested her de-scent; she seemed to weigh less than my sodden hat. I set her upon the grass, forgetting in my alarm to let go of her slender waist.

"Unhand me," said she, and I followed her through the gap in the hedge, where Midnight awaited. He snorted most expressively when he spied my condition, or rather smelled it. There being no other travelers in sight, Gruntle emerged from the hedge, his wings a-chatter, and landed on the saddle.

"A lot of good you did," said I, venting my wrath at the tiny fel-low. "Leaving a defenseless princess to fortune's whimsy. And who was that blackguard with the club?"

Before anyone could answer me, perforce we continued down the road, for the bull roared ceaselessly on the other side of the hedge. Once we had gotten past his domain and reached a shallow stream that bubbled across the road—this was before the ways were improved with culverts—I rinsed myself off and Princess Morgana retailed their adventures.

"After you left," she began, "we waited a while so that our steps should not catch us up with thine, if perchance you had taken this way and not the other. Then we set forth, Gruntle in his stealthy way and me upon the high road. Traveling afoot is weary work. Willum has gone ahead to recruit assistance to our cause. I thought myself well disguised, for none took an interest in me."

"Well disguised?" I cried. The only change in her appearance that I could see was her embroidered dress was a little plainer and there was an ordinary mobcap on her head instead of the silvery net.

"I was mistaken," she allowed. "For that scalawag with the stick came over a gate and matched his pace to mine, walking a little behind me. For a mile it was thus, and my fears were ever mounting. Twice, thrice, and again I almost cried for Gruntle to assist me, but if my father had employed that brute to capture me, resorting to magic would reveal where we were to the rest of his minions. Instead I spake some harsh words, though I don't recall them at this moment—"

"I do," interjected Gruntle. "Where a princess learnt such words I ain't aware, but they'd a' made the One-Eyed Duchess blush. 'Thou ventricose fustilarian*,' said she, and that was the least of it. 'I'll have thy worm-poisoned soul stretched on the rack of eternity, thou grobian bog-born rapscallion,' said she also. 'Mayest thou drown in the icy darkness of the void where sleeps the Elden Kingdom,' said she as well, and more besides. . . ."

"That will do," said Morgana, modestly, and Gruntle raised his lumpen hat and fell silent, his face red. She continued, "The remainder of the tale thou may easily guess: That unpleasant man

---

* Ventricose fustilarian: herring-gutted stinkard.

pursued me, and I ducked through the very gap in the hedge through which you came, and there was the bull. I ran to the tree, the ruffian ran after me, and then we perched like mockingbirds until you arrived."

"You think he was not a common bandit?" I asked when the tale was finished. "The ways are infested with such folk."

"After I had spoken hastily to him, he called me 'your Royal Highness,'" Morgana said. "Not in a satirical way, but most contemptuously; I think he knew me for what I am."

"We'll ride together, then, for Midnight can bear us both with ease. It makes a strange sight, a foreign girl and a waterlogged squire sharing a champion horse, but there's nothing else for it. We must get away from here."

Before she mounted, the princess, seeking the best disguise for herself, threw her strange cloak on and off a number of times, on each occasion changing her appearance: First the pig-nosed woman, then a plain yellow-haired girl with freckles, followed by a very old nun, a very tall washerwoman, a Turkish dancing girl, and a Gypsy. It was the last incarnation we settled upon. It changed her appearance the least; her dark looks and almost-green olive skin remained the same, if a trifle less vivid, but now she wore somber over-stitched skirts, silver hoops in her ears, and a red kerchief about her head. Gypsies being an alien race at that time, any strangeness in her comportment might be forgiven as part of the Travelers'* customs.

So it was; we boarded Midnight and trotted away, and there was no further talk of separating the party that day. Princess Morgana had proved to herself how little she knew of the ways of men, and I had proved myself a fool.

---

* Traveler: Gypsy. Also Romani or Romany.

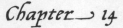

THE UNLUCKY LUNCHEON

ON WE rode. It was not gallantry on my part, pray understand, that caused me to ally my cause with hers. I found myself enchanted with the princess, it is true. But she was an enchantress, so that was to be expected. Rather, I understood after our separate misadventures that we would be better served together, at least for a short while.

It was my intention that we should part as soon as it was practical—and hers, as well. Having learned that Ireland was a free Faerie state, my plan to emigrate to France, *not* Ireland, was cemented in place. (I didn't know then that France had six such free states within its borders, but that's another story.) My own flight must wait. Knowing the risk the princess faced, and having seen how quickly she got into trouble, it was unthinkable that I should leave her side before she was delivered into friendly hands. It was simply good manners.

We had gone but a few miles when Willum returned, accompanied by a third feyín, who would not show herself to me. Her name was Violets, and she spoke only once or twice in my presence, always from a place of concealment. She was determined not to break the Eldritch Law any more than she must. Gruntle addressed her as "cousin," so these creatures had families much like our own.

First Willum spake to the princess in some other language, presumably the Faerie speech, with much pointing this way and that. Presumably he was telling her what he'd learned of her pursuers, and where we would meet with allies, and so on. She listened closely and interjected questions at certain points, also in the strange tongue. Then it was my turn.

"Captain Sterne, what wants to stretch your neck, has gone haring off eastward," Willum reported to me. "My mates are following him, and they'll dash off a bee if anything changes. Apparently the captain thinks you're so cunning you'd double back and return to your original route, knowing he'd follow thee to the west because he *thinks* you'd go east, and therefore west, but east, and so forth. North and south didn't come up. Which goes to show you're more cunning than he because you're not actually cunning at all. Which is clever."

I took him at his word. Then he, Gruntle, and Violets flew off ahead to scout the road for dangers. For a while we rode in peace.

"How does that cloak of yours work?" I asked the princess, after a long silence.

At first she didn't respond to my question. "I wonder—" said I.

"Forgive me," she replied. "Thou didst not use the correct form of address, so I did not realize to whom thou spoke."

"My apologies," I said. "But I can't very well call you HRH Morgana, Princess of Faerie, can I? Somewhat gives the disguise away."

"Call me Morgana, for the nonce."

"And you may call me Kit."

"It's all very new to me," she said, sounding regretful. "I scarcely know my own privilege. I've never had to do anything for myself. Even magic. Unlike my feyín companions, I must use enchanted objects to achieve my caprizels—that's our word for magical effects."

"So the cloak is a bit of portable magic, then."

"It's called a jaguundi. I was given it for serpicore hunting many years ago. As you must know, the serpicore is slow to fix upon a target for its venom, so merely changing your appearance is enough to baffle it."

"Yes, of course," I said.

"And now my cloak provest useful for disguises in the First Realm. But the best disguise for me will be a change of habits. Prithee tell me when I betray my upbringing. I shall not take offense."

"Very kind of you," said I, and offered an immediate suggestion. "Here's one for starters: you might try speaking in a less . . . archaic manner. I mean no criticism, naturally. But it does stand out. 'Thee' and 'thou' went out with King James."

"Shouldst discourse in *common* speech?" said she, amazed.

"It does have the virtue of being more common."

"Thus shall it be."

This brief conversation left me feeling light-headed. At first I thought it was the effect of hunger; I'd eaten little enough the past couple of days and was altogether gutfoundered. But instead, I began to realize Morgana was exerting some sort of charm upon me, as I had suspected. I found her every word delightful and interesting, her every gesture graceful, from the inquiring tilt of her head to the feather-light tread of her foot. I resolved to resist this effect. It must be, I reasoned, like the warming influence of a hearth that lulls the drowsy person to doze, soon to tumble into the embers of the fire. Morgana's company was warming, but I must not be lulled to sleep.

The journey to the Irish Sea would take weeks on foot and horseback. We were headed roughly northward. For some miles our way was uneventful; it seemed that the ruffian had not reported directly back to Morgana's father, or if he had, the pursuit had not yet caught us up. Presumably Captain Sterne continued on his way to the east.

Once, when I chanced to look at butterflies flitting above a cot-

tage garden, I thought I saw Violets in the foliage for a moment, dressed like the other wee people, with the addition of a flower on her head—but it was impossible to be sure.

The weather was changing, for there were blue-gray clouds on the horizon and mare's tails above, which warned we could be in for a soaking before long—by then, I hoped, Morgana would be with the sympathizers to her cause, and I'd be on my roundabout way to Dover.

"I'm going to ask you another question, if I may," said I, after we had gone another mile or two in silence.

"Pray do," Morgana said.

"Willum keeps mentioning bees. It's my impression you use them to send messages."

"That's right. I don't know why you manlings don't do it."

"Do you tie a small message to its leg, or do you write directly upon the bee?"

Morgana laughed at this. In fact she laughed until bright tears ran down her face and we had to dismount from the saddle lest she fall from the horse.

Willum and Gruntle returned, alerted by some mysterious instinct, and demanded to know what was the matter.

"You've made her cry, you bounder!" Willum shouted, and pointed at my feet. A moment later I was covered in stinging ants.

"I'm laughing," Morgana said, and laughed all the harder because I was leaping up and down, shrieking and beating at my legs.

Willum called the insects off; they flowed back to the ground and returned to their ant business as if nothing had happened. "My apologies," said Willum.

"You might learn to control your temper," I suggested, deeply embarrassed by the spectacle I had made. "Is anyone hungry?" I added, because Gruntle was walking around in the middle of the road, eating the ant casualties.

❦   ❦   ❦

I took us down a couple of obscure lanes and found another road to throw off any persons, natural or supernatural, who might be tracking us. We sat to lunch outside a tavern by a river, in a place concealed among lavender bushes. We could not eat within the public house; in most respectable establishments, Gypsies were not permitted to enter. I first suggested Morgana change her appearance to something else, but she insisted she would stay a Gypsy for the duration of the journey, regardless of what people thought.

Willum delighted in the meal—game pie, cheese, and biscuits— of which he ate an extraordinary amount despite his size; Gruntle wasn't having any of "that fancy foreign muck" and contented himself with wood lice from beneath the log on which we sat. Violets did not show herself. Gruntle claimed she was eating something she brought with her.

Across the river, storm clouds were piling high, but it was sunny on our side. A couple of fishermen walked past, and the feyín vanished, as was their habit. Morgana said this was called "doing a ruck-ins," and couldn't explain how it was accomplished. It was a sort of instinct, like blinking of the eyes. Upon his reappearance, Willum said the age at which feyín infants* learned the trick was a nightmare, because they would sometimes disappear for weeks on end.

Morgana's feet required tending before we resumed our journey; I would have bound her blisters with a bit of cloth, but Gruntle had some sort of healing comprimaunt that solved the problem. This magic was performed with hand gestures. While her shoes were off, I saw that Morgana's toes were not entirely human in configu-ration—as with the feyín's feet, her first toe started much farther

---

* The word Willum used in the original manuscript was *nymphs*, which is the feyín term for *infant*.

down the foot than her other toes, almost like a thumb. This sort of thing was what made her so fascinating—in the greatest of beauties there is always a touch of the uncanny.

Not being required, I strolled a little distance away and took the opportunity to examine my master's map. There upon the route was the frog, which could stand for my encounter with the bull's pond, or collectively for all the plunges I'd taken that day. In the latter case, the frog represented *me*. The next illustration showed a flower with an arrow through it, and the one after that a horse with a spear through it. I rather hoped this last wasn't meant to indicate Midnight. I'm not much for riddles.

I was studying these scribbles by the riverbank when I felt a sting upon my neck. With an oath I rubbed the injured spot, thinking a bee had sent me a message in the traditional manner. Instead I discovered a tiny arrow, the size of a tooth-pick, had sunk itself into my skin.

"What the deuce—" I exclaimed, examining the object. Then a horn sounded.

"Pixies!" cried Violets, and I saw her leap out of the lavender bushes from the place in which she'd been concealed, not far from where I stood. "This way," she called to me, and flew straight for the place Morgana and the others were. Ere she reached them, she fell to the ground, half a dozen of the same arrows bristling from her back. There was a small *pop*, and Violets disappeared in a puff of dust. Where she had lain, there fluttered three gray moths, which flitted away as if they'd always been moths, and nothing more. Master Rattle had sketched a flower transfixed by an arrow upon the map. If only I had guessed it was a violet!

I crashed through the shrubbery and found the rest of my party on their feet, looking about in alarm. Moments later, a hail of arrows came from the foliage about us. They pricked me like needles. Willum dived behind me, but Gruntle ran to shield the princess. Morgana swept her fist through the air, and the missiles were diverted around us, as if striking an invisible dome of glass.

"I didn't know I could do that," she cried, and sprinted for Midnight. I ran after her, Willum and Gruntle flying beside me. A moment later I'd thrown Morgana onto the saddle, and a swarm of feyín even smaller than Willum and Gruntle came buzzing out of the grass, firing their arrows from quivers slung between their wings. I didn't see them very clearly, for I was climbing into the stirrups myself, but they looked naked, with green skins, and they had the wings of birds, not insects.

"Get into the saddlebag!" I cried to Willum and Gruntle, but then I saw Gruntle fall. He was wounded, an arrow having torn through one of his wings. He tried to fly, but cried out and fell to the ground again. I sprang out of the saddle, beyond the range of Morgana's protective spell, and immediately felt the bite of a score of the tiny missiles. My mind began to whirl. This must have been the fate of the bandits who waylaid Morgana's coach: a cloud of maddening arrows. But I scooped up the wounded feyín, tossed him into the saddlebag after Willum, and we were riding away within moments, pursued by the swarm.

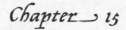

Chapter 15

THE BRIDGE

I F YOU have never ridden a great horse, you cannot know what speed feels like. Should men ever learn to fly like the feyín or harness steam-piston engines to a carriage, perhaps then there will be some way to run faster than Midnight. But on that day, there was no swifter creature in the world.

I dashed the arrows from my skin as we went. Morgana, seated sidesaddle in front of me, weighed little more than a child, and I was not a large man, so the horse was scarcely burdened as he fled down lanes and across fields of whispering corn. The sheer strength of him drew tears of exhilaration from my eyes as we soared across the bosom of England. Even the supremely self-possessed Morgana loosed a cry of delight as the mighty horse ran.

We hadn't had time to discuss a plan, but there was little need of one. Ahead of us was the River T_____. The water was too deep and wide to ford, but there was a broad stone bridge that Morgana could manage, although she would be deprived of her strength while upon it. I could not imagine being unable to cross a body of flowing water—these creatures had such powers, and yet such weaknesses!

But if my companions would find the water an obstacle, our

[*The Bridge Over the River T——*]

pursuers would have less luck—they didn't have a human guide to get them across.

The river was in sight—the bridge in sight—and Morgana realized where I was taking her. "I cannot cross! It's too wide!" She struggled as if to leap clear of the horse, and I threw my arm about her.

"You're as human as I, or nearly so," I replied. "Draw courage from your mother's blood."

The abutment of the bridge was directly before us. There were shrubs around the end of the structure. To my inexpressible horror, a dozen goblings sprang out of them, their stumplike legs churning up the road. Their pikes formed an impenetrable gate as they lined up against us, and I could not help but recall the fateful drawing on the map—a horse pierced through and through!

"All is lost!" Willum cried. But seeing the silvery metal spears arrayed in our path, an inspiration came to me. With scarcely a rod* between us, I plunged my hand into my pocket and dredged up a great fistful of my master's gold sovereigns.

Midnight's nose was almost among the lances and the map within a handsbreadth of coming true when I flung the coins full in the gobling's faces. I might as well have thrown vitriol at them. The creatures screamed and dived out of our path; where the gold smote them, it burst apart, and each fragment burned into their flesh, wreathing them in noxious smoke. One of the goblings tumbled down the bank and into the water with a shriek I will not forget as long as I live.

We were through the scrimmage. On we rode across the span. An unfortunate traveler with his nose in a book had to throw himself out of the way, and I think a fisherman was propelled off the sidewall and into the river. Morgana swooned in my

* Rod: about five meters.

arms—the power of the water was too much for her. At the far end of the bridge was a checkpoint manned by two redcoat soldiers who were too distant to have seen the goblings for what they were, but not too far to hear the commotion. They stood at port arms to stop us. There was a tollbooth there, so I guessed they were not a part of Captain Sterne's detachment, but ordinary soldiers. It would not go well if they stopped us in any case, so I kept Midnight at a full run and cried, "Her father is after me! If you see an angry Gypsy, don't spare the ball and powder!"

So saying, I flung another handful of gold at the soldiers, with the opposite result: They sprang not away from the coins, but toward them, laughing at my desperate plight as they filled their pockets.

"Take that!" I cried, and meant it. They troubled us not at all as we sped past.

We had safely crossed the bridge despite enemies on both ends, and it had only cost me the annual salary of a chaplain, about thirty guineas.

We tore down the road. Midnight was nearly blown. Horses will run until they die, if they have to, so the rider must not drive them beyond endurance. I slowed him as soon as it seemed we were not pursued across the water. It began to rain.

A very sick-looking Willum, suffering from the influence of the river, crawled out of the saddlebag and made his way forward. There he performed a comprimaunt that somewhat revived Morgana. The cool rain upon her face also helped.

"We lost Gruntle on the far side of the river," he said. "Poor chap panicked when he saw the water coming and jumped out of the saddlebag. I'll never forgive myself for not stopping him."

"I'll go back for him straight away," said I.

"He's probably dead," said Willum, and a pale, dreary light gleamed from his breeches. "Lot of goblings just then."

"Those moths," said I, my thoughts on the slain Violets. "Is that what you become when you die?"

"They're called *brails*," said Willum. "Without the magic in us, we're just moths. Violets was a great soul; she became three brails when she went. Gruntle must be an entire choir of them."

He was choked with emotion.

"This is what we humans get up to all the time, you know," I said. "We 'manlings.' It's always war and killing with us. Gruntle was right about that."

Morgana hung her head. "My father proposeth to make such foul business a permanent occupation for the entire kingdom of Faerie. I feared this alliance with the human king for my own happiness, but now I have seen one of my father's own subjects—my people—die before my very eyes," she said, her voice almost as small as Willum's. "Had I confronted him when first he made his plans, had I refused on the spot, this might not have happened—"

"It wouldn't have worked, would it?" I said. "Your father doesn't listen to you, I suspect."

"He is the King," said she, straightening up proudly, and I saw again that regal flash of defiance in her eye: "Our ancient blood holds more wisdom than mere words." Then the severe look was gone and she shook her head. "I am sorry to speak thus to thee. I've got mingled in my veins the summer heat of manlings and the winter's blood of the Danann Trolkvinde Arian. They take turns making a fool of me."

She fell silent again, and wept into her hands. It wasn't her fault she was a princess, and as far as I was concerned, she was on the right side of this business. From what I had seen, Faerie magic was exceedingly powerful. Combine that with mankind's imperial ambitions and it seemed to me there would never again be peace in any corner of the world. Take one of our warships and teach it to fly: Could not such a vessel rule the land, sea, and sky? Equip its cannon with deadly comprimaunts of fire: Could not such weapons topple the mightiest fortification? Now put a man such as Captain Sterne in command of them, and watch the countryside turn to ash. The very idea chilled my marrows.

There was no sign of our pursuers, so I dismounted and led the panting horse. Willum stayed behind to wait near the bridge, in faint hope that Gruntle might yet make his way across the water.

Morgana and I came, after half an hour, to a small village of thirty cottages with a church no bigger than the stables at the Manse. The homes looked jolly, even in the rain: They were bewigged in thatch and had whitewashed walls and boxes of bright flowers at the windows. Strange to think I had jumped Midnight through the roof of such a cottage not long before. There was a small public house at the far end of the village, which I thought might offer the miserable Morgana some warmth, at least. As we approached it, I saw there was a mail-post before the door, and at the foot of the mail-post a brassbound trunk. Upon the trunk sat a yellow-haired young woman, as damp as the rest of us. Beside her sat a threadbare and equally damp baboon.

"Lily?" said I.

Chapter 16

DESIGNS UPON WOMEN'S HEARTS

I DOUBT THERE is a man in the world who has sorrowed as a woman can sorrow, be she half Faerie or entirely from Liverpool, as Lily was. For it was she, at the very bottom of the selfsame pool of misery in which I'd so often seen her bathe when I was a small boy, like a clumsy pearl diver always dropping the same oyster overboard and plunging down after it again.

When I spoke her name, she looked up sharply. When she saw it was I, her face dissolved into fresh tears like a wrung sponge. Now I had two weeping women, one upon either hand, with whom to contend. At a loss for what else to do, I suggested we get in out of the rain.

In the snug of the public house, which was a room about ten feet square, with a hearth half as large to warm it, we sat with our backs to the streaming windows and our faces to the fire. The landlord did not know what to make of me, as you can imagine—had I broken *both* their hearts? But why the ape? His imagination must have composed tales around the four of us that would have daunted Shakespeare's powers of invention. But he made no complaint over the presence of a Gypsy girl, and for that I was most grateful.

I convinced my bedraggled feminine companions to take a little restorative: for Morgana, a hot toddy of whisky and Spanish lemon, and for Lily, gin and water. I had a dish of piping hot coffee to ward off a chill, as I'd had many cold baths that day. Morgana had never before consumed alcohol, so the effect was an immediate improvement in her spirits. Lily, on the other hand, required several infusions. Once her sobs abated, she told us her tale—with increasing emphasis as her thirst was increasingly quenched.

The baboon, as you have probably guessed, was my old friend Fred, late of Trombonio's Traveling Wonder Show. He had fallen to Lily's care after the troupe was disbanded, and when the white-faced and black-hearted clown had (inevitably) joined the crowded ranks of Lily's faithless ex-suitors, she had taken the creature with her.

"Me and Fred, we've been a-tramping since. 'E's such a comfort, holdin' of my hand and offerin' me dead mice, but it's no use. I can't stop my misery up."

After this latest heartbreak, she had decided she could endure no more of life upon the road, and had determined to fall upon the mercy of her only living relative, an uncle. This person, of advanced age and sharp opinions, made his home at the margin of the very hamlet to which we had come. He had once been the master of a show that played at the hippodrome outside Finchley for fifteen years, and toured Europe. Disaster ended the show, but the uncle had cannily put away sufficient fortune for the rest of his years.

The reason we found Lily sitting irresolute in the rain was because all was not well between her and the uncle. Truth to tell, it could scarcely have been worse. Lily's decision to take up performing, which her uncle denounced vehemently since his forced retirement, had driven a wedge between them. He was her only relative by that time, but had no kinship to offer her unless she abandoned the trade. In defiance, she toured as a high-rope dancer, having vowed never to give up performing—and never to return.

"But this latest romance done me in," she said, slurring her words a trifle. "That d___ Pierrot with his lovely big eyes and strong hands, I thought he was the one to make a honest woman of me. Things went grand for nearly a year—four months at least. Or anyway it was a number of weeks. But then he strayed, and strayed again, and ere I knows it, it's me he's straying with, and him affianced to somebody else!"

With this, she broke down sobbing, and Morgana, moved to tears by sympathy and a Faerie inability to command whisky, also wept. So when the landlord entered to see if I wanted a doctor for them, in desperation I told him to bring some cheese and fruit for us, and oats for Midnight. Fred and I shared the meal, and by the time we were done, the women had regained their composure.

"Anyroads," continued Lily, refreshed after the crying, "here I am at his doorstep, and haven't the courage to knock upon the door. My uncle hated me, said he. Never wanted to set eyes on me again, said he. I'd come to ruin, said he as well. Here I am, ruined just like he said I'd be, and between my pride and his, I'm afraid to say hello."

She managed not to weep, but dabbed at her eyes continuously. Morgana was all sighs, with one hand pressed to her bosom, eyes rolled heavenward. You'd think she'd never heard such a sorry tale, to look at her. In any case, I looked at Fred, and he at me, and neither of us had any idea what to say. Fred outlasted me, so eventually I spoke.

"Dearest Lily," said I. "Since ever I've known you, you have suffered these reversals. Every man to whom you attach your affections is, as you inevitably discover, a cad of the lowest sort. And yet there is always another, and always much the same. Perhaps your uncle is a different sort of man, who will have changed his heart for better, not worse? Such men are made, you know. We are not only rakes and rapscallions."

"Oh, Kit," she cried, and threw her arms about my neck. "You're the only true gent I ever knew, but only a boy before. Now that you're a proper fellow, have you not grown callous like all the other men of my acquaintance?"

"I should hope not," said I, thrown into disarray by her pretty speech. "That is to say, I haven't tried it."

"He will, you know," Lily said to Morgana. "They all do. Wait and see: My uncle will cast me off his door-stoop without a kind word. Our Kit will be rid of me as quickly as he can, because he's got designs on *you*, my dearie. Then I'll be alone, except for Fred, and he's not a gentleman, he's a *Papio anubis*. I can't marry *him*."

About halfway through this statement Morgana suddenly became alert, and her eyes were bent upon me with singular intensity, like the rays of a dark lantern with a green lens*. I did wish to be rid of Lily as quickly as I could, so she was half right. But I didn't have designs on the princess. Or did I? The word *designs* was simply too general. I found Morgana charming and interesting, yes. And of course she was bewitchingly beautiful. But that hardly constituted a design. Now here was Morgana with her eyes blazing like emeralds on a fire, and me with no idea what to say. Because all things being equal, I could see having designs on her, if I didn't precisely have designs *yet*. So I didn't want to deny it more than was absolutely necessary.

But, thought I, and all but shook my head, like a drugged man, *this is her magic working on me*. For all I knew, I wasn't even fond of her. It could just be an unknown comprimaunt of hers. Some magic was done with gestures, and some with but a glance. Of the most subtle magic, there was no outward sign at all.

Thus reminded, I found my tongue: "Lily, I assure you, I am at

---

* A dark lantern was a kind of early flashlight. Unlike most lanterns of the period, the light was directional, rather than diffuse, its beam shining from an aperture in an otherwise opaque canister. The opening was sometimes fitted with a colored lens for signaling.

this young lady's service, but I have no unspoken designs upon her. My intentions precisely match her own."

"Oooh," cried Lily, now delighted, "are you and her engaged for to be married?"

I felt flames rise up my cheeks and chap them red, and blustered, "I didn't say that! We are on the same business, that's all." Morgana's eyes drilled into me like gimlets.

"Oh." Lily was disappointed. Our story obviously wasn't as tragically romantic as hers.

"But," I added, "My friend here is fleeing an unwanted engagement herself. It's quite the opposite of your problem, which is suitors fleeing you."

Lily began weeping again, and I realized she had every right to be upset. I hadn't spoken in quite the most politic way. "That is to say, what I mean," I gabbled, "is—"

"That's quite enough, Mr. Bristol," Morgana said in what must have been her best royal court princess voice—it was so haughty, it struck me dumb—and then she addressed Lily, as kind as could be: "Let's go up to your uncle's house and *make* him take you in, shall we? I think he owes thee an apology."

And with that, she rose, helped Lily to her feet, and guided her to the front door of the public house. Fred and I exchanged mute glances, then rushed out after them.

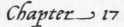

THE THREE QUESTIONS

L ILY'S UNCLE must have put away a good deal of money, because his house was nearly as large as the Rattle Manse and in immaculate condition. The rain drummed down on a roof of firm slates, the windows were shut tight against the spray, and a red door with golden flowers painted upon it stood fast before us. There hung the knocker, and there stood Lily, but nothing happened for a very long time. Fred, Midnight, and I sheltered under a mulberry tree while Morgana and Lily bravely faced the door.

At last, it was Morgana who took up the knocker and clapped it thrice upon the plate. We could hear the *rap-rap-rap* echo through the house. Someone was at home; there was a fire in the parlor and lamps lit elsewhere at windows.

A maid of about Lily's age opened the door. She looked strikingly like Lily, in fact, with yellow hair, although her figure was more plenitudinous abaft, due to a less active career. "Good afternoon," she said, sternly. "Can I help you?"

Lily started weeping again, so Morgana explained the situation over Lily's shoulder to the puzzled maid. "This is Lily, the niece of Mr.— What's his name?"

"Cornelius Puggle," said Lily, through her tears.

"This is Mr. Puggle's niece," Morgana continued. "She's been cruelly abandoned, and Mr. Puggle was the first to do it, though not the last. It is time he made some reparation for his coldhearted behavior, and take her in."

The maid took a long time about it, but eventually said, "You'd better come in, then. The monkey can stay in the barn with the horse."

The maid, whose name was Prudence, took us into the parlor once we'd wrung ourselves out somewhat. Morgana retained her cloak, which by some trick was dry not only inside but outside, too, the moment she entered the house. Lily and I stood and tanned our backsides by the fire until we might have outshone Willum. Morgana and Prudence seated themselves decorously in chairs. I observed that Morgana's features and costume had changed in some subtle way that made her look more English and less Romany, without any particular alteration I could identify.

Then Prudence revealed she was not a maid.

"I am Mr. Puggle's nurse and caretaker," she said. "You are not the first person to come here making claim upon his avuncular affections; I have interviewed no fewer than twenty-three nieces in the last five years. In each case, the young ladies proved to be mistaken about the relationship."

"But—but why would anyone lay claim to be me?" cried Lily. "Uncle Cornelius *hates* me."

"He hated his niece ten years ago when she ran away. But as every girl with an eye to his fortune knows, Cornelius Puggle underwent a change of heart almost the minute she left. Since then he has tirelessly sought the girl out, and his agents have even located her for brief periods, but always she evaded them. And during all these years, never once did she come to his door. It was his greatest wish to beg her forgiveness. Tragically, he has succumbed to senility, and so that interview can never be fulfilled. But while he still retained some of his wits, he entrusted me with three secrets that only his true niece could know. No one has correctly answered these questions since ever I came to this house."

"How could you not have known about this change of heart?" I asked Lily, incredulous as I was.

"I'm ashamed to tell," said Lily, and I think she really was.

"You'd better out with it, then," I cried, "for your ignorance doesn't sound very likely."

Lily shook her head. "Any time anyone would mention my uncle, I would do this"—here she thrust her fingers into her ears—"and say, 'Rhubarb, rhubarb, rhubarb,' over and over again until they stopped speaking. I wouldn't hear a word about him. It drove my last fiancé mad. That's the truth, and I'm very ashamed of it."

"Well," said Prudence, "perhaps you would be so kind as to answer the questions with which Mr. Puggle entrusted me, and we can see you on your way."

Morgana and I were fairly craning our necks with curiosity. Our eyes met several times, and her earlier fury at me was gone. Now she looked altogether swept up in the excitement of this unexpected drama.

"First," said Prudence, standing grandly by the door with one hand on a spinning chart-globe of the known world, "what was the name of Mr. Puggle's pet goldfish?"

Lily laughed. "It didn't have a name. He didn't believe animals ought to have names as they hadn't any souls."

"I see," said Prudence.

"Was she correct?" Morgana blurted out, in a very human manner.

"All in good time, young lady," said Prudence. *Young lady!* thought I. *She's older than your grandmother!* But Prudence turned to Lily again and said, "What is the name of this rug?"

We all looked down at our feet, and there was a great blonde animal skin with short, coarse hair, the skin covered in the sort of tattoos that sailors get, of ships and knotted ropes and birds on the wing. You can imagine my surprise when I recognized it myself!

"Frieda!" Lily and I cried at the very same instant. We stepped off the rug right away. It didn't seem decent to stand on a deceased colleague.

"That's your answer?" Prudence said.

"Who else could it be?" Lily reasoned. "Frieda the Tattooed Camel. I think my own name's wrote on there somewhere, pricked in hindia hink."

"I'll vouch for old Frieda myself," said I. "I know she's got that one right."

"Unfortunately," said Prudence, "Frieda the Tattooed Camel is fairly well known, and therefore this has proven the weakest of the three questions. Several women have gotten it right, none of them the niece. Now here is the third question: How wide is forty-two?"

Well, that question stopped me cold. The others hadn't been riddles. This one sounded to me like a trick—something a Faerie might come up with. Morgana and I raised our brows together, and I could see she was as confused as I, although prettier at it.

But Lily, after only a moment's thought, snapped her fingers and said, "As wide as a circus-ring. Forty-two feet. Uncle Cornelius had a hippodrome, you see, and it was designed after Philip Astley's trick-riding circus in London*. So the horse-circuit, or circus, was forty-two feet across."

There was a long, tense silence. The rain beat at the windows and the flames beat at the coals, but the four occupants of that

---

* Astley's circus ring was not premiered until 1768, some years after the date of these events. Lily must have been referring to an early prototype. But the earliest known ring of Astley's design was sixty-two feet in diameter, so this may also be a slip of Kit's memory, as the events herein were recorded after the fact. As an interesting side note, Charles Dibdin, himself a famous equestrian, jealously mentions in a letter that "Ph'p Astley, Kitt Brystol, and divers others didd ride at Waterloo to muche acklaimme"; we may assume therefore that Philip Astley and Kit knew each other.

room were absolutely silent. Then Prudence spun the globe beneath her fingers once, twice, and again, as if each revolution represented one question.

"I'm sorry," she said. "You had better go."

❖   ❖   ❖

A large and ominous footman saw us to the door. We sloshed our way around to the barn, which communicated with the house by a passageway on the upper story. Lily was so miserable, gin-soaked, and worn with sorrow she could hardly walk, and Morgana, although by far the least sturdy of the pair, was bearing her up. Midnight and Fred were standing inside the barn door, Fred tickling Midnight's nostrils with a wisp of straw.

"We should at least wait out the storm in here," Morgana said. "Th'art both soaked."

"That footman means us no good," I said. "If we're not out of here in five minutes, he'll throw us out. My master could have thrashed him, but not I."

I wanted to find the stairs inside the barn and rush up there into the back of the house straightaway, to introduce Lily to her uncle; but according to Prudence he hadn't any wits left and would not recognize his own mother, let alone a wayward niece from ten years before. In fact, I had earlier attempted to go up the stairs inside the house itself, but the footman—a burly, red-haired fellow with enormous arms and a lace jabot—had emerged from a back room and escorted us out bodily.

Yet when I found a steep flight of steps at the rear of the barn and prepared to mount them, it was Lily who said, "Don't trouble him."

"But you answered the questions correctly. You said so!" I cried.

"I could have been lying," Lily said. "I could have lied about this entire business."

But you didn't lie, Lily," I protested. "I've known you since I was a small boy and can assure you, if you knew how to lie you wouldn't have suffered so many romantic disappointments!"

That got Lily weeping again. I gave up. While Morgana tried to console her, I put the saddle back on Midnight.

Then I turned to them, very serious now: "Lily, there's something you should know. I wasn't going to trouble you with it, because I thought you'd soon be reunited with your uncle. However, things have changed. There's little time. Morgana, who has been your constant companion the last two hours, is fleeing an unsuitable arrangement, as I told you. But there's more to it. The instigator of the situation has a lot of armed and dangerous servants, who are in pursuit of her. We must make the shore of the Irish Sea without being detected by them, or all is lost. So we cannot take you with us. I'll accompany you back to the village, but then we must part ways. . . . Oh goodness, look. A bee."

For just as I was finishing up my speech, I spied a solitary bee walking crookedly atop a tack-box near the door.

"Yes I *know*," said a disembodied voice, seething with frustration. "I've been trying to read it ever since you came barging in here!"

With that, Willum appeared from atop a beam over the barn doors. "Your Royal Highness? Yes, I know. I just did another ruckins in front of a mortal in *direct* defiance of the eighth verse of the tenth chapter of the Eldritch Law. But I have simply *got to read that bee*!"

Chapter 18

THE IMPRESARIO'S FLIGHT

LILY, WHO had run out of other emotional effects to achieve, screamed at the top of her lungs and fainted. Morgana didn't say a word, instead fixing Willum with the same cruel stare she'd given me in the snug of the public house. Then she turned her attention to reviving Lily.

Willum, for his part, flitted down to the tack-box. "You were standing directly in my line of sight," he snarled at me, and then bent down to examine the bee's erratic course, left-right-up-down in various patterns. "Go back to the beginning, you daft insect!" he cried.

I didn't see any change in what the bee was doing; it resembled a very small quadrille.* But presently Willum looked up, his face and bottom shining with hope, and said, "It's Gruntle! He's alive, but can't fly. He hid from the goblings at the far edge of the river and got across on a dung cart. Now he's in a farmyard, and he can't get away on foot because there's a dirty great cat prowling around. We must get to him!"

---

* Quadrille: A French square dance popular at balls.

"The *bee* said all that?" I spluttered.

"They're good for a couple of long paragraphs. Now come on, we need a human to get rid of the cat and collect Gruntle. He's not a mile away. But we must hurry!"

"And hurry we shall," said a high, wheezing voice above us.

Everyone turned to look, except Lily, who was still unconscious. On the upper-story hayloft, a door stood ajar that must have opened on the passage to the house. I saw wallpaper within. Before the door stood a thin, bent man with a white fringe of hair and white mustaches. He wore a soup-stained nightshirt and house-slippers. "I distinctly heard a feminine cry," said he. "Hitch up that fine horse to the wagon, and let us away!"

"Uncle Cornelius?" Lily murmured as her eyelids fluttered open. "Is it you?"

"Great wheels of Parmesan cheese, is that young Myrtle?" the old man cried, and clambered down the steps to the ground floor of the barn. "Myrtle, the fire-breathing tiger-woman! Bless my barometer, it's good to see you. Now listen to me, there's no time to waste. We'll introduce ourselves properly later on, but that wicked nursemaid and her henchman—*henchman*, I say—will discover my absence in no time at all. Raise the stays, young man, and let's get ready."

With that, the old gentleman hopped to the back of the barn—he had a strange, springing walk, his knees always bent—and grasped a large tarpaulin of canvas. This he dragged aside, revealing behind it a Burton wagon* of what later became known as the *Romanichal vardo* type: a little home on wheels of exquisite craftsmanship, elaborately carved, painted in red and green with cream-colored wheels, and all picked out in gold. Emblazoned on both sides in ornate golden letters was PUGGLE'S SPECTACULAR.

---

* Anachronisms have been introduced into Kit's description of the wagon for clarity's sake; in fact this was probably the first specimen of such a vehicle ever made, and may have served as a model for later examples.

[*A Most Extraordinary Conveyance*]

"Young man! Move!" he barked, and I sprang into motion. Despite his age and condition, the gentleman knew how to command.

"What art thou doing?" Morgana demanded as I struggled to get Midnight into the wagon traces.

"Escaping," said I. "Mr. Puggle, for this must be he, has an idea, and I have a plan—and they amount to the same thing."

The horse-furniture of the caravan possessed more straps and buckles than the cart at the Manse, but the principle was the same, and in a minute or two the great horse was casting me looks of disgust as he took his first few steps as a beast of burden. Meanwhile, Mr. Puggle had gone up the steps at the back of the wagon. We heard him rummaging around inside. He emerged at the front and took his place in the driver's seat, a transformed man.

He was dressed to the waist in a splendid if timeworn Prussian hussar's uniform that matched the wagon, with a tall bearskin hat and plume upon his head. The nightshirt hung out below his gold-frogged tunic, and his slippers completed the ensemble.

"Away with us!" he cried, and because he seemed so determined, and we needed so much to get away, and the red-haired footman was stomping across the side-yard with his arms in the air, we all tumbled into the caravan. I took up the reins, flicked the outraged Midnight forward, and we lurched out into the rain.

The footman had to fling himself aside from our path, and sprawled in the mud. It was good to see someone else do it for once. A moment later we were through the gate. At the front door of the house, Prudence the nursemaid appeared, shaking her fists and demanding the return of her patient. Midnight turned his nose toward the village, Mr. Puggle struck up a warbling old marching song in a mixture of Italian, French, and Spanish, and Puggle's Spectacular was on the road.

My plan was fairly simple: We would drop the poor old gentleman off at the public house, commandeer his wagon, and use it to escape *en masse* until such time as less conspicuous transport could be arranged. Our only stop would be to release Gruntle from his torment, wherever he was, and then we'd take a variety of side roads to evade pursuit. The vehicle, being unexpected, was unlikely to rouse the suspicions of any of our foes. Mr. Puggle, unaware of the betrayal I planned, was in perfect spirits.

But the nursemaid had pursued us into the street with an umbrella, shouting, "Kidnappers!" at the fullest extent of her voice, which was considerable. So it was that doors flew open at every cottage, and the cry was taken up by one and all. Men came out of their houses, stamping into their boots with greatcoats thrown over their heads, and took up the chase themselves. In a matter of a minute, half the village was in pursuit, with "Kidnappers!" ringing from every throat.

There was no stopping at the public house. Mr. Puggle, hereafter known as Uncle Cornelius, was coming along.

Fortune was with us: We outstripped our pursuers on foot, after which Willum sat on my shoulder and directed us toward Gruntle's location. This took us down obscure paths and lanes, the wagon rocking outrageously over the poor, muddy ways. Our pursuers were quick to find horses, and we heard them galloping up and down the better-traveled roads not too far distant. I have never been so grateful for the privacy of tall hedgerows as then. By now they were shouting accusations of murder, abduction, arson, and similar crimes, so there could be no hope of mercy should we be apprehended. But none of them spied us through the thickets, and then we were behind a row of hills.

"Is this the road to France?" inquired Uncle Cornelius.

"Yes," said I. "The Irish part of France."

"And is that your parrot?" he asked, indicating Willum, who had abandoned the eighth verse of the tenth chapter entirely, as far as present company was concerned.

"I won him at cards from the One-Eyed Duchess," I said.

"Mad as a March hare," the old gentleman said, clapping me on the other shoulder. "My sort of person."

A short while later we arrived at the scene of Gruntle's captivity.

It was a mean place, the farm buildings as
low and narrow as they could be and still
serve some purpose, with stone walls
piled up all around the yard. I halted the
wagon out of sight around a bend in the
track, and Willum and I proceeded on
foot—he on my hat, to be precise. There
being nobody about at that time of day,
we were not accosted by the occupants,
and so found our way to the piggery at the back, where a large
tomcat missing half his tail was crouched in front of an overturned
firkin. I shooed the cat away, upended the little cask, and there
found Gruntle, as miserable a sight as one could possibly behold.

"I owes you my life, Master Kit," said Gruntle. "I shan't rest until
your kindness is repaid."

I picked him up and placed him upon my shoulder, and we
walked back to the caravan. Willum embraced his friend the entire distance.

"You made that look so easy," Willum said to me with frank
admiration. Perhaps it was my nettlesome pride working again,
but I did not point out that it *was* so easy. I coaxed the unhappy
Midnight back into motion and we were on our way.

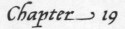

Chapter 19

SAVED BY GILT

I MUST INTERRUPT the narrative, which in any case for a time consists only of our wagon lurching along narrow lanes, to describe this extraordinary conveyance. Residential caravans were common enough; they served as home and office for salesmen of patent goods, elixirs, and similar items no one would purchase from reputable premises. Gypsies lived in them their whole lives, and the more popular traveling shows had such caravans for the comfort of their performers. The troupe with which I had toured slept in barns and hayricks, but we dreamed of such luxury. However, the ones I'd seen always had canvas roofs stretched over hoops of ash or iron, being otherwise common hay wains.

This particular specimen was of a far more deliberate design, with a superstructure of wood resembling an outsized stage-coach. It had been outfitted to Uncle Cornelius' exact specifications many years before, and had remained fully stocked with all of its equipment because he had been intending for years to do one last grand tour with an imaginary team of performers which (for reasons he could not understand) never came to collect him until today. He thought the delay might be due to his conniving nursemaid, Prudence Fingers. He and I sat up in front behind the foot-board on a good cushioned seat with a carved and gilded baldaquin or canopy over our heads, which kept off the worst of the weather.

During a brief stop while Willum scouted the roads ahead, I took a tour of the wagon's narrow interior. There was a door be-hind the driving-seat that communicated with the apart-ment inside: Immediately within, there was a sleeping compartment that would accommodate four people, so long as they were packed in like salted hams in a cask. The space was tall, but exceedingly narrow. Next there hung a heavy curtain, and behind that, a combination storage space, kitchen, and sitting-room, so ingeniously fitted with cabinets and hinged panels that it could be converted from one purpose to the next with little effort. There were small cur-tained windows in the sides, a door at the back with steps beneath it, and a bowed roof over all of it that resembled the hull of a boat. The comparison was fair: Uncle Cornelius had employed a shipfitter to construct the upper parts of the wagon.

There was one difficulty involving this fine vehicle: If either of the feyín came too close to the golden decorations, a bright spark would jump between them and the metal leafing. I learned many interesting curses while they learned to avoid this. Luckily their small size meant they could escape this phenomenon with a little care. It had no effect on Morgana. I expect this was due to her half-human heritage.

The rain slackened, but continued to fall. Poor weather was welcome: it would discourage pursuit. In any case, I was less con-cerned with Captain Sterne and his like than with supernatural agents at this stage of our exploits. Man, I had come to understand, was the noisiest and least stealthy creature in the world, and since my falling-in with the feyín, who seemed to possess senses as acute as nature (or supernature) could provide, I doubted our party should ever be surprised by human ambush. But those miniature arrows with their needle tips—I could not forget that every leaf might conceal a host of savage little bowmen with the power to drive men mad. I feared them almost more than goblings and trolls.

It was Lily who demanded we stop, poking her head through the front door. We were nowhere in particular, among groves of young trees spaced well apart, with glades of grass and flowers between them. I guided Midnight off the road and into a stand of woods that formed a rough ring with a clearing in the middle. There we stopped, at the edge of the trees.

"I want to see to this little one's wing," Lily said. "It's broken, but I know not how badly, for I know nothing about wings."

Lily's introduction to Willum had been a terrible shock, but she was a girl accustomed to shocks, and had grown fond of the Faeries almost immediately, calling them "dear wee pets" and similar sobriquets. She tenderly held up Gruntle, who despite his pain looked rather pleased.

"I'm bein' ministered to by a human lady," he said to me, and grinned foolishly.

One of his wings—which as you will recall stuck out to the sides, after the manner of a dragonfly—was dreadfully torn, like the sail of a windmill struck by a thunderbolt. He had three more wings, but as he told us, "them's the steerin' one." So without it he could only go in circles.

Lily thought she could devise some kind of temporary repair until a feyín *shamaan* could have a look at it; the injury was beyond the comprimaunts of anyone present to heal. Lily and Morgana consulted together on the problem in the back of the wagon, with Gruntle basking in the attention as if it were summer sunshine.

Fred the baboon ascended to the roof and watched the scenery with his close-set red eyes. He did not seem to mind the rain at all; perhaps his costume of weskit and spatterdashes* provided suffi-

---

* Spatterdashes: spats, shoe covers.

cient shelter. When last I had met him, his fur was already salted with age. Now his head was white and the rest of him silver—except for a single gold earring, which well suited his complexion. I didn't know how many years such creatures could expect to survive. Fred, it seemed to me, was old by anyone's standards. Except the macrobian (or long-lived) Faeries, of course.

I tended to Midnight, who required a deal more soothing than usual. His brute muscles seemed to have settled into the unaccustomed work without soreness, but his pride was dreadfully inflamed by the demotion to pack animal. I fed him a few pieces of ten-year-old sugar from the wagon's kitchen cupboard and explained to him in great detail—as horse-lovers will do—the reasons for this indignity, and why he was the true hero of our adventures, and how fond I was of him, qui-tam horse* or not. How much of it he understood, I do not know, but he understood the strokes and kisses upon his nose.

The tireless Willum snipped his way into the cloudy sky to look for enemies, which left only mad old Uncle Cornelius idle. He fixed his eye upon me, of course.

"François," said he, thinking I was some long-lost colleague, "I don't like where we've stopped. There are banditti on the road. And that young acrobat in the 'van has seriously injured himself. The ladies will bind his wounds, but he might be ruined professionally. I don't see how he can put his full weight upon that limb any longer. And us here in Italy! Where shall we find a replacement, and what shall we do with the poor boy?"

"I know not, sir," said I. "The show must go on, of course."

"Naturally!" Uncle Cornelius said. "A fellow my age must keep busy. If I didn't have these exhibitions to put on, I daresay I'd be senile within a fortnight. If only my niece Lily was here—she's a tender nurse, and could also take the place of that unfortunate lad. But she seems to have gone somewhere."

---

* Qui-tam horse: can be ridden, can also draw a vehicle.

I thought this might be an opportunity to encourage his memory, so I said, "Why, Lily? She's right inside the wagon. You'll know her by her yellow curls, Mr. Puggle."

But the old man shook his head, and several tears fell into his whiskers. "She's not my Lily," he said, in the most tragical tones. "Lily vowed never to return."

I might have tried again, but from the sky there came a piping cry, and Willum dived like a sparrowhawk faster than the rain could fall. He tumbled to the wet ground and sprang up, shouting, "Goblings aloft! Goblings aloft!" Then he flew around the back of the wagon to convey the news within.

"The bedouins, is it?" Cornelius cried. "I knew they'd find us eventually. Heathens, man! They'll take no prisoners but the women, and for them it's the harem! We must escape."

"It's worse than bedouins," said I. "I have a pistol within; can you shoot?"

"Can I shoot! I am an expert at trick-shooting—did I not perform for the crown of Austria this last week? Uncork a bottle, snuff a candle, and knock an egg off a showgirl's head, all with pistols, and that is just the matinee!"

I decided not to give him a weapon, lest he attempt any of these feats, and hurried him up into the caravan. He protested all the while, accusing me of showing the white feather to the enemy. Within the wagon, I glimpsed a row of pale and frightened faces; only Morgana spoke.

"The goblings have taken to the air. Hide yourselves."

I hadn't any idea what that meant. Were not goblings assigned to the ground, and pixies to the air? But I retrieved my gun. Then I ran to Midnight and released him from the traces. I slapped his backside to get him out of the clearing. He capered away readily enough, glad to be free of the wagon. Then was I alone, with the light rain coming down, the dripping leaves of the trees, and the phantoms of mist scudding between their trunks.

I heard a sound. It was a keening, blood-stopping shriek, high in the air. If you can imagine the hunting cry of an eagle mingled with the scratch of fingernails upon a slate, but a thousand times louder, that is what I heard. It would have shivered the scales off a fish. I drew my pistol and watched the low clouds; the sound had come from directly above. A second scream followed the first, and then another, overlapping it; there were several of the things, descending rapidly. Whatever were approaching, they were large, swift, and in an evil temper.

Call it a triumph of caution over boldness, but I decided not to stand and fight them on the open ground. Rather, I concealed myself beneath the wagon, pistol trained through the spokes of the front wheel.

I fancied it was caution, but in truth it was terror—I near bewrayed myself. Nor was my fear without foundation. For I had scarcely thrown myself beneath the axles when six dark shapes resolved themselves in the clouds, increasing in density and size as they plummeted toward the earth. Great iron-gray wings were thrown wide to arrest their descent, webbed with leathery skin like those of immense bats, but fringed with long black feathers outstretched as if to claw the air apart.

The creatures were supremely cruel in appearance. They had the feathered heads and necks of eagles, with vicious yellow beaks and yellow eyes, and the limbs and trunks of lions, but dark-furred. Their tails were hairless and writhing. I thought they must be gryphons of legend. Even after they thumped to the ground—I felt the earth shake beneath me—their wings continued to beat, and would have borne them aloft again except their hooked black talons gripped the soil so deeply they were anchored where they stood.

Worse yet, they had not arrived unburdened: upon their backs rode red-clad goblings, armed with quivers of javelins slung over their backs. The foremost and chief gobling wore a crested helmet and brandished a blackened scimitar—there was something in his arrogant bearing that reminded me of Captain Sterne.

"You!" the gobling chief cried, his voice like a cave. "Where are they?"

I pressed myself in the most craven fashion into the grass, but the monster was not addressing me. The other goblings drew out javelins and readied to throw, but they were all pointed at something ten feet above my head. Fred! I had forgotten him in the general alarum. He must still be on the roof. The goblings clearly did not know one primate from another. I knew I should defend him, but I was too afraid to move.

"*Je suis désolé,*" a low, nasal voice replied. "*Je ne parle pas anglais.*"*

Despite my terror I was puzzled by the source of the voice. It couldn't have been Fred, of course. But there wasn't anyone else. I felt the breath of the monster's wings blowing across the grass into my face; they stank of cats and wet feathers and rotten meat. Then a third voice entered the conversation, and I feared disaster was upon us all.

"Great balls of marzipan," Uncle Cornelius exclaimed, descending from the back of the wagon. I saw his thin bare legs shuffle around to the gobling's side of the caravan, slippers flapping; then the rest of him, first the bedshirt and then the hussar's uniform, came into view as he advanced cheerfully toward the wing-riding goblings. He stopped just out of range of the foremost gryphon's jaws. "You certainly arrived in style."

"Where is the Princess?" the gobling chief snarled.

"Which princess? It has been my pleasure to perform before the crowned heads of France, Italy, Austria, the Ottoman Empire, Russia, Liechtenstein, Spain, Sweden, Belgium, Germany, and some chap from Morocco. In every court, there was a brace of princesses at the very least. I recall fifteen in Spain."

Uncle Cornelius did not seem to find anything intimidating in the appearance of the goblings or their mounts; despite my fear, I

---

* "I'm sorry, I don't speak English."

wondered what he saw when he looked upon them. Did he imagine cavalry on fine horses? Or was everything around him so enriched by phantasms that the genuine article didn't stand out? The gobling chief seemed to be considering the same question.

"Do not dissemble, mortal. Our scouts found her scent at your nest of stone. This is your nest of wheels. We smells her. The Princess is here."

"You must mean Princess Onahtah. The Iroquois girl from the American colonies. She isn't really a princess, you know. But if you could smell anybody it would be her. The English food didn't agree with her, you see," Uncle Cornelius said. "I don't know where she's gotten to, though. Bless my brass binnacle, I haven't seen her in days."

The gryphons were growing increasingly agitated, and the goblings became more and more irritated as the interview wore on. If any one of them made move to throw his javelin, I'd shoot that one. None of the creatures had seen me, nor looked in my direction.

"Ludovico," Cornelius said, now addressing the baboon on the roof. "Have you seen the princess? No? Cat got your tongue?"

"Search the cart!" the chief gobling snarled.

Two of his companions climbed down—the gryphons clacked their beaks hungrily at them—and advanced on the wagon. I kept the barrel of my pistol trained on them both. It would take but the additional weight of a feather on the trigger, and the hammer would fall. But before they had gotten within arm's reach of the coachwork, there was a flash of golden light, and the goblings stumbled backward, pawing at their eyes.

"It's gold," one cried. "The thing is covered in real gold!"

At the sight of these creatures flung back by the gilding upon the wagon, the most improbable thing happened: A plan of future action sprang into my mind, and I knew how we should (with luck) get Morgana to Ireland and preserve the lives of our merry companions, if we but survived this interview.

The chief of the goblings, meanwhile, raged and swore evil punishments if the others did not breach the interior of the vehicle, but though his underlings came at it four times—the last at a full run—the blaze of gold threw them back. They simply could not endure the reaction to the stuff. The very air around us stank like a Leyden jar full of the mysterious fluid they call electricity.

"What on earth are your chaps doing?" Uncle Cornelius inquired, after the fourth attempt. The gobling troops were crawling half senseless on the ground by now, level with my eye. I could see the details of their complexions, which resembled the skins of rhinoceroses, composed of overlapping plates of calloused leather. Their eyes were more like nail heads than anything else, and the glimpse I got between their jaws evoked the broken ribs of a carcass rather than teeth in a mouth.

"You and the Frenchman travel alone?" the chief demanded of Cornelius, when it became clear his troop would not be searching the wagon.

"It's just myself and François," Uncle Cornelius agreed. The old man looked about him, but not up at the ape—I saw with a fresh shock that by François he meant not the baboon, but me. If he called me out, all was lost. By luck he had forgotten where I was, and a moment later the gobling's interrogation faltered, for a strange fog seemed to blossom in midair among us out of nowhere, as thick as new cream, swirling as it grew. It was icy cold, sucking greedily at the heat of the world.

From the moment this phenomenon appeared, the chief gobling was evidently frightened. That such monsters could be afraid, I knew from witnessing how they responded to rushing water and gold coins. But this was an altogether new sort of fear. His mission was forgotten. Even the gryphons began to champ and shudder, twisting their long necks about like eels as the vapor spread around them, a phantom's shroud. The gobling soldiers hurried back to their mounts.

With much shouting and beating of gryphon skulls with

javelin ends, the monsters were persuaded to turn their wings skyward again—but the weird fog coiled about their limbs like serpents, growing in opacity and strength until the entire flying party was swallowed up. It might as well have been wrapped in sailcloth, for not so much as a shadow escaped. I could hear the goblings shouting and the gryphons keening within the miasma for a few moments, and then the cloud that had consumed them shrank inward upon itself. It collapsed into a writhing ball—cannon smoke going backward down an invisible bore—and disappeared into thin air, leaving behind only a scattering of violet sparks. The creatures were gone, consumed by it.

I crawled from beneath the wagon the instant they were out of view.

"Who the deuce are you?" said Uncle Cornelius to me. "And why is there an ape on my roof?"

"I'm Herring of Canterbury.* It's ape day," said I, and heartily embraced the old fellow. "You, sir, are magnificent. The flower of our age."

The world was growing warm again.

Lily and Morgana emerged from the wagon. Lily ran straight to her uncle, who looked dazed and ill from his recent adventure. Morgana, I was gratified to see, ran straight to me, although Willum and Gruntle marched across the ground behind her, watching every tree and stone for further attackers. The princess didn't enfold me in her arms, but took my hands and rewarded me with sparkling eyes and more than half a smile.

"Are you hurt?" she asked.

"Only worried," I said, and whistled sharply for Midnight. "If the King knows where we are, and how we travel, then it is but a matter of minutes before the pixies and so forth descend upon us again. We must flee for our lives."

---

* Thomas Herring, Archbishop of Canterbury 1747–1757.

"Those were not the king's goblings," she said, pressing her fingers to her brow. By the storm clouds that drew across her face I saw that she was contemplating some new hardship.

"Then to whom do we owe the displeasure?"

"The scourge of Faerie," Willum groaned. "Mistress of the Black Planet."

"The one-eyed pirate queen what rules the gulfs," Gruntle wailed, falling to his knees for dramatic effect.

"The Duchess of the Red Seas," said Morgana, keeping her voice steady, if a trifle strained. "One and the same. I know not how she learned what road we are on—she may have heard of our escape across the river and connected it with the highly public kidnapping of Mr. Puggle. A simple matter to scout all the likely routes away from that place, if one has a strike of gryphons* at one's disposal. Even now, Kit, the Duchess may not be certain this *is* the party she seeks, for the old man gave nothing away. But you are correct. We must leave immediately. My father's servants will have detected the arrival of the Duchess's gryphons. They weren't precisely . . . subtle."

In a trice we were back on the road. Midnight seemed to have forgotten his reluctance to draw the load; it was all I could do to stop him charging off with us at top speed. Man and beast, we wanted as much distance as possible between us and that unholy meeting-place.

---

* A group of gryphons is called a strike. A juvenile gryphon is called a kite.

Chapter 20

THE BEST CONCEALMENT

WE CAMPED that night in the remotest spot from which we could still get anywhere else. All around was gorse and heather. I chose the place because it was sheltered on one side by a large rock, twice the size of an ordinary house, that overhung the ground sufficiently to create a sort of cave. The rain had stopped, so shelter wasn't required, but it would make our campfire less visible from the air, and give us something to put our backs against if we were attacked in the dark hours. Near to hand was one of those ancient, eerie constructions of giant stones, like a door lintel; the druids of old must have come to this place, perhaps building their fires in the selfsame location we did.

🏵   🏵   🏵

During the drive I'd taken the reins so that Uncle Cornelius could rest; he was still affected by the afternoon's adventure. Morgana climbed through the door behind the coachman's seat and settled primly at my side, careful not to allow so much as a fold of her skirts to touch me. She seemed shy, for a person so accustomed to command. I thought she must feel terribly alone in the world, being altogether in it, but not quite of it. And in such company! An ape, a madman, an acrobat, and an amateur thief were her worldly companions.

For a span of time she did not speak, and I came to understand that whatever matters weighed upon her mind, she knew not where to begin. So I thought to mention something that weighed upon my own.

"Morgana, you have magical strengths, do you not?"

"I do, but they're untried. I haven't any idea of their extent, as I have always been discouraged from using them."

"But you can do bits of conjuring like Magda?"

"She taught me what she could before she was banished betwixt the worlds. Little enough. I have nothing one could call skill at it."

"If I may advise you, the sooner the better to determine the extent of your powers, and the methods of employing them. The entire time those ghastly gryphon-birds were upon us I was wishing most fervently I'd a caprizel or two to fling at them. We could use another spell-caster, I think."

Morgana sighed and wrung her hands in her lap, causing blue sparks to fly from between her fingers. When she saw this, she huffed and sat upon her hands instead.

"You are right, Kit," she said. "Power comes from strength. If I am to oppose my father's might, I shall need to learn the application of what talents slumber within me. Be they great or small."

Seeing her spirits sag under the weight of this resolution, I changed the subject to the other matter that most oppressed my mind.

"Pray tell me of this formidable Duchess," said I. "If there is a new enemy upon the field, I would know her strengths as well."

For a while she said nothing, but rocked with the caravan over the rutted way, her eyes gazing into some remote distance above Midnight's haunches. Then she found her voice, as if reciting an old tale.

"In the Faerie world, we have oceans. Not as in this world, filling the low places; ours soar among the spaces between worlds. They are sometimes like rivers, sometimes cliffs, or betimes a great bowl stretching overhead."

I had seen something like that in a vision, once. It had been the first moment our eyes met.

"Unlike here, *our* waters hold no terror for us," she continued, "except one. That's the Duchess of the Red Seas. Magda told me tales of her when I was small. I presume nursemaids tell tales to children here, as well?"

"Never to me," said I, truthfully. "Although sometimes the orphan-master told us hot water was soup, which is a tale of a kind. But do go on. I would learn as much as I can about this fearsome creature."

Morgana seemed to enjoy the story, once she'd got the rhythm of it. "According to legend long ago, the Duchess was a Faerie royal, like me, but a warrior as well. Those days were troubled, for the War of Stone and Light was raging across our worlds. She was fearless and bold, and won many a battle. But then in her pride she challenged a foe too great for her. He was an ogre, Hrimthur, half son of the Elden People. He slew her army and felled her to the ground, but did not kill her. Instead, for spite, he plucked out her eye and drew out her soul from between her empty lids."

"And she survived?" I cried.

"That was the cruelest part of his revenge: His triumph complete, Hrimthur released the Duchess, neither dead nor alive, and after that she was a wild thing. Without a soul, she could know no home. She could know no happiness. She could not even know who she was. So she took to the seas, where no home is. She took to destruction, which costs much and is worth nothing. And she took the title of Duchess of the Red Seas, which is no name at all."

"That sounds—pardon me—but that sounds like a fairy story," I said.

"Of course it is," Morgana replied.

I realized then that she didn't know we told our children stories of her people, in much the same way they did theirs. I might explain that some other time, when her mood was less volatile.

"So your father the King seeks to capture you, and for some reason this Duchess wishes to do the same thing. But I gather she is not in your father's employ?"

"No," said Morgana. "They are enemies. Had the Duchess not been robbed of her soul in defeat, she might herself rule Faerie. She is, according to legend, my great-great-great-great-aunt, sister to Snaremink the First, father of my lineage."

"Right. So why does she desire your capture enough to lob a flock of gryphons at us? I'm not much on court intrigues, but she must have a purpose in it."

"I know not," Morgana said, sunk in thought. "She cannot cross between the worlds herself, for to do the ruckins requires a soul. The best she could manage would be a sort of phantom. But she can send her minions after us. It is them we must watch for. If there's good news in it, it's that her efforts will surely collide with my father's, and the two of them may hinder each other to our advantage. It is possible."

"What if," I ventured, having cudgeled my brains for some scrap of wisdom that might improve our situation, or at least impress the princess, "she wishes to capture you for a hostage, because your father has something she wants?"

"He has nothing she wants," she said. "He hasn't got her soul. That's been lost for a dozen millennia, by your calendar. Anything else she desires, she simply takes, and the Black Planet swallows what's left over."

"I say, Faerie sounds a jolly place," said I. Morgana didn't reply, lost in her own thoughts.

After a time she returned to the present, favored me with her half smile, and said, "Thank you for taking my part in this business. I wanted nothing to do with you, at first. Now I don't know what I would do without you."

So saying, she blushed prettily and went back inside the snug of the wagon, whence I soon heard feminine laughter. Lily had a tonic effect on everyone when she was in good spirits. Morgana's words had a tonic effect upon me.

I spent the remaining hours it took to drive us to the remote place examining my recently conceived plan. Nothing Morgana had said dissuaded me from the notion. It was a terrible idea, speaking plainly, but it was also the only scheme that made the most of our party's strengths and the least of its weaknesses.

There were two keys to the program: the first was our caravan, which had proven impregnable to goblings, although feyín could come and go from it easily enough, as long as they didn't touch the gold decorations, and Morgana (being a halfsie) wasn't affected by the metal. That made our humble conveyance a rolling fortress.

The second key was our unusual assortment of talents.

$$ \text{\maltese} \qquad \text{\maltese} \qquad \text{\maltese} $$

At sundown, with our encampment made beside the enormous stone, Lily cooked oat porridge from the cupboard, enriched by a rabbit caught by Fred. Gruntle—irritable since his wing had been repaired with paste and parchment—was horrified by this dexterous piece of poaching, and closely inspected the deceased cony to make sure it wasn't anybody he knew. I was astonished that Fred had been so civilized as to return with his game, rather than eat it "on the hoof," so to speak; he had nothing to gain by his generosity. But so he did.

As twilight fell, I saw the baboon and Gruntle contentedly eating ants out of a hill together, so there were no hard feelings between them on the rabbit's account.

Meanwhile, I attended to Midnight. His disgust with the situation was palpable. I plied him with grass and oats and a good brushing, and told him how clever and noble and handsome he was.

Then I took myself apart from the others to study my ex-master's will by the light of a candle-stump. It wasn't of any practical use, for we had already strayed beyond its borders, but I was interested to see if the last few drawings upon it matched our recent adventures. Had Magda predicted everything correctly? In addition, I was feeling sentimental, and wished to remember my master by the pen strokes he'd made upon the map.

The entire drawing had changed.

"Morgana," I said, returning to the circle of firelight. Darkness was now full upon us. "If I could trouble you for a minute or two?"

The Princess was no longer so stiff and formal as when we'd first met—and not just because she'd been advised against it as a matter of disguise. Her adventures had placed her firmly among the doings and customs of we manlings, and I suppose the human side of her was enjoying a newfound liberty. While she had once sat always as if upon a throne, no matter what the accommodations, with her back straight, her head erect, and her hands folded before her, now she was all elbows and knees upon the ground, sprawling comfortably. I suspected Lily's influence may have been exerting itself, as much as anything else. She was an informal soul.

When I spoke to her, Morgana immediately adopted a more regal posture, and rose decorously at my request.

"I've got my eye on you," Willum said to me from atop a heap of firewood drying by the blaze.

Morgana and I retired a little distance from the others. I didn't want to reveal the peculiar change in the map to anyone else, in case it was something dangerous. I showed her the sheet of paper, holding the candle close.

"Do you see it?" said I. "The entire thing has changed. You can just see the edge of the old map, here at the bottom, but this is an entirely new drawing otherwise. And the little ciphers have changed, although they're still penned in my master's hand. I'd call it witchcraft, but I'll warrant that's stating the obvious."

"'Tis witchcraft," Morgana said, peering closely at the page. "Magda's work, this is. I thought it was but an ordinary drawing when first I saw it; there are no witchmarks upon it. But this is a borigium, a caster's map. It would take hours to enchant such an object into being, and yet you said you took it from your master's lifeless hand, with the ink scarcely dry?"

"That's right," said I, confounded. But then, "Do you know—I recall something now. The day I met the old witch, when we parted, it went from afternoon to night, and from one place to another, in what seemed to me the blink of an eye. It didn't bother Midnight, but I was sore disconcerted at the time. Could she have—"

"That's the very chance she needed," Morgana said. "She must have hexed you out of time, prepared this borigium, and then hexed you back. Midnight wasn't bothered because he carried you to the new spot himself, in the usual way. He saw time pass, and thought nothing of it. You were little more than a dressmaker's dummy until Magda lifted the spell."

"But I first saw it before she could have touched it," I protested.

"The original drawings were indeed your master's work. He was telling you what Magda had warned him would happen, but he didn't dare label it. It's the Eldritch Law, verse six of chapter two: 'Of Faerie, make no record.' Magda must have warned him."

"But what can the purpose of this be?" I couldn't imagine what the witch had in mind—the map hadn't been of much practical use.

"If we had only known what you possessed, it should have saved us no end of trouble," Morgana said.

"I wasn't hiding it," I said, defensively.

"I didn't say you were! By the Starlit Falls, you *are* a sensitive fellow, Kit Bristol. All I mean is that I have myself been a fool for not recognizing this object for what it is. You see, with a borigium we receive warning of what's to come.

"The reason it has all changed since your master sketched it is because circumstances have changed. Some things came to pass. That's what the drawings indicate: events to come. Others did not. These new illustrations tell us of events that could lie ahead. They may occur and they may not occur, but we can guide our course by them, like stars glimpsed through the dark clouds."

She swept a stray lock of black hair from her brow, and it fell back. So she took off her Gypsy kerchief and rearranged her hair, in such a very human and womanly way it was a delight to behold. I half expected her hair would brush itself by magic, but it tangled as hair ought to do.

"Why are you staring at me?" she asked, without seeing that I did so.

"I'm not," I said.

"But you were."

"I wasn't staring, I was looking." And a pretty poor defense it was. Most of the time, I couldn't tell whether to be glad or irritated by her, so I was both, in rapid succession. "Anyway," I went on, rather more gruffly than necessary, "there's only one symbol on that map which hasn't changed. The last one is a hanged man. It has remained a hanged man since the first, and I don't like the look of it."

"It will change," she said, but didn't sound very confident. "Nor are we certain that it represents you."

"It looks like me," I said, although in truth it was just a featureless stick-figure.

"Let us see what we can decipher," Morgana suggested. She touched the map with her slender fingers. "This is our route northward. The first of the drawings here at the edge shows our unusual carriage; that's clear enough. I am thankful that Mr. Puggle used real gold, and not Dutch metal, to decorate his wagon, or we would all be captured or slain. The next sketch is a girl standing upon one foot, holding a spear, I think."

"I'd have said it's a tight-rope dancer," I ventured.

"A what?" Morgana had probably seen every wonder genuine magic could devise, but apparently she'd never seen an aerialist in action.

I explained the general principle to her, and how it was the very thing Lily did for a living, when there was a living to be had doing it (income being intermittent in the performing arts). Then we moved on to the next drawing: a face inside an oval with a loop hanging below it. Following that, as near as either of us could tell, was a portcullis, a barred castle gate.

The following sketches we made no sense of; they looked like meaningless doodles. Morgana explained that too many things were now uncertain, so the future couldn't be scryed that far ahead. *All except the man in the noose*, thought I.

"Now that we know what this map is, I am encouraged to hope we might end our adventures better than we started," Morgana said, when we had studied every inch of the paper. "But I cannot understand why the next event on our map shows Lily on a walking-rope. Is it so important that she give a demonstration, or does it refer to her in a general way, accomplishing some action?"

I thought I had some idea of that, based upon my plan, but forbore telling her of it yet.

We returned to the circle of light thrown by the campfire. Poor old Uncle Cornelius, though recovered from his shock, had fallen asleep and was snoring lustily through his mustaches inside the cabin. It was no wonder: By his own account he'd toured all of Europe since morning.

Gruntle was toasting crickets in the coals, but the primary dish was the porridge, which everyone consumed with appetite, although it wasn't very flavorful, there being no salt in the larder. Morgana seemed reluctant even to taste it at first, but hunger got the better of her. She was accustomed to more delicate fare. I vowed we would lay in a stock of food if we remained with the wagon for more than another day or two. And I intended we should. It was time to discuss my plan.

"We have had quite an exciting day," I said, when all were done eating. "And for some of us, several of them. I know that I intended to end my part in it yesterday; yet here I am, and it would be folly to leave this business unfinished. We're well on the way to our goal, and everyone has played some part in getting us here."

"Hear, hear," said Willum, and flashed his posterior on and off.

"Well done one and all," Gruntle said around a mouthful of insect.

"I'm having ever so much fun," Lily said. "My happiness would be complete if only Uncle Cornelius were to recognize me for just one minute."

"Perhaps he will, soon enough," Morgana said.

"No good him knowing you if it's not in front of that nurse-maid," Willum observed. "You've a considerable fortune before you, and that nervy woman has it locked away."

"Oh," said Lily, "I care nothing for that. I just want to have my uncle's mind clear for long enough to tell him I'm sorry for breakin' of his heart, that's all. Can't one of you magical folk enchant him back to health?"

"Regretfully not," Morgana said. "Alike among your people and mine, the mind cannot be cured of its ills. My own father, King Elgeron—his very soul sickens. He lusts for power in the manling's world, and even gold, although he cannot touch it. He envies me my human blood for that alone, I think. If he could but hold gold in his fist as I can, he would bury himself in it."

Morgana's eyes were now moist, and Lily's brimming. They fell into each other's arms and sighed up a gale of feminine misery, as full of sobs as a plum duff is full of currants. I hadn't meant to make everyone weep again, so I steered the conversation back to the topic on my mind as soon as they had recovered themselves.

"Speaking of your father, or that is to say, of the topic of our journey, in which he is obviously implicated, I have a plan."

The women having exhausted their tears, I was given every-one's full attention. Even Fred seemed to be listening from his perch atop one of the wagon wheels. I wondered again at the phrase of French I had heard that day, and puzzled over whence it had come. Surely not *Fred*.

"We have among us," I began, "three magicians, an aerialist, and a trick rider—myself, that is—with a fine horse. We have in addition a gentleman once numbered among the greatest impresarios of his day. We have a caravan, ideal in every respect for life upon the road, its property-chests stuffed to bursting with everything one might require to stage a modest spectacle."

"We know that," Lily said. "What do you plan to do, sell us to a novelty collector for boat fare?"

"I intend," said I, getting to the meat of the matter, "to go on a tour of England, from here to the Irish Sea, traveling not in secrecy but full upon the open road, and to put on merry performances at every stop along the way."

There was a silence that gave to me the feeling of stepping off a high place in the darkness, not knowing what lay below. All eyes were turned upon me, and every face was an unreadable mask (except Gruntle's, which was characteristically blank).

Then Morgana spoke. "You suggest we conceal ourselves in the crowd."

"We make our own crowds, and hide behind them," Lily added.

"We hide in plain sight," I agreed, relief flooding through me that they understood.

"What a load of steaming—" began Willum, but Gruntle piped up.

"I likes that idear. We found a merry Punch-theater inside one of the cupboards this arternoon. Willum and me can dress up as puppets and do plays for the childerns, and begging pardon to her Royal Highness, beside the several verses of them Eldritch Laws we're like to break, but we could use our comprimaunts to get them fancy effects what no other show has. Why, our old whiskered gentleman—he could talk the fish out of the trees, he's that good with words, like. He can do the tellin' of the shows, we do the showin', and by the ears of the stone wocklebear, nobody will dare bother us! We'll be too famoust."

This speech positively stupefied Willum; he might as well have been hexed out of time by Magda. It may have been the longest statement Gruntle had made in a century.

"Just so," I agreed, before Willum could gather his objections.

"If we're popular, it will be that much more difficult to attack us. We'll be noticed; there will be human eyes upon us much of the time, and that will make it difficult for those blasted pixies to strike. Your Eldritch Laws could be useful, for once."

"But you forget our entanglements in the *human* world," said Morgana. "The very minute we show ourselves in public, that vindictive captain of yours may become interested, or word will get back to Prudence Fingers and her swain at Mr. Puggle's estate. Then undoubtedly there will be some human intervention in our scheme."

"She'll have the magistrate on us," I admitted. "I though we could paint a different name on the wagon."

I didn't share my thoughts about Captain Sterne. If he came for me, I'd have to make a run for it, that was all. The others could carry on without me well enough, I hoped. The hanged man.

"I don't think we need worry ourselves about Prudence Fingers," Lily said, tapping her forehead. "A cunning piece of business, is she. With Uncle Cornelius out of the way, she can have him declared missing and take over his property until such time as he returns—never, with luck to her. It's perfect—she's above suspicion and gets all the benefit. So she'll not be eager to find him now, thinks I."

This was an unexpectedly profound insight from simple Lily—but then, I supposed, she knew well enough how a *female* mind worked. It was *men* she didn't understand.

"I remain unconvinced," Morgana said, staring into the fire, the light transformed to gems in her eyes. "The business with your uncle, Lily, is one matter, and not a fatal one. My father's minions are quite another, and the Duchess another yet. Our chief obstacle remains the Faerie loyalists, who are searching for us with thousands of eyes. Should they find us, we shall have no rest or safety and our downfall is assured. If we make ourselves plainly known, as must be the case were we to perform in public, some magical creature will discover us before the first show is done, and we'll be captured before the second show begins."

We all became quiet a while after that. I poked at the embers of the fire, and Willum's bottom flickered like a rushlight. Then the missing element of our scheme came clear into my mind.

"Your people," I said, addressing the Faeries, "find human technology impressive, am I correct?"

"If by 'impressive' thou mean'st 'stupid,' then yes," Morgana grumbled.

But Willum's posterior lit up handsomely. "Of course we do. The canals! What a triumph! Ships on the ocean, wheels, cannon, cathedrals, ironworks, woolen mills, pickled eggs—these are mighty feats."

"And yet," I continued, grateful that Willum, at least, would hear me out, "you laugh uproariously at our attempts to do things such as conjuring, or training brute animals to do our bidding. Even what Lily does you find unimpressive."

"They don't, does they? Well I never," said Lily. "Little ingrates is what they are."

"It's nowt personal-like," Gruntle broke in. "We can make pigs play the 'arpsichord, if we likes, and make neliphaunts walk upon two legs. We can dance on cobwebs and fly through the air. As for magic—well, nuffink personal to manling-kind, but you're doin' it wrong. That's all."

"But don't you see?" I said, rising to my feet in my excitement. "If we do precisely the things the Faeries aren't interested in, they won't suspect us for a moment! They'll take one glance and say, 'Oh, another miserable bunch of talentless, entirely human fools,' and leave us quite alone!"

"I think I begin to understand," Morgana said, and her eyes were full of merriment now. She smiled at me, and I saw that when she smiled fully, she had only one dimple, because her mouth came up higher on one side than the other. But while I was falling into her eyes, she was still speaking: "What you suggest is we perform only human tricks and feats. No eldritch magic at all, no comprimaunts or caprizels. Our foes will look on our efforts with such scorn they will discount us!"

"Precisely my meaning," I said. "Faeries will think we're beneath suspicion, and humans will think we're above it."

"Brilliant," Morgana said, and snapped her fingers at the fire. It burst up in a great green ball of flames, the coals flew up in a red spray, and all at once the light winked out. "I'm sorry," said she, in the sudden darkness. "I didn't know I could do that, either."

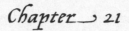

Chapter 21

PLAY-PRACTICE

FOR A few days, we divided our time between fleeing and rehearsing. Once, we heard gryphons screaming in the sky, but at a great distance; we spent the afternoon concealed inside a hay-barn, to be certain we were not detected. On another occasion Willum was scouting ahead and spied pixies upon our route, so we took another road that led us long astray. All the while, bees came and went, Morgana keeping up so busy a correspondence with sympathizers to her cause that I thought it might have a measurable effect on the supply of honey that season.

Part of our collective disguise was the appearance of leisure. If we raced at speed across the countryside, it would be evident that we were either fleeing someone or rushing somewhere. The former would arouse the suspicion of the human king's forces, and the latter would arouse the suspicion of the Faerie king's forces. So we took our time about it, stopping in the afternoons to practice our performances. These pauses allowed Morgana time to concentrate on her bees, as well. She didn't need play-practice in order to read palms, or so I thought.

The order of business was as follows: We would halt the caravan in some secluded place, preferably near flowing water so that there would be a defensive barrier against attack on one side. Then, while I freed Midnight from the harness, Lily would secure a rope between two trees, a couple of hands above the ground. Uncle Cornelius would set up the puppet theater. Willum and Gruntle would don their costumes, the hand puppets.

I observed that the feyín's wings could curl up like overcooked bacon if they wished to get them out of the way, until they resembled a rucksack on their backs. Gruntle's injured wing would not curl, but it was flexible enough to lie along his side, so it wasn't a hindrance to wearing the puppets.

While everyone readied for their parts, I'd saddle Midnight—he would frisk like a colt at the sight of the leathers—and guide him to a level, clear patch of ground about the correct size for a riding-ring. The reason trick-riders go in circles is because the horse, in galloping, leans toward the center; this makes it easier for the rider not to be flung off. It also creates a full ring for the audience to stand in, which earns more pennies. But the primary advantage is defeating the effect of gravitation, at least a little bit.

🜚   🜚   🜚

On the occasion of our first practice, during an afternoon halt, Midnight and I started out with simple things, riding around and around. The horse thought I'd gone mad. We had lovely countryside on every hand, and here we were pelting about in circles. But he soon got the hang of it, and seemed to find me scampering across his back rather interesting. I practiced hanging from the stirrups, standing in the saddle, and mounting and dismounting at a run, leaping across his back like a Minoan bull-dancer of ancient times. Midnight practiced not tossing his head or kicking up his heels at inopportune moments.

I love horses, and the riding of them, as I believe this narrative reveals. But to return to the old trade after a long interval, and to find it still fresh in my mind (if not my body), awakened such a joy in me that I wanted to ride all the way around the world. Instead we rode around the ring, man and beast discovering a new partnership. It wasn't until we cantered to a stop after that first practice that we discovered the rest of the troupe had ceased what they were doing to watch us.

I'm proud to say that the first applause to ring out for Puggle's Spectacular was earned by Midnight and I. That it was our fellow performers doing the cheering diminished the delight of it not one whit.

❦   ❦   ❦

That same evening, we made camp in the corner of a field with a brook along one side and a wood on the other. There was a crust of ruined monastery in the middle of the field—whether the result of the Tudors or Cromwell, I knew not. Until my recent adventures I hadn't noticed how many ruins were scattered about the English countryside. It was like Rome with more sheep.

I set Midnight to graze, then sat on a monastery stone to watch Willum and Gruntle, who had elected to continue practicing their show beside the fire. They dispensed with the pup-pet theater, performing on the ground, which meant their legs were visible below the skirts of the puppet costumes. Willum took the part of Punch and Gruntle took every other role. The overall effect was of watching ugly dolls hop about on very thin legs.

"Act three, scene three, the prison," Willum cried from within Punch's head. "Enter Gruntle as Jack Ketch."

"Not as the doctor?" Gruntle demanded, for he was costumed as the doctor.

"The doctor is dead by act three, scene three. That's why it's set in the prison, thou lummox."

"And because Mr. Punch slain 'is wife and child."

"Right, but the doctor is deceased at this time. You're Jack Ketch," Willum explained, his voice getting higher as he grew more irritated. "Why would a doctor hang a fellow? What sort of a doctor would he be?"

"A Hippocratic oaf," said Gruntle. "I done a joke."

Willum struck his companion over the head with his Punchstick and there was an interlude of boxing, but as neither of them could see anything more than their opponent's feet, no telling blows were landed.

"'Oo plays the constabule, then? There be a constabule in this scene," Gruntle inquired once the fisticuffs were ended.

"We'll cut that role. Ketch can do both parts."

"Oh good," Gruntle said. "I ain't learnt the constabule part norhow."

"But you have committed the Jack Ketch bits to memory?"

"No."

They went on like this for a considerable period of time, never quite getting to the point of rehearsing the scene.

Fred was prodding the fire, Uncle Cornelius was peeling potatoes he'd bought from a farmer, and Lily was inside the wagon, doing what women do when they're doing things men don't know about, whatever those are. Morgana was in conference with some bushes at the edge of the wood, within which I presumed there must be concealed some feyín. Or, for all I knew, she might be talking to the bushes.

"Fetch me the salt, will you?" Uncle Cornelius asked me. "It's in the grease cask on the other side of the wagon." Salt! I sprang to my feet and went straight to the wagon. We hadn't had salt since our escape. Lovely salt. Unfortunately, the cask contained axle-grease, as it was intended to do. So I got out the brush and greased the axles.

This meant that I was bent below the little window in the side of the wagon, and so heard Lily's voice from within.

"I *am* a pretty girl," said she. "You're very kind. Nowt like a fine princess, pr'aps, but for a common sort I'm uncommon 'andsome."

My curiosity piqued, I stole a peep through the window. Had her garments been disarranged I'd have perished of shame, but she was entirely decent, sitting on a tiny stool at the tiny table beneath the tiny looking glass hanging on the bulkhead within. I could not see the glass, but I could well see Lily simpering and tossing her curls at it.

"It's a bafflement to me why that young Kit makes eyes like fried eggs at that slip of a girl when there's a woman under full sail at his very helbow," she whispered to the glass. My ears burned so hot I worried they'd light up like Willum's bottom. I ducked down again and scuttled away from the wagon, bent double like a porter carrying an invisible trunk. It was in this undignified posture that I collided with Morgana.

"What, pray tell, are you doing?" she inquired.

I stood up straight, my ears reaching boiling temperature. "I was hastening across the grass," said I.

"You were a-spying on Lily," she said. "I saw you at it."

"I wasn't spying. I was overhearing."

"With your eyes bent upon the open window?"

"Well," I gabbled, "I was overhearing and overseeing, but she's perfectly decent. It's just that I heard her speaking, and looked in to see whom she spake to, and there being nobody within but her, I hastened away."

"I see," Morgana said, in such a way that I was convinced she did *not* see.

"Why must you think the worst of me?" said I.

"I do not," said she. "I think very well of you."

"Then go you to that window and listen to the one-sided conversation in there. As a favor to me, whom you esteem so much."

Morgana cast such a skeptical look upon me that I found myself studying the night sky, unable to meet her eyes. But at length she crossed the sward on silent feet and stood below the window—she was so diminutive she need not crouch—and listened a while. I stood at a remove, to avoid any further suggestion of impropriety. Morgana returned to my side, one hand clapped over her mouth.

"She's merely talking to herself," she said, and a giggle escaped from beneath her hand.

"So I said."

"It is a privilege of our sex to talk to our reflections," she said, her amusement gone. "Like players, we must rehearse our parts, for we have by far the more demanding role."

But a week before, Morgana had been a stranger to the ways of man. Now she was an expert in the ways of woman. I bent at the waist and clapped my hat over my breast.

"Why dost thou bow thine head?" she asked, reverting to her accustomed speech—an indication she was growing angry with me.

"You grow more human with every passing day," said I, "and yet more mysterious than ever. I daresay you shall make a great queen."

She rolled her eyes but couldn't think of a rejoinder. Instead, she snatched away my hat and pulled it down over my eyes. At this moment, Uncle Cornelius announced the potatoes had boiled, and we rushed to the fireside, Lily, Morgana, and all. I was the last to arrive because I couldn't get my hat off.

☙ ☙ ☙

The next day was uneventful, except for a detour to avoid a nest of goblings of which Willum had got word from a friend. One of Violets' cousins, he told me. Faerie folk had very large families because they lived so long. The death of one of them was a momentous matter for the same reason.

That evening we made camp a little way from a village of timbered cottages, in a dell full of rushing streams and tall curling ferns. There wasn't any level ground sufficient for Midnight and I to practice our act, so we had the night off; I went into the hamlet and bought ham, bread, cheese, salt, and pepper from a farm. Thus equipped, we could make any meal a feast.

Lily took a halfhearted turn or two on her rope, then installed herself inside the wagon as soon as the sun went down. Morgana puzzled over the tarot cards with which Uncle Cornelius had supplied her from the property box. He tried to explain their various meanings, but got it all completely wrong. For example, he identified *l'Epape*, the Pope, as an onion-seller with a building on his head. In my previous life as a performer I had seen enough fortune-telling with cards to describe the main suits, and resolved to clarify matters for Morgana later on.

The feyín argued and came to blows, and between bouts rehearsed their puppet show. As far as I could determine, they had added a character modeled after the One-Eyed Duchess who went about shouting antiroyalist slogans. Fred watched them gravely.

Uncle Cornelius seemed to enjoy cooking, and he was reasonably skilled at it, except he put twigs in the ham soup. I'd gotten through a bowl of it, along with some cheese and bread, when it occurred to me that Lily hadn't joined us at the meal.

"Is she at the looking glass again?" I inquired of Morgana.

"I know not," said she, and went to look into the wagon. I saw that her bowl was empty and wondered if she'd eaten the twigs as well. Uncle Cornelius was in the middle of an instructive anecdote about a Chinese dignitary in a Parisian bathhouse when we heard voices raised in distress.

Everyone rushed to the wagon.

". . . I was merely coming to see that you were well," Morgana was protesting.

"I can care for myself, Your 'ighness," Lily rejoined.

"Lily!" said I, having reached the doorway first. The two of them stood inside the cabin, their noses almost touching, for there was little enough space, and Lily's features were bent into an expression of malice I'd not seen on them before. Morgana looked mostly surprised.

"Well," said Lily, "the cavalry comes. This one 'ere—I know what she is. And such a fine one! Goin' about the countryside with a troupe of hacrobats when her people are suff'rin, puttin' her own safekeeping ahead of everyone else. Risking *your* neck, Kit, for 'ers! You, what never done wrong when I was stealin' spoons and climbing through windows, blameless Kit, turned banditti for this bold girl! Whistlin' Jack, I never!"

So saying, she turned on her heel as emphatically as possible in so small a room and rushed past the rest of us down the steps. She pelted off into the night, wreathed in sobs.

"What a performance," Uncle Cornelius said. "My niece Lily would never have made such a fuss as that girl. I miss her terribly."

"Willum," said I to the wee fellow, who stood upon my shoulder, "make sure no harm comes to her, will you?"

"Me!" he cried. "I'm going to hex her silly. I've got a lovely comprimaunt that will give her flaming boils, and I intend to use it. The *brass* of that woman!"

"No!" Morgana said. "She's not to blame. That's not the Lily I've grown so fond of these past few days. Lay not a finger upon her or risk my displeasure."

"Please keep her safe," I repeated. Willum, though his bottom blazed red as the setting sun, bowed to Morgana and I in turn, tipped his hat to Uncle Cornelius, and flitted into the night.

"I don't trust these Belgians. I'd better find her," the old man said, and followed Willum outside. Fred followed *him*. It was just as likely we'd lose Uncle Cornelius as well, unless he was watched.

"Morgana," said I, and knelt before the afflicted princess, whose entire being radiated misery.

"I am not hurt by her words," she said, swallowing back tears. "I am hurt by the truth of it. Here I am in this gilded wagon, fleeing my responsibility to my father one minute and my responsibility to my people the next! And the while, bee after bee tells me the pixies have raided a dozen Faerie rings, clipped the wings of innocent feyín to make them tell where I am, and goblings roam everywhere, stealing cows and sheep and making mischief for manlings. Oh, the tales I have read in just the last few hours!"

"But that's not your responsibility. It's your father's irresponsibility, I should think," said I.

"Whom else is his daughter?"

"I've no mother or father. Does that remove all responsibility from me? But there's another matter here. I never told Lily you were of royal blood, nor what our mission is. Yet she called you 'Highness' and divines your people are suffering. Unless she can read bees, someone told her this."

"No," said Morgana. "I am certain she used title with me ironically. I am prone, when tested, to put on courtly airs. Thou hast been the brunt of it often enough. As for the suffering of my people, she's seen what happened to Gruntle, wounded for my sake, and she has heard Willum's warnings of fey folk lying in wait on the road ahead. She's got a good brain, does Lily. She merely put the buttons through the button-holes and guessed my plight."

The tears fairly poured down Morgana's face, and her voice was in knots when she spake, but she sat bravely erect and held her head high. Gruntle climbed up on the table beneath the looking glass and reached timidly out to take Morgana's hand. Or the end of her little finger, at least.

"Truth is, ma'am," he said, "we common folk been a-sufferin' many a year, be it in Faerie or be it 'ere in Ningaland. There were a time, like, when we done our magic to freeze the ponds and drop the leaves in winter, then bloom the buds and fatten up the ninsects in springe, all for the love on it."

"And I love you for it," said she, smiling through her sorrow to see the little fellow so concerned.

But Gruntle wasn't done. "Then we begun ter get *directives*, as might be. Fail a crop 'ere, dry up a river there. Pizen those wells and sicken these 'orses. *Mischievin'*, it were. Decrees from King Elgeron. We was meddlin' in manling affairs! I wot not what thy old pater had in mind wi' it, but no good, I'll be bound."

"Her father has been manipulating the affairs of England?" I blurted out.

"In a manner, sir. In a manner," said Gruntle. "By Faerie ways."

"Your entire society is founded upon agriculture," Morgana said to me. "It's a simple matter for a king who rules the seasons and conjures up the weather to make of you what he will."

"By Jove," I cried. "Then what's his purpose?"

"It is that very question I have been trying to answer. But with only half my resolve, for it is escape from marriage that has been uppermost in my thoughts. I *have* been a selfish creature."

Here, she hung her head. I was near overcome by a desire to shower her with kisses and embrace her trembling frame in my arms, to press her to my bosom until my weskit was soaked with tears.

But I did nothing except rise to my feet and say to Gruntle,

"There's a pitcher of fresh milk and a box of oolong in that cupboard. If you could make use of your comprimaunts to boil some water for a pot of tea, I think both ladies may require it."

Of the reunion of Morgana and Lily late that night, I will only say that there was much hurt, many tears, and then all the embraces I'd forborne to make were visited upon both of them by each other. Morgana never kissed anyone, perhaps because of her high station, but she clung to Lily as fiercely as a mother to her babe. They mutually apologized for their behavior and vowed eternal friendship and so forth, and drank a great deal of tea together and of consequence couldn't sleep.

That night I couldn't sleep, either. As usual, I spent the dark hours stretched out upon the driver's seat of the caravan to guard the door. I was tormented by the thought of Morgana's kisses. Were they merely rare, or had the species gone extinct?

Chapter 22

THE TORTOISE COMB

AN UNEVENTFUL day passed, and another. A couple of small boys watched me practice my trick-riding with Midnight one afternoon, and cheered whenever things went wrong, in the way boys do. But they were most impressed and complimented me on my horsemanship, and Midnight on his excellence as a horse.

The larder of the wagon, through judicious stops at farmhouses and sorties into marketplaces in small villages, was bursting with victuals: sausages and eggs, fruit, bread, cheese in several varieties, a pin of beer*, and a loaf of sugar. Luxury! I could almost have traveled in this fashion for the rest of my life.

On the third afternoon following the falling out of Lily and Morgana, it was Lily once again who broke the peace. She had been behaving strangely ever since the Duchess's gryphons confronted us, but I thought this marked her as more sensible than the rest of us; one would have to be mad not to have been affected by such a fright. But she seemed different, somehow.

---

* Pin: a cask containing 4.5 imperial gallons, or half a firkin.

I was reminded of a colorful sword-swallowing acquaintance from my youth: He was a dedicated scoundrel, a pickpocket, and a rake, when he wasn't consuming fencing foils. Then one day he followed a young lady to a meeting of the Quakers, and thereafter devoted the rest of his life to good works and the young lady, in equal measure. From that time onward there was never a more sobersided, boring fellow in all of England. I'm told the lady ran off with a serjeant of the marines.

Lily had something of his aspect: She would sigh, and her eyes would gaze off into the distance, and she'd forget to answer questions. I would have thought her deeply in love, except there wasn't anyone to be in love with except me, and I wasn't her sort of man. But it wasn't a happy state she was in. It seemed almost as if she were pining for someone who had not come to claim her.

That afternoon, we stopped in a quiet place overlooking a forest of oak. I required some time to repair a broken trunnion-pin on the wagon, in which effort I was joined by Willum and Gruntle, who found mechanical things fascinating. Fred went about collecting grubs, Morgana studied the tarot cards and received bees, and Uncle Cornelius conversed with a wild pony that had come to inspect Midnight.

Lily was within the wagon. As I was beneath it, I could hear her moving about, and thought little of it. But then there was a sort of barking sound, and rapid footfalls, and the back door was flung open.

"'Oo's got it!" Lily shouted.

"Got what?" Uncle Cornelius asked.

"My comb! My good tortoise comb!"

"You can't comb a tortoise," Gruntle said. "Bain't got no hairs on 'em."

"The manlings have a very famous story about a tortoise and hair," Willum pointed out. They began to argue over what Lily meant. I crawled out from under the wagon to find it out for myself.

"My loverly comb," Lily said, weeping at me. "Gift from a hadmirer, it is, and the one thing of value what I possess. Now it's gone!"

"None here can have taken it," I said. "Nor would they. The wee fellows have been with me ere we stopped, Morgana's 'round the other end of the wagon, and your uncle has been discussing the architecture of Seville with that pony over there."

"Well it wasn't Fred, if that's what you mean," said Lily.

"I wasn't suggesting Fred took your comb. I forgot to mention him, that's all. He's on the roof, making a salad with worms in."

"There's but one here who might take an interest in a pretty thing like my comb," Lily said, her eyes narrow. "One what misses fine things, pr'aps, or don't know the value of 'em, raised among riches as might be."

"Lily, stop. This is beneath you," I said, and took her by the shoulders. "You are not yourself these past few days."

There was a strange light in her eyes, and it occurred to me that she could be going mad. It ran in families, after all. I noticed her uncle stayed beside the horses, picking wildflowers. He might be insane, but he knew when to keep out of something.

Morgana came around the wagon, tucking her cards away.

"Wert thou speaking of me?" she said, and fixed Lily with a glare that would have slain me on the spot.

"I *was*," Lily huffed. "This gentleman 'ere seems to think my fine tortoise comb walked off all by itself, and I was thinking, you being of the female persuasion like myself, that you might have some idea where it's gone to."

Morgana had no idea what Lily meant by this. "Art thou saying it's been enchanted so that only a woman might find it?"

"Only a particular individual woman of my acquaintance, to be precise." Lily sneered. "One what has access to the little table in there and might have thought I wouldn't miss a bit of shell. But I *did* miss it, and I'd like to know where it is!"

With this, Lily thrust her fingers into the Gypsy sash wrapped around the top of Morgana's skirts, sending the tarot fluttering all about us. I was astounded, and caught up her wrists. Morgana was briefly shocked, and then outraged, and threw up her hand, with the heel of her palm first. There was a flash and a bang and Lily flew several paces and tumbled to the ground, confounded.

Willum and Gruntle emerged from under the wagon. Gruntle went on foot to Lily, she being conveniently located on the ground, and Willum flew up and perched beside Morgana.

"What ho?" said Willum.

The fury washed out of Morgana as suddenly as it had poured in. There were bright blushes on her cheeks, but she was more sorry for the magical blow than upset that Lily had accused her, I think. Still, she was so thoroughly hurt by the accusation her friend had made that she didn't offer her a hand to get her back on her feet. Instead, she ran off a little way and sat down beside the pony, arms folded. Uncle Cornelius offered her a bouquet of flowers. She gave it a sharp look and the blooms wilted and turned brown.

"I don't know what caprizel she tooken, but she tooken it right between the eyes," Gruntle said. "She's comin' 'round, though. No 'arm done, I think." Lily was struggling to sit up.

"How came I here?" she gasped. The strange look was gone from her face. She was my good Lily again.

"You lost your tortoise comb," said I, helping her to rise. "You made a rather unkind accusation. I suggest you owe your friend Morgana an apology."

"Gorblimey, my head ain't half spinning," Lily remarked, and sat heavily on the step of the wagon. The apology would have to wait. But as she sat down, Willum emerged from inside.

"This comb of yours, it's a sort of red and black thing with teeth? Bit like a batwhale's baleen?"

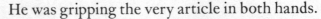

He was gripping the very article in both hands.

"*There* it is!" Lily cried, and took it from him. "Oh, you're a pet. Thank you so much. I'd kiss you but I might swallow your head," she added, and tucked the comb into the bun of yellow hair at the back of her head.

"Never fear," said Willum. "Confirmed bachelor, I am." With

this, he flitted away to see to Morgana and inform her the crisis had passed.

"Willum," I called after him. He paused in his flight like a hummingbird. "Where exactly did you find the comb?"

"It was on the table beneath the looking glass," said he. "Right in plain sight. Don't know how she missed it."

While everyone else worked on the problem of reuniting the two upset ladies, I went inside the wagon and stared at the little table. It was an ordinary thing, with ordinary things upon it: a pot of mustard, some scraps of paper, a quill, a jar of ink, and a dish of skin cream made of goose fat. It would be difficult to miss something such as a hair comb in that assortment.

Then my eye fell upon the looking glass that hung on the bulkhead above it. A chill crept over me. It was a common sort of mirror of the type tinkers sell, a circle of glass backed with silver and framed in wood. There wasn't anything to cause me unease. But when I looked into it and saw my reflection there, I had the distinct feeling that something was inside it, peering through the eyes of my image, regarding me with malevolent will.

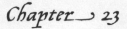

THE FELL REFLECTION

AT LAST we were one day's march away from a market town where we might stage our inaugural performance of Puggle's Spectacular. It was the evening of that penultimate night when things reached a head with Lily, and a bizarre discovery was made.

Lily and Morgana weren't speaking to each other since the disagreement of the previous afternoon. I was unable to account for Lily's behavior.

Morgana climbed up beside me during the last march of the day, still careful not to let her skirts touch me. For a while she stared at her fingers, absentmindedly snapping them now and again, each time sending sparks whirling through the air.

I was about to break the silence (or rather, the clop of hooves, the creak of the wagon frame, the croak of the harness, the rattle of the wheels, and the squeaking of the axles) when she began to speak, very quietly so that she should not be overheard from within.

"What Lily said is true," she began. "I have been selfish, and the plight of my people has come second to my own interests."

My first instinct was to babble denials, to say her interests *were* the interests of her people, and that she was making great sacrifices and so on. But that's not what I said.

"I cannot tell that, for I know nothing of your people, but what you do next is what matters most," is what came out when I spoke.

"You understand me well, Kit," she said, which was not at all what I'd expected. I thought I'd made an appalling blunder.

"Well, I mean—"

"I feel as if my entire life has been a mistake until now, or founded on one. I have drifted like a cypril leaf upon a stream, floating along on privilege and obligation. Did you know, until I met Lily, I'd never had a friend? Never in all my decades. And now that I have one, I'm neglecting the vital affairs of Faerie because we've had a tiff."

"If you've never had a friend, then you know not what happens between them," I said.

"Do they often fight?"

"Sometimes. And sometimes not. It is a matter of the mutual characters of the friends, and thus each friendship is as different as it is alike, the same as people."

"I'm only just learning people. Lily broke my heart into two pieces when she said those things, because they were cruel, and spiteful, and true. Now I scarcely understand whether we're still friends, or if we're not. And I don't understand how Lily seems to have changed so! Or is it me? Have I changed in ways of which I am unaware? Do people change without knowing it?"

"People become who they are without knowing they do so. After that, when we change we usually have some sense of it. That's what puzzles me. This isn't the Lily I know. She's not herself. And yet she seems altogether unaware of it."

"So it's not entirely me?" Morgana said, with a pathetic note of hope in her voice.

"You're doing very well—for a princess," I said. *That* was the wrong thing to say.

Morgana stared at me awhile with her mouth pursed, then ducked back inside the wagon without another word. I cursed myself: What right had I to tell anyone else about friendship? *I* clearly hadn't any idea how it was done. At least Midnight liked me.

$ $ $

We camped in a rather sinister gorge that night, for we had heard the faraway cry of a gryphon not long after Morgana stopped speaking to me. The walls of the gorge overhung the cart track at the bottom, and there were tall trees there. These would hinder attack from above. Our stopping-place was near the far end of the gorge, so if there was pursuit on foot we might escape that way. Still, it was not an ideal place to stop, and certainly it was an unhappy vale. The trees were gaunt and narrow, the stone walls of the gorge blackened with mildew and perpetually damp. There was no undergrowth, only moss. I doubted the sun shone into that place for more than an hour or two in the day.

Nightfall came with a deep darkness. We elected not to light a fire, as the walls of the gorge would light up and make our resting-place uncommonly visible, but stumbled about with bits of candle in our hands. The feyín had no trouble at all—they could see fairly well at night to begin with, but in addition, their hind ends provided them with enough light to read by, if they could read. Perhaps Willum could.

Our agreed-upon sleeping arrangement placed the ladies in the front room with the bunks. Uncle Cornelius, Fred, and the feyín slept in the back room—the old man on the floor, the ape in a drawer, and the feyín anywhere they pleased. I slept outside on the driver's seat.

In practice, however, Willum slept outside the wagon, huddled inside one of the rear side lamps with his feet hanging out the door. He didn't like either end of the vehicle to go unguarded.

So that night, Fred went a-hunting as soon as it was dark. The rest of us, listless and uneasy, whiled away our time at trifles, eating a cold meal, each of us alone.

When things began to happen, Uncle Cornelius was in the back compartment of the wagon, writing a memoir. Willum was sitting in his lamp, impersonating a candle. Lily was in the bunk compartment, Gruntle I knew not where. I was cleaning Midnight's hooves by candlelight.

A little distance away, Morgana was whispering up a nearby tree. She issued what sounded like the sort of orders one gives to couriers. She kept repeating passages as if to help someone memorize a phrase, but I couldn't hear what she said, only the tone of her voice. I supposed she was talking to feyín—but why? Then it came to me. I knew there was a flaw in the bee-mail system! Bees are a diurnal species. No messages at night!

I was just finishing up the third hoof when the door of the wagon swung open, spilling light across the ground. Lily was in the doorway.

"Morgana," said she. "My sweet Morgana. How I've missed your company. Come, I wish to give you a gift. To make up for my terrible behavior."

Morgana turned from her whispering. She was as surprised as I.

"A gift? I desire only to enjoy your good opinion. That is gift enough," she said, and delivered one last command to whomever was in the branches of the tree. She stepped into the tail of the light from the door, so that it seemed to form a glowing pathway between them.

"Oh please, dear," Lily implored. " 'Tis human to give presents as tokens of our love."

"Only," said Morgana, "if I may give you a present in return."

Given Morgana's mood, it wouldn't have surprised me if she'd handed Lily a purse of plenty—and left her on a moor somewhere, wealthy and alone. I'd altogether forgotten about Midnight's feet, so interested was I in this turn of events.

"We shall exchange tokens of our affection, then. And you'll forgive me if you will, and as I pray," Lily said. Morgana hesitated only a moment, then walked up the illuminated path to the door and mounted the steps. The door clapped shut behind her, the light was snipped off, and I stood there by the glow of my tallow wondering what on earth had come over Lily of late. She seemed to swing between extremes, like a pendulum.

I'd returned to Midnight's hooves, and was describing features of tomorrow's performance to him, when I heard a distinct *thump* from the wagon.

"The deuce!" cried Uncle Cornelius from within his compartment.

Then there was a scream of terror, and I ran like blazes for the door.

The latch was locked. I could not lift it. Inside the wagon there were sounds of a struggle, and the entire conveyance rocked on its frame.

"Morgana!" I cried, and "Lily!" for good measure.

Willum streaked around the corner of the wagon and clung to the nose of a carved sphinx aside the door, to which I was now applying my shoulder.

"Back door is sealed," he panted. "None of my comprimaunts will open it!"

"Try the windows," said I, for they were too small to admit me, but ample for him.

"Sealed as well. The entire boat's been hexed!"

"Gruntle?"

"He was with me. He's trying to find a way in from underneath."

"We simply must get in," I cried, for the sounds of struggle were renewed. I distinctly heard Morgana shouting in pain, and Lily's voice was unrecognizable, growling and cursing.

Just then, who should come hurtling out of the darkness but Fred, a pheasant in his jaws.

Without breaking his four-legged stride, he spat the bird out, flung himself into the air, and crashed through the side-window like a cliff-diver plunging into a puddle.

There was a tremendous noise within, a chorus of shrill screams, and a moment later the latch was lifted and I nearly tore the door from its hinges in my frenzy to gain entrance to the compartment.

Fred threw himself outside with as much haste as I threw myself inside, and in a trice I saw why. Evil had entered our snug refuge.

There was chaos within. Every article of furniture had been overturned and the floor was strewn with wreckage. Lily and Morgana were struggling desperately. Their clothes were torn and their hair awry. Lily was stretched across the floor, gripping Morgana's ankle, trying to pull her toward the door. Morgana was at the back of the cabin, struggling with her hip against the table and her hands pressed to the bulkhead, trying to push herself away, but some force was dragging her against it. In the opening of the bulkhead leading to Cornelius's compartment was the old gentleman himself, sprawled on the floor with the heavy curtain pulled down over him.

In the first instant I could not understand the meaning of the tableau. But then, as Morgana twisted and fought, I saw there was something between her and the wall.

It was a human arm.

The limb gleamed strangely, glittering in the light of the swaying lamps. It was a woman's arm, the fingers knotted in Morgana's hair. A strong woman, for I saw muscles flexing beneath its shining skin, dragging Morgana inexorably toward the looking glass.

It was this from which the arm had emerged, like a serpent slithering from a hole. I saw that the crown of Morgana's head was only a handsbreadth from the plane of the mirror, the disembodied arm drawing her into its depths. There wasn't an instant to lose.

I clambered over Lily's prostrate form and grabbed Morgana's hair, closer to her head than the mirror-surfaced hand. I felt the fingers of it, hard and cold. Like glass. With all my strength, I pulled. Morgana cried out, and it wrenched my heart to hear her pain. But the strength of that arm was incredible.

"Willum!" cried I. "Can you enter?"

"I cannot," he shouted. "The caprizel still holds!"

There had to be another way. "Lily! Find the scissors, or my razor. We must cut off her hair!"

But Lily could do nothing, for she had knocked herself senseless against the corner of the stool. Morgana writhed like a speared fish, I strained against the apparition in the looking glass to no avail, and nothing seemed possible.

But then—it was a looking glass. Unless there was some mirrored creature on the other side of the bulkhead, reaching through, then the magical effect ended at the silver behind the glass. I dared free one hand from Morgana's hair and grasped the frame of the looking glass. It was perfectly free, attached only by a nail. I pulled it from the wall.

In a trice, the mighty strength in the arm was rendered useless; without the bulkhead to anchor it, it hung from Morgana's head uselessly. Still clinging to the frame of the glass, I carried the thing to the door, with Morgana in tow behind me. Now those uncanny fingers were crawling up through her hair, trying to reach her head—to crush it, or for what purpose, I knew not. Snatching up a fragment of porcelain from a broken teacup, I slashed at the princess's hair, chopping away at it in the very narrow space between scalp and mirrored fingers. I could see my own reflection in the hand, distorted and flung back in countless facets.

Then it was free. There was a painful popping sound as I tore the remaining strands from Morgana's head, and I had the looking glass in my hands with the arm projecting from it. Morgana fell back across Lily, clutching her injured scalp, her strength gone.

I dashed down the steps of the wagon. The shining hand was clutching at me now. For an instant, I looked into the glass and saw a green face glaring out from *behind* the arm. It was a woman's face, with flaming red hair that leapt up, and across one eye was strapped a patch of black leather. Such hatred I saw in the remaining eye! It froze my blood.

I flung the grotesque object into the darkness. It sparkled as it flew, the arm flailing, fingers outstretched. I saw black clumps of Morgana's hair fluttering along behind it.

I was back inside before the thing had even struck the ground, and scooped up Morgana. I bore her outside and stretched her out upon the moss, where Willum and Gruntle immediately deployed their reviving comprimaunts upon her. Meanwhile, I went straight back inside for Lily, from whose brow blood was flowing. By the time I had her outside as well, Uncle Cornelius had managed to untangle himself from the curtain, and shuffled through the wrack of the interior to the door.

"Reminds me of Russia," said he, surveying the scene. "I was courting a countess when another countess of my acquaintance came along, and the waiting chamber looked much the same as this when they were done discussing the matter."

Then he fixed his old eye upon me. "Careful of women's hearts, young Petrovio. When they crack, the world cracks with them."

By now my every limb was quaking, in that way that follows when a brush with death is averted. Fred was beneath the wagon, looking on with his red eyes wide. Lily was in a trance, her eyes rolled up behind open lids.

"See to her head, will you?" I implored her uncle. He complied with admirable speed.

Morgana's eyes drooped and she mumbled behind her teeth; Willum and Gruntle plied her with so many enchantments that her skin flickered purple and green.

Then, all in a moment, she sat up straight and pointed directly at me.

"Destroy the phantolorum!" she wailed, and fell back, unconscious.

"You 'eard 'er!" Gruntle shouted in his piping voice. "Busticate the phantorolium!"

"What, pray, is a phantolorum?" I was, as always, bewildered.

"That blinkin' mirror," Willum said. "It's not done with us."

I hurried into the darkness in the direction I'd thrown the

thing, stumbling over root and rock, nearly blind. Dead branches scratched at me. I fell on my face before I'd gone very far, tripped by a rotten log. It wasn't long before I was almost out of sight of the wagon. I had hurled the accursed looking glass as far as I could, but it seemed impossible that I had not yet encountered it. I could not throw *this* far.

Had it gone into the branches of a tree, and hung there now like some glass bat? Or had it burrowed beneath the springy turf of moss underfoot?

Then I spied a wink of light up ahead, and another, and as I got closer, I saw it. The glittering arm was dragging itself along the moss like a wounded animal, the looking glass forming a backing to the place where it would otherwise have shown the anatomy of a severed limb. It betrayed no evidence of tiring, this disembodied arm. How did one destroy such a thing, especially when it possessed demoniacal strength?

I circled 'round until I was in its path.

"Stop," said I. "You have done all the damage you can."

I wasn't expecting a response. To my horror, there came one. It was Lily, shouting at the top of her voice from back at the caravan.

"You'll dance in your guts for this, lubber!" she cried. But it wasn't her voice. It was another, hoarse and powerful, the cry of a woman accustomed to command. As she shouted, the arm at my feet shook its fist, then pointed straight at my head.

I'd had enough of this. I raised my boot-heel and brought it down upon the looking glass. It shattered to pieces, and the arm did the same, bursting apart in a spray of bright shards. The fragments themselves broke apart, until there was nothing. For the first time in my recent adventures, I was profoundly grateful for those fine boots, red turndowns or not.

There came a lingering wail from Lily—first in the fierce accents that had delivered the threat, then trailing off until it was Lily's own girlish voice. This cry echoed off the walls of the gorge for a very long time, and the quiet that came after it was as deep as a mountain lake.

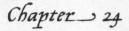

Chapter 24

LILY'S DREAM

THE NEXT morning, both Lily and Morgana seemed perfectly well, despite their misadventure. I say perfectly well, but Morgana's hair was chopped off in the roughest fashion at the top, her scalp visible in the midst of it. Lily had an enormous purple bruise at her temple, and both of them were bedizened with cuts and scratches. By mutual agreement the entire cast had spent the night outside the wagon, in case there was some further enchantment laid upon it. The curtain that had trapped Uncle Cornelius was pressed into duty as a tent. Morgana and Lily lay within, holding hands like sisters. The rest of us huddled beneath blankets and coats, except Fred.

This ape, the hero of the night, resumed his post atop the wagon. He was unperturbed by the events of the evening, and ate the entire pheasant raw. If he knew what he had accomplished, I could not tell. But it was to his valiant actions that we owed Morgana's life.

🐟 🐟 🐟

Shortly after dawn we decamped, following a close inspection of the wagon by the feyín for any vestiges of enchantment upon it.

They found none, so we swept out the debris and carried on our way. Morgana's head was bound in her Gypsy kerchief, so none would observe the unusual cut of her hair. We broke our fast at a little inn, or rather, in the yard of the little inn, for they wouldn't let us inside in our condition. It was no matter to us. We feasted on hot coffee and warm bread and felt the wholesome meal drive away the otherworldly chill that had visited us in the dreary gorge.

We didn't discuss what had happened until we were on the road again with the sun well up and the birds singing their beaks off. The opportunity came when we halted briefly that Willum might scout the way ahead.

Uncle Cornelius set to making an inventory of damages, to be presented to the chieftain of the Tartars; he intended to demand compensation. The rest of us gathered at the back step.

"Are you telling me," asked Lily, "that it's Wednesday?"

"Indeed it is," said I. You came over all peculiar some days ago, and since then a number of memorable incidents have occurred. You can't recall anything of it?"

"Not I," said Lily. The last I remember I was sittin' at the looking glass—it might have been Saturday—inspecting of my complexion, as girls do. Then it's a dream after that. I dreamt my reflection was a-speaking back to me, and we had a lovely chat. It was ever so flattering."

"To be expected," said Gruntle. "You're a beautiful womanling." Then he blushed so much his bottom lit up pink.

She curtsied to him, then continued her recollection. "'Ave you ever had one of them dreams that seems perfectly real, so that waking is all confusion, because you thought yourself awake already? This was the other way about. I thought it was all a dream, but seems it was *happening*. I begun to have regular chats with the looking glass, and it told me terrible things about you, Morgana, some what I didn't understand about politics and royal obligations, and some what I understood only too well."

Here, she looked at me from beneath her pale eyelashes, and it was her turn to blush. I was mystified as to what she meant, but decided it was probably best not to know.

"In this dream, me and the mirror were fast friends, and I came to understand a lady lived inside it, and only borrowed my reflection to speak through. We had ever so many chats about things, and I found I wasn't much interested in poor suffering Morgana any longer. This seemed to upset the mirror-lady. She loved to *talk* about you. But she didn't *love* you, that was clear. It pizened my thinkin', it did."

Here she shyly reached out to Morgana, and the princess took her hand with both of her own and smiled the sad half smile. Lily continued, addressing her friend: "I remember there was a bit in the dream about my tortoise comb, for I couldn't find it, and the lady in the mirror thought she'd seen you take it. You know, from 'er side of the glass. But she must have been mistook, for it turned up soon enough. Then I don't remember anything until last night."

"You need not go on, if it distresses you," said Morgana, when she saw tears spill down Lily's scratched cheek.

"I'd take it as a favor to confess the whole dream," said Lily, "if you can bear to hear it. Last night I remember sitting at the looking glass as I'd been doing, and *this* time, the lady reached through. Her arm was all of a mirror as I recall. A nightmare, tell the truth. But at the time she said such things as I thought was kindness itself. She said I ought to give dear Morgana my tortoise comb as an offering of friendship, and set her down before the glass to see how well it suited her lovely black hair. She took my hand in hers, as you done with mine."

All of us were thrilled with horror at the idea of Lily's slender fingers clasped in that hard, cold grip. Morgana let go of Lily, as if her own hands might turn to glass.

"Well, there it is. I took of 'er advice, called you inside, and bade you sit before the glass. Do you know, I don't think I've ever seen you do it before?"

"In truth," said Morgana, "my appearance means nothing at all to me, for I am disguised."

"That hexplains it, then," said Lily. "Though I think I'd know you well enough without it. Anyroads, you know the rest. It weren't a dream after all. When you sat down and looked into the glass and that arm come snaking out and caught you by the hair, I must have awoke, for I was all confusion. I recall a struggle, and Fred come rushing through the window, and then there was a tap on my nut and I suppose I dreamed proper, after that."

So saying, Lily sat on the bottom step of the wagon, nearly crushing the admiring Gruntle.

"There you have it," said I. "Nothing makes plain sense anymore, the world has gone mad, and I'm fair certain we are *all* asleep. There can be no other explanation."

But Morgana began to pace, a few steps away and a few steps back, pinching her chin with her fingers. Then she addressed Lily.

"Didst thou—did you, that is—call Kit a lubber?"

"I don't recall," said Lily.

"She did," said I. "And correctly, for I've never been to sea."

"All is clear," Morgana cried. "Few can conjure with such power, and only one speaks like a sailor. Lily, you were possessed by the One-Eyed Duchess. That you survived the experience speaks well of your spirit and everyone else's quick actions.

"We call such enchanted objects 'phantolorums,'*" she went on. "They are used to communicate between the worlds. I should have thought of it myself. The looking glass was backed in silver, of course. The fey metal. It was like a porthole penetrating the cage of gold that kept us safe. She discovered it, and used it to attract your attention and enchant you, Lily. She would have preferred to lure *me* before it, but I had no reason to look into the glass, and so did not.

---

* There are two known phantolorums in the world today: One is the Kudara Kannon, an ancient camphor-wood statue of the Buddha now housed in the Tokyo National Museum's Horyuji Treasures gallery; it has been inactive for four hundred and fifty years. The other is a single page in the Book of Armagh, housed in the library at Trinity College, Dublin. The page purportedly depicts four evangelists. They are in fact denizens of Faerie. This phantolorum is still active.

She might not have had the same power over me in any case. So she gained a confederate, taking over your will."

"That's narsty," Lily observed. "I owe her a clip on the bonce."

"I daresay," Morgana agreed. "So in amongst us was this phantolorum. The episode with the comb must have been some error on her part; she almost lost control of you. I suspect she intended to poison your mind against me, so that you would eagerly help her to pull me through, rather than resist the attempt."

"Pull you through!" I cried. "You wouldn't even fit through that glass! That crawling arm filled up the frame."

"She didn't require my entire body, Kit. What she wanted was only my soul."

The implications of this made me ill. Had the Duchess succeeded, we would have rushed into the wagon and found Morgana lifeless, and Lily all battered and bloody upon the floor, and we would have assumed the worst—that Lily had slain her dear friend!

"You understand the implications of this," Morgana said to me, and I had again that uneasy sense that she had read my mind. "When Lily misplaced her comb, the enmity with which the Duchess had divided us burst out *outside* the caravan, where she could make no use of it. But she is cunning. She was able to turn the incident to her advantage and use the selfsame comb to lure me before the looking glass, after all. The rest you know."

"What a diabolical cow," said I, and was immediately ashamed. Speak ill of one woman and you speak ill of them all, as Master Rattle had once observed. "That is, how cruel of her. How entirely wicked."

"She hasn't a soul of her own, you know," Morgana said. I think she felt sympathy for the creature who had almost slain her. "You recall the Duchess is my great-great-great-great-aunt. That means our souls come from the same lode. She could take mine and be almost entirely restored . . . *That's* why she wanted to capture me! Of course!"

"I don't understand it," said I.

"I don't understand *any*thing," said Lily.

"When the Duchess sent her gryphons after us, she hoped to carry me back to Faerie through her agents, for she cannot cross over herself without a soul. This much we knew. Frustrated in the attempt, she changed tactics, and tried to lure me before the phantolorum and drag out my soul.

"Her purpose is clear to me now: Marriage unites the souls of the betrothed. She needs mine *before the wedding takes place*, or it's of little use to her, stuck to another. So it's become a race between my father and the Duchess to capture my soul."

"We're in the race as well," said I. "Where is Willum? We must away!"

❀ ❀ ❀

The remainder of the day passed without event as far as our party was concerned, but things were happening abroad in the land. Morgana received a bee from a sympathizer some ten leagues behind us that said a mad English officer was scouring the countryside for a whistling highwayman matching my description. I was reminded that I had practiced my riding with Midnight in places where people could watch, and cursed myself for a fool. Still, thirty miles of poor roads and winding lanes was a safe distance, in those days. As long as we didn't tarry, we could be well away across the sea ere he caught us up.

Later, she received another bee with the interesting intelligence that there had been a fight between two parties of goblings. The combatants had been wearing the crest of the Faerie king on one side, and the Duchess of the Red Seas on the other. So fierce was the combat that a manling had heard the noise and seen what transpired. The local feyín, thinking of the Eldritch Law, had confused his mind so that he thought he'd dreamed the whole thing. I wonder now how many of our dreams are thus produced.

During a brief pause in the middle of the day, Morgana asked to look at the enchanted map.

"It's come true," said she, examining the illustrations along the route. "There is Lily on the rope, but I think it meant she would perform a balancing act of a different kind. And the sketch after it with a face inside an oval is a looking glass, and now that things have come to pass, I can recognize Lily in the reflection. Look you—the road ahead winds along as ours does, and there is the portcullis gate. But were not the looking glass and the gate beside each other? Now there is another drawing between them."

"I don't like this map," said I, glancing at the hanged man. "It laughs at us but doesn't inform us."

"We aren't using it properly," Morgana said. "Ordinarily they are studied by scryers and sages, who can find portents in every line. I don't have that knowledge."

"But if there is a new picture added in, does that not mean we have changed our fate in some way?"

"Or someone else has. It represents a complication."

We put our heads together to look at the new picture. I could smell her hair, like rain. Which meant she could smell mine. I imagined my hair must smell like my hat, which object had endured the tortures of the damned. Without thinking, I leaned away a trifle, to avoid offending her nose.

"You smell like your horse," she said. A dozen protests sprang to my lips, but I spake not.

She puzzled over the drawing awhile, and then held it before my eyes. "Does that not look like Magda?"

It did indeed. A hook-nosed, hook-chinned creature with a hump, weazened and bent.

"I'd like to see her again," said I. "I have many questions to ask her, and I miss little Demon acutely. He's a fine pup. You would like him."

"I know him well," Morgana said. "A fine pup, and a formidable one." There must have been two dogs by that name, I thought. How could she know *my* Demon? Unless Magda had told her of him, of course. Still, *formidable* might be the very *last* word to describe Demon—or the second to last after *tall*.

※　※　※

Within pistol-shot of the town where we were to perform, Uncle Cornelius called a halt. He wished to go over our equipment and make all ready. This we did, and it was agreed that we would dine early, in case the show went so poorly that we felt obligated to flee town in the night.

Morgana was all nerves again. She didn't eat any supper. Lily cajoled her and made light of our worries, even going so far as to offer Morgana the tortoise comb.

"It's just a bit of cow horn, really," Lily said. "I got it from a suitor, and only keeps it from sentimentalist value. But 'e's in the past and your hair's a mare's nest, so you 'ave it. When it grows back in you can wear it proud."

"When it grows back in?" Morgana said.

"Only yesterday it was shorn right down to the scalp on your crown, 'adn't you noticed? Our Kit's no barber."

By way of response, Morgana untied the kerchief from around her brow, and a waterfall of dark, shining hair came down. It was completely restored, with no evidence of my hasty tonsuring. But I observed a narrow band of white among the black, sweeping back from her temple.

"I'll be," Lily exclaimed. "That's magic, that is!"

"*My* magic," said Willum, freshly returned from scouting the area around the town. He puffed out his chest and looked rather pleased. "Ordinarily I only use that comprimaunt to inflict mange on badgers, but do it backwards and you get some lovely tresses. I had to repeat it three times," he added, giving me a dark look.

Still, even with the comb tucked into her piled-up hair for good luck, Morgana could not escape worrying. Eventually she sat by herself on an overturned butter-churn, and I thought it was my turn to attempt to improve her mood.

"We're safe from attack," said I. "No enemies for miles about. Willum said there are some pixies, but they haven't been pressed into the king's service. They're just ordinary miniature green flying people. If our collective disguise as Puggle's Spectacular is effective, they won't think twice about us. It's an excellent test of our scheme, I think."

Morgana shook her head and squeezed her eyes shut.

"It's not enemies I fear," she said. "It's going before the manling crowd to read fortunes."

I'd completely forgotten about the tarot deck. "Shall I describe the cards?" I asked. "We can pretend you're reading my future."

"No," said she. "I worry the card of death will come up."

"Right," I said. "Never mind the cards, then. Just take the palm like this"—here I extended my hand—"and run your finger along the lines. Hem and haw, then say whatever seems good to you. The less instructive you can be, the better people will like it."

She took my hand, and when her fingertips traced the lines on my palm, sparks flew up. We both laughed at that. Then she composed herself and tried again, her face grave.

Without warning, the world vanished around me, and I saw another of those visions such as had visited me when first we met.

I saw a terrifying beast wreathed in red flames, its head all jaws and teeth, plunging into combat with a vast dragon. There was a bloody battlefield beneath a sky full of enormous stars, or moons, I knew not which. I saw a fearsome black orb of immense size that belched smoke and fire and flew through the air, swallowing entire planets.

The next thing I saw was Morgana and Lily looking down at me with the ordinary afternoon sky above them. I was lying upon the ground.

"You fainted," said Morgana.

"He's suffering from nerves, I expect," said Lily. "It used to happen to 'im right before a performance when he was small."

Chapter 25

PUGGLE'S SPECTACULAR

Ladies, Gentlemen, and Urchins Underfoot," cried Uncle Cornelius, "what you are about to witness is a distillation of wonders from all my years touring the world. This is not the most lavish show, nor the largest; I shall not fill your ears with unfounded claims. What I bring to you is a sampling of delectable delights, made portable enough to fit within the confines of our motley wain, with which we have beguiled the very crowns of Europe and the world. And they paid more than tuppence, rest assured."

The old gentleman went on in this manner for some time, his voice, if not as loud as it once was, still equally persuasive. We had entreated him to complete his costume from the waist down, so now he wore riding breeches and turned-down boots lined with yellow calfskin, as well as a fine wooden theatrical sword.

We had determined the order of the performances based upon their likelihood of success, putting the weakest ones in the middle. Consequently Lily and Fred went on first, with a comical turn. Then I would perform some poorly rehearsed equestrian feats upon Midnight. Uncle Cornelius would deliver a humorous monologue about the Caliph of Arabee, and Lily would go on again to do her tightrope routine for the finale. Simultaneously with all of these events, Willum and Gruntle would put on their puppet show, and Morgana would sit on the back step of the wagon, pretending to read fortunes.

Cornelius would oversee everything and make certain we delivered a few pennies' worth of entertainment before the day was done.

We had decided to separate Morgana and the feyín from the main show in order that they might keep a lookout for Faerie agents. Morgana, particularly, was concerned about pixies—if the wagon was left unattended, they could get past the gold-leaf decorations and ill-repaired window just as well as Willum and Gruntle, for they were even smaller, and once concealed inside could cause us immeasurable trouble. But all of us hoped fervently they'd never discover we were persons of interest.

🜊   🜊   🜊

We stopped the caravan on the village green opposite the marketplace of the town we had selected, and Uncle Cornelius immediately demonstrated that he might be a little hazy about what year it was and whose company he was in, but he had forgotten not a whit of his experience doing shows.

"Ah, Beauregard," said he, to my latest incarnation. "Just the fellow I wished to speak to. I have considered the arrangements and they are to be thus: if we arrange the tightrope there, between those two trees, we can park the 'van directly behind to act as a backdrop; and then we can place the bank, or stage platform, here at the side, at a slight angle so everyone can see. We'll need four casks of hogshead size and a dozen planks for this purpose.

"Then we shall put down straw in a circle forty-two feet in diameter, no more and no less, to cover the riding-ground directly beneath the tightrope. You can measure the circle precisely by attaching a twenty-one foot string to a stake; simply walk around the full compass with the string extended, and there's your riding-ring. But you know all this, Beau. I don't know why I'm telling you. I suppose I'm just anxious because the Sultan will be attending."

I did as he directed. He barked up a crowd, collected pennies, and the show began.

Lily, who had only missed a few days of performance time during her retirement from the trade, was superb. She teased laughter from the crowd with Fred's assistance; he was a droll and heartwarming clown despite his two-inch fangs. Thus was sympathy established for the yellow-haired beauty. Then I came around from behind the wagon, riding upon Midnight. We hadn't rehearsed properly, but our desperate flight cross-country had taught us perfect harmony between rider and mount.

Midnight discharged his duties with excellent form. I, however, made a mess of things, and the crowd was against me until I tumbled off while attempting to stand in the saddle. There came a great gasp of horror from the audience. Now, just as my skill with a sword was mostly defensive, my finest skill upon a horse was falling off.

Long experience had taught me to roll through the impact with the straw-strewn ground. This I did, with no harm to my person. But when I stood up, the crowd groaning with concern, I made a great show of being wracked with agony. Thereafter, when I mounted the beast again, I could do no wrong—there's nothing like the possibility of a broken neck to warm up a crowd.

Cornelius's monologue was uproariously funny, the highlight of the show to that point. It had been an amusing patter when he was younger, I am sure. Now that he was absolutely mad, however, he kept adding in nonsensical flights of fancy, getting names wrong, forgetting his place in the story, and addressing an imaginary boy at the side of the stage who insisted on interrupting him. The entire crowd was doubled up and weeping with laughter by the time he was done. Although our better knowledge of his pitiable condition robbed his performance of mirth for we troupe-mates, we were as glad as any for the uproarious applause he received.

The final act could not have been better. Lily ascended to the tightrope, some twenty feet from the turf, on a loose end of the same strand that hung to the ground. Then I threw a cane up to her, as I had done so many times in my childhood. There was the sketch on the map! She used the cane as a balancing staff, and made a great deal of work out of shuffling to the middle of the swaying span. This was deliberate. She could, if she wished, *run* across a rope blind drunk and reading a book. With the audience's sympathies already aroused by her charming drollery with Fred, and then by her hesitant and fearful progress along the slender perch, she could have plucked the petals off a daisy and the entire crowd would have thought her brilliant.

However, she gave them everything she had (as was her custom in all matters). My own eyes swam with admiration for her courage and skill. She did cartwheels and somersaults, and danced upon the gyring rope as if it were the floor of the Palais Ballroom. She even walked upon her hands, revealing enough of her hind limbs to get every gentleman in the crowd perspiring freely. At the end of Lily's turn upon the rope, she struck a pose and called over the heads of the onlookers for me to bring Midnight around for the "old plunge," as she called it.

I didn't want to make the attempt—I'd lost my touch with it completely—but she begged me, and the crowd demanded it, and at last I rode Midnight directly beneath her position, and stood upon the saddle with my arms stretched upward. Lily, now hanging by her hands from the rope, released her hold and plummeted into my arms. Luck was with us, and I didn't drop her or fall off the horse. We cantered around the ring to general applause, and I hadn't so enjoyed myself in two years.

"Extraordinary!" said Uncle Cornelius to Lily, when the crowd had dispersed. "Young lady, you are a natural talent, perfected by hard work. I have only known one better, and that was my niece, Lily, whom I scorned terribly, and who left my life years ago. If she was here—ah, but she is not. If only angels would deliver her to me, then you should see a proud gentleman begging upon his knees to be forgiven. But I'm being rude, and now my eyes are wet with tears, and I suppose I *am* just a mad old fool."

Lily met this speech with implorations: "I *am* your Lily," and, "Don't you know me, Uncle?"

She devolved into misery when the old man asked her, but a minute later, "Did you not enjoy the show, ma'amoiselle? If not, I shall allow you admittance to the audience free of cost upon the occasion of our next performance."

All did not go perfectly. There were impediments to the success of the show other than my own incompetence, which I heard about later that evening when the market had closed up and we were sojourning in a farmer's field before a good campfire, with an enormous feast of market-fresh delicacies roasting upon it, and a jug of ale passing around.

The first difficulty involved Gruntle, who, minutes before the Punch-theater curtains were to part, was overcome by a terrible case of stage fright. The poor fellow was beside himself. Willum had reminded him they would never be visible, even for a moment, and it was just playacting for children, like when the feyín enchanted ladybirds for their own young to distract them from doing ruckinses. Willum tried everything to keep his companion from paralysis. Gruntle thought he was going to be sick. Then the curtains parted, and Gruntle took courage and went on.

Had a child crept close to the puppet theater and whisked aside the painted tapestry that formed the enclosure for the puppeteer's legs, he would have been surprised to discover there were no legs within, nor any puppeteer. Fortunately, no child was so precocious. Instead, the crisis arose when Willum and Gruntle started out as Punch and Judy, and made a terrible mess of it; they were heckled by infants.

Uncle Cornelius, between his own turns, had an opportunity to observe. He saw the feyín lurching their puppet costumes about, shouting in shrill voices in just the way all such shows are done. It looked very like any other puppet show, but lacked the slightest spark of fun.

So he went up behind the theater and whispered, "Tell 'em any story you like, lads, but it's got to be a story you believe. Put your own life into it. They'll like that well enough."

This could have been a disaster, if the Faeries had taken him at his literal word, for they might have exposed the entire subterfuge. We would have been beset by pixies inside the half hour. But humble Gruntle was inspired; he took the lead. In no time, he was clad in a dragon-puppet costume, and breathing fire of orange yarn at the brave highwayman, secretly the son of a noble family (Willum inside a Dick Turpin puppet), who must also battle a large spider, Punch, a soldier, and a genuine stuffed rat before he won the princess's hand.

Below is rendered a sample of the performance that day.

The scene: a typical Punch-theater with curtains framing the proscenium, the performance area being about two feet square, with an apron suitable for hand puppets. The backdrop is a painted country scene. A score of children sit before the theater.

Dick Turpin rises into view.

DICK TURPIN

Right ho, list thee well, you rotten little scoundrels. I am in fact the famous highwayman Whistling Ja—No . . . er . . . em . . .

[There is a pause while he struggles to think of a name.]

DICK TURPIN

Not Whistling ahem. Er . . . Whispering Jane. Rather . . . Shivering Jim? No no no no . . . My name is Sniveling Git!

[Roar of laughter from crowd]

DICK TURPIN

No, no, I said that wrong. I meant to say . . . erm . . .

[Various unsavory suggestions from the crowd]

DICK TURPIN

You! You in front there, with the tooth missing. One more remark like that and I'll give you a clout up your earhole you won't soon forget!

[Further threats are interrupted by a voice issuing from out of sight below the apron.]

SPIDER

(loud whisper)

Thundering Clive.

DICK TURPIN

Thundering Clive? Who the blazes is that, thou mutton-witted aphid-muncher?

[A large SPIDER rises until just visible at the bottom of the stage, prodding Dick Turpin with a hairy leg.]

SPIDER

'You are, mate.

DICK TURPIN

Oh, you mean— . . . YES! That's my name, for I am Thundering Clive, fearsome pirate.

SPIDER

Highwayman.

THUNDERING CLIVE

Where!

SPIDER

You are. A highwayman.

[Peals of laughter from audience]

THUNDERING CLIVE

The next one of you delinquents laughs at my suffering, you're in for a smiting.

[The spider emerges into full view, bows to the audience.]

SPIDER

> But after all, 'ere we are, you adventurin' about like what you do, and up jumps me, this great urgly spider, and says I'm going to bite yon princess on the head. Now what are you going to do, Clive?

THUNDERING CLIVE

> By the Barbary Ape of the Forgotten Moon! Have at you, thou rancid villain!

[Thundering Clive strikes the spider across the head with some violence. The spider, enraged, beats at Clive with its nine or ten legs.]

SPIDER

> Quit hittin' me so 'ard! Take that, and these!

[A furious battle rages across the stage. Then Clive drops out of sight and returns with a REDCOAT SOLDIER puppet, permanently attached to a musket with fixed bayonet. He uses this weapon to jab at the spider.]

THUNDERING CLIVE

> How do you like that! Taste cold steel, Tegenaria gigantea!

SPIDER

> Right, you're for it, mate.

[The somewhat tattered spider dips out of view, during which time Clive accidentally drops the redcoat puppet in front of the theater and has to implore a scurvy child of four years to return it.]

[Meanwhile, hook-nosed PUNCH has risen into view behind Clive, wielding a club.]

[Punch insists on speaking with the whistling voice of the traditional character, which requires a kazoolike device called a swazzle inserted in the mouth. As the swazzle is for human-sized mouths, nothing Punch says can be deciphered.]

PUNCH

> (unintelligible cry)

[Shouted warnings from thoroughly amused children]

[Punch gives the highwayman a good thump on the head.]

THUNDERING CLIVE

Attack from behind!

[Thundering Clive and Punch proceed to beat each other until Punch's chin falls off.]

The best laughs were got when Willum's temper overboiled and he fell out of character and began to shout at Gruntle. The latter party, meanwhile, revealed a talent for storytelling that had all the children in the audience clamoring with delight. As soon as the performance had ended, Uncle Cornelius pretended to escort the puppet-master within the theater back to the wagon; in truth he was carrying the entire apparatus.

I had the opportunity to watch a bit of the performance, and laughed aloud. Then a rare flash of inspiration came to me, and I drew the map out of my coat. The hunched figure in the new drawing wasn't Magda at all. It was the puppet Punch!

The final difficulty in our première performance taught Morgana a thing or two about human nature. She sat on the caravan's back step with her crystal ball (a lump of glass) and Gypsy costume (she had made her nose longer and more prominent for the occasion, some little adjustment with the jaguundi cloak).

She did not have the power of seeing the future the way Magda did, but as I had explained to her beforehand, a fortune-teller does not tell the fortune of tomorrow, but of today. So when she began taking customers, mostly women come to town to do their marketing, she saw glimpses, in that uncanny way she had, of their innermost hopes and fears. She addressed these directly.

This went very poorly. Her customers didn't want to hear whom their husbands found prettier than them, or learn their children were just as badly behaved as they feared. She was spoiling her patrons' illusions about themselves.

"You're a witch!" one of the women cried.

"Not yet. I'm too young," said Morgana. The woman ran away wailing.

After that, Morgana didn't want to tell fortunes any longer. But Uncle Cornelius whispered in her ear, and she went from a state of misery to one of inspiration. She had only one customer left, a shy girl with a stammer. She informed the girl that she would come, ere long, into good luck, love, and money. The girl scampered away in a state of great excitement. Within minutes, Morgana had a queue stretched halfway around the riding-ring, and was pronounced a genuine soothsayer, consorting with the very spirits of the aether.

❧ ❧ ❧

There had been no sign of magical persons the entire day, and although a couple of soldiers stopped to watch Lily's aerial act, they didn't take any interest in me. Like the fellows I had enriched at the bridge, they were ordinary king's men. Once Captain Sterne followed our trail to this place, as he surely would, I didn't doubt they would remember the trick-rider on the beautiful black horse well enough. But as long as we stayed ahead, our subterfuge might work: It seemed our little troupe's greatest disguise was indeed the open air.

Chapter 26

A BRIEF AND HAPPY IDYLL

I T IS a regrettable feature of storytelling that the happy parts must generally be left out, or the tale becomes dull. Forgive me for omitting an account of the carefree days we spent upon the road, except to describe them in summary form, with a discursion into one unpleasant occasion.

We made our way northwest by short stages, stopping wherever our little Spectacular might draw a crowd. We were sometimes in the company of other troupes, and sometimes by ourselves; many a stimulating adventure was had, and many a triumph won, all within the compass of our show. I don't think Lily or I had ever enjoyed such success—I had enough gold to keep us all, but in the end we earned enough copper to pay for our fare, without the slightest touch on my pocket.

The wagon was the sun, and we its satellites. Along we went, through rain and shine. There were good roads and bad. Midnight seemed happy in his new role: He would condescend to pull the wagon if he could later canter around the ring to cries of admiration. The friendships between us all were cemented (all but one, which I shall explain shortly).

Uncle Cornelius was the happiest man alive, returned to his glory before senescence* took him, and mingling daily with imaginary kings. He delighted in the company of Lily, whom he often said reminded him uncommonly much of his niece; but Lily herself—whom he called Julie, or Meg, or Emma, or Saphira, or a host of other people's names—was always found wanting, for she had not all the excellent qualities of the Lily he carried with him in his mind.

Willum and Gruntle continued to argue, but found great joy in their theatrical partnership, and Gruntle's wing knit back together with the help of daily healing comprimaunts performed by Willum. Morgana and Lily, meanwhile, as different a pair as nature could devise, their friendship strengthened by adversity, grew fonder of each other by the day. Lily taught Morgana everything there was to know about human strengths and weaknesses, which she was adept at mixing in perfect proportion. I think Morgana, for her part, showed Lily how to be more confident in herself, lending her a little royal dignity.

The only friendship that seemed to gain no strength from experience was that between Morgana and myself. It was always thus: We would enjoy some mutual occasion that ought to have thrown us closer together, and then something would occur that seemed to widen the gulf even more. It put me in a terrible state of agitation, at times; I knew not why, unless it was a desire to be popular with princesses, or to have pretty Faerie halfsies think me admirable. The worst of these occasions began as a harmless mistake, and burgeoned into a tempest.

※ ※ ※

We had a day without any performances to do, wending our way between two towns, and upon our halt happened to camp somewhere in the vicinity of a beehive. Consequently, there were many

* Senescence: old age and decrepitude.

of the industrious little creatures about. Morgana was constantly occupied with them.

"Cannot bees be intercepted by spies?" I asked while one such creature spelled out its message on the back of her hand.

"No, for they will reveal their messages to none but the recipient."

"Even on pain of death?"

"Bees live in numbers, not alone. They care little for their own lives, if the rest live."

"Admirable quality," said I, and sat upon a stone. A lance of pain shot up the part of me that doesn't light up, and I sprang to my feet.

"Pixies!" I cried.

Willum soared into view, casting caprizels in all directions.

"Into the wagon!" Morgana cried, and Lily and Uncle Cornelius, at least, complied. Fred bared his teeth, crouched on the roof of the wagon. We waited for the onslaught of arrows, Morgana with her hands up to ward them off with magic.

Nothing happened. The air hummed with drowsy bees, not pixie arrows.

Willum alighted on the stone I'd recently vacated, and examined its surface.

"Not pixies," said he. "You sat upon a bee."

"By the Six Sisters!" Morgana shouted at me. "Thou manling blunderoon!"

She wouldn't speak to me, nor accept my apologies. I'd not only slain the bee, but erased its message, which was part of some fey negotiation.

🐝　🐝　🐝

Disgraced, I retreated to the far side of the wagon and told my troubles to Midnight. Willum took pity on me, I suspect, for he took up a post between the horse's ears and began to describe his ongoing efforts to recruit local feyín to our cause. According to him, the wee people, feyín and pixies, were the only Faeries who lived most of the time in the First Realm. Could we but recruit enough of them to the revolutionary cause, King Elgeron would be isolated in the Middle Kingdom and his human alliances made moot.

Since our adventures began, he had been flitting about, always far from our route, to pass word to his relatives about the cause. He had thousands of relatives, and word spread quickly. But few would commit to it, fearing raids by the royalist pixie bands such as had slain Violets. As we spoke of these matters, a bee alighted in a flower not far from us.

"How do I send someone a bee?" I asked, watching the insect at its work.

Willum rolled his eyes at my simplicity. "It's simple. First get its attention, and then tell it your message. Then tell it who the message is for. Off it goes," he said, as if to a child.

"So I could tell this bee," I said, pointing to a bee, "'Dear Princess Morgana, you enchant me,' and then say, 'Take this to Princess Morgana,' and it would do so? Simple as that?"

I composed this message ironically, for Morgana and I were not speaking.

"Yes, but that's not the right sort of bee," Willum said.

"How do I know the right kind of bee?"

"By its accent," he said, and, bored with my ignorance, flew away.

🐝　🐝　🐝

Not an hour later, having practiced some riding tricks with Midnight and Lily, I returned to the wagon for some tea, and found Morgana sitting alone inside, her eyes downcast.

"You and Lily," said she, "get along so very well."

"Yes," said I, defensively. "It's because she's predictable, and I'm not very bright. It's the formula for happiness."

"You're far more clever than you believe," she said. "Twisting a princess up in knots is no easy feat."

Well, I thought I was in for another argument, and filled my chest with air to expend upon my defense, but the sharp words didn't come. Instead, she looked up at me and smiled her radiant, secret smile, the one that bewitched me. I thought to myself, *This must be what warm toast feels like when butter melts into it.*

Her smile turned quizzical. "Toast?" she said.

Once again I turned red with such force my face felt as if it might burst.

"Can you read my mind?" I fairly shouted. "I've been meaning to ask, but I was afraid of the answer."

Morgana looked surprised, and a little hurt. "I don't *read* your mind, I *receive* things from it. You just sent me a picture of buttered toast. I love buttered toast the best of all manling food."

"Oh curse my britches!" I said. "I was just admiring your smile, and an image of buttered toast came into my head, that's all."

She laughed outright at my indignation, slapping her knees in an unprincesslike manner she had learned from Lily. "Well, I think it's lovely," she said. "Thank you. And thanks for the bee."

"The *bee*?" I said. My veins filled up with icy water.

"Yes. I wonder about you, Kit. Sometimes I think you hate me, and other times you send me pictures of buttered toast. You're just the most delightful bundle of contradictions."

In rapid succession, my insides turned into snow, and then feathers, and then they fell into the ocean and sank. I realized what must have happened—another bee, adjacent to the one I had addressed, and of the correct type, had heard my message, presumed I was speaking to it, and delivered the message to the party named. I searched for words to say, but my mouth was so dry, my tongue was like a mummified baboon in the middle of the Sahara Desert.

Morgana couldn't look me in the eye, luckily. She was studiously examining the ground at her feet, her cheeks blushing prettily like copper pennies. "That bee came as quite a surprise, to be honest," she said.

"W-w-w-w-well," I croaked, "I apologize."

Now she looked up, and transfixed me with those leaf-green eyes. "Don't apologize. I said it was lovely. I'm not only a princess anymore. I'm trying to learn how to be a young woman. I've never had a proper love letter like that. It's not permitted, unless a Faerie prince wished to do it. And Faerie princes don't. They're unromantic."

"*Love* letter!" I blurted out. "*Romantic!* Good lord!"

Naturally, Morgana took this outburst in precisely the wrong way. She sprang to her feet with her brows bent down in angry strokes.

"Was it just some kind of *jest* to thee? Didst I amuse thee with my confession? How *dast* thou! I have relinquished my crown, but within this bosom yet beats the heart of a princess, and I will not have anyone mock my heart's generosity! Get out of my *sight*."

And, just to make doubly sure, she got out of *my* sight. She stomped into the sleeping compartment and threw the curtain across. I stumbled outside and clung to the wheel of the wagon for support. There I must have stood for ten minutes at least, entirely thunderstruck.

Morgana had gone from warm to cold, thrice, in such a very short time, and I had done the same in alternating sequence, that I hardly knew what to think. So I thought nothing, but listened to the swarm of tale-telling bees in my head.

I understood little about women, and less about Morgana, but I'd learned something after all. The Faerie Princess might have lived half a century in years, but she was no older, nor much wiser, than I.

Chapter 27

TOASTING THE STEWARD

S O IT was that the days and leagues alike went by the way, and although there were many incidents, none went so badly as to be included in this history, except to record that Morgana remained both Scylla and Charybdis, and I the most inept Odysseus imaginable.*

After another week or so, we were less than three day's journey from Liverpool, Lily's place of birth. There she had an ex-suitor in the fishing trade; his boat could take us across the Irish Sea to Cork, where there was an independent Faerie council to which Morgana could address her plight. The Faeries, one and all, spent their entire waking hours dreading that sea passage.

Even as Morgana let fall her cool Faerie nobility and became increasingly human in her behavior—picking up a wealth of insights from her fortune-telling, besides the feminine mannerisms she learned from Lily—she also became more commanding. One night, she and Willum went out into the darkness and did not

---

* Scylla and Charybdis were the original 'rock and a hard place,' crushing ships that passed between them. Odysseus managed to survive the experience.

return until dawn. I doubt Lily slept for worry. I know I did not. But when they returned with the pink of dawn, she wore a garland of flowers woven about her brow, and the jaguundi was not the travel-stained homespun of her disguise, but white and silken, shimmering in the pale light. Her true features, not the subtle living mask, were upon her face.

"There has been a council," said she. "I am Steward now, caretaker to the Faerie people in this region. It is a lesser role than king, but these folk believe the King has gone mad. So I am now the highest authority here."

"Congratulations," I said, for I knew not the correct thing to say.

Willum told me that our traveling subterfuge was working very well—the Faerie people thereabouts knew not how their princess traveled. But they did know she was abroad in the land, against King Elgeron's wishes, that the planned marriage was in disarray, and that she would defy her father to the end. There was a tremendous uproar among the magical folk, but to the humans in our party it seemed nothing at all was happening. We saw only pleasant summer days and heard no more than birds and insects.

When the sun had set on that same day, I was composing myself for sleep on the seat of the wagon when Willum appeared at my elbow and tugged on my sleeve.

"You awake?" he inquired. I assured him I was.

"Thing is, me and some lads, we're celebrating Morgana's stewardship. And they don't believe I'm mates with a manling. So I was wondering if you might like to come along. There will be refreshments." Such yearning was in his voice that I could not refuse.

🦋　🦋　🦋

It seemed as if I walked for miles in the dark, with Willum fluttering from branch to twig and twig to stone, telling me which way to go. He was keenly excited, I think. We were in a wood of very old trees. At length we came to an open space among them in which stood a "Faerie ring," a rough circle of toadstools. I didn't see any evidence of an entertainment going on. It was perfectly still, except for the distant cry of a fox.

"Right. This is him," Willum said.

Of a sudden, there were lights all around me. Some were feyín bottoms, but most were flowers that had been enchanted to glow like candles, so that they cast their color over the scene. The ring of toadstools was populated with a dozen little winged people—pixies among them—all regarding me with wide eyes. Gruntle stood at the fore, flexing his mended wing.

"Look what the cat drug in!" he shouted. "Old Leather-End!*"

"The Eldritch Law—" one of the others said.

"Not tonight, Bunkle," said another. "Tonight we're rebels."

"Greetings," said I. "I am Kit. Thank you for the invitation."

It took a while for them to grow accustomed to a human being in their midst, with rather a lot of ruckinses if I moved too suddenly, but eventually they wee behaving as I suppose the feyín do—at parties, in any case. These wee country folk had simple fare laid out on leaves, and ample drink scooped from a hollowed-out melon. I didn't partake of the food, which tended toward roasted larvae, but the drink, called glump, was quite pleasant, and there were countless toasts to Morgana's health. I could have consumed the entire supply of glump in a few swallows, but sipped it as they did, from the caps of acorns.

"Glump's made from the melon its own self," said Willum. He'd had so much of the stuff his nose had begun to light up, too. "Caprizel on the inside, leave the outside alone, and a week later it's melon brandy. Stand back, Granny!"

I paid particular attention to the pixies, which were so elusive

---

* Leather-End is a popular character in Faerie stories, a hapless human farmer who goes to great lengths to destroy the feyín on his property, always with disastrous results. The name "Leather-End" is derived from the fact that humans have ordinary skin in the parts where feyín are luminous.

but influential in faerie matters. They were various shades of green, and smaller than the feyín, with feathered hummingbird wings; they were clad only in fur loin-clouts, and carried bows and arrows. I saw that they had very sharp teeth and eyes tilted almost upright, like a cat's.

There were some speeches made toward the middle of the event. They were in the feyín's own tongue, but I heard Morgana's name repeated many times, always with great gravity, insofar as those present were capable of it in their melon-fueled condition. These concluded with a song of which her name formed part of the refrain, and some of the little people about me wept to hear it. Then, to lift the mood, there was a backside-lighting contest.

"We're all takin' turns seein' who can wish Princess Morgana the best luck," Gruntle said, his bottom-light winking slyly. "Mine was rather good—wished her a endless supply of the juiciest beetles with the tenderest shells. She's Steward now, you know. Got to earn that one, cain't be a-born to it."

Although the gathering was a merry one, with many cheerful songs sung and much clapping, I detected fear among these people, and not just fear of me. There were a few posted outside the light, I saw, and they neither ate nor drank, but watched the shadows. And once, when a badger waddled past, all the lights went out and I was alone in the dark, surrounded by toadstools. The wee people didn't return until the animal was well out of sight.

"Badger," Willum explained. "Can't be too careful. They're moody beasts. Do you know," he went on, trying to throw his tiny arm around my shoulders, "don't tell the Princess, but did you see the white in her hair?"

"I did," said I. "It must have been from the shock of that accursed phantolorum thing."

"It's not that at all. Badgers, mate. Like I told you, I used a reverse badger comprimaunt on her hair. Well! It came in with a badger stripe. Don't mention it to her. Lucky she's not vain—I think I can sort it out before she discovers it."

🎵   🎵   🎵

I awoke the next morn refreshed, my head full of Faerie songs. Willum seemed somewhat ill; I suspect he was overhung from the glump. Gruntle could not rise at all, but remained abed inside a woolen mitten.

The party had revealed to me that there was a busy world of magic beneath our very noses. From some of the conversations among the feyín at the event, I learned that Faerie villages had been raided by pixie bands. The pixies who had attended the party were of a different sort from the ones that swarmed. They were a solitary breed, each keeping to itself much of the time, and were known to play little tricks on manlings to amuse themselves, but also to pay them kindnesses. They were appalled by the behavior of their more collaborative and violent cousins.

The raids, according to pixies, had not the effect the Faerie King desired—instead of frightening his people, it infuriated them. Among those present there had been talk of a general strike. If the wedding went forward, there would scarcely be a flower that bloomed in all England, except by luck—apparently the feyín had considerable influence in that area.

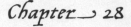

Chapter 28

THE SIGILANTUM

I N O N E place, a day or two later, we saw cruel evidence of a pixie raid. We passed through a grove of fine horse chestnut trees and the air beneath the leafy canopy was thick with smoke. There was an uncommon number of moths flitting about, winking like stars in the strips of sunlight that came down through the foliage.

"By the whiskers of the Sleeping Mountain," Willum said, and bid us stop the wagon.

The feyín flew up among the branches overhead and for some minutes searched all about; for what, I did not know. Morgana stood a little way apart from the rest of us, leaning against the bole of a mighty tree. Then Gruntle flew down to her feet and cast an armful of tiny arrows upon the leaf mold.

"Not a soul left alive," said he, and walked back to the caravan with his wings drooping.

Then Willum also descended from the canopy; in his arms was a pair of shining Faerie wings similar to his own. He was furious.

"You see these?" he cried. "Cut off! Those pixie brutes! They're torturing folk now."

With that, he spoke some words in a foreign tongue and performed the fire-comprimaunt upon the wings, and they disappeared in a puff of green smoke. Then he flew into the wagon, pulling his hair. For her part, Morgana wept.

"It is my fault that these good folk have died," she said. "Didst I but marry as my father demands—"

I put my arm around her and spake useless words of comfort for a time, and then Lily did the same, to better effect, pointing out that lives given for a noble cause were never lost, but a cause abandoned was no better than an unmarked grave for those who died in its name. There's wisdom to be found in all heads. Lily was as foolish as I, but only in ways that would cause trouble to herself, never others.

With such thoughts, and with lamentations for the feyín dead, my mind was occupied. There were thousands of brail-moths flittering about us—what I had at first taken for smoke was but the dust of their myriad wings.

Now I bent my eyes upon the ground, and there saw signs of struggle all about—the moss underfoot was torn, stems of wood flowers broken, leaves cut and pierced as if by miniature knives, which they may well have been. And the pixie arrows were everywhere. Even as I looked upon them, I saw they were turning, becoming needles, as from a pine tree. Only the most observant eye would mark them, and wonder how came pine-leaves to lie beneath a stand of chestnuts.

Then a glitter of bright metal caught my attention. I strode to the place, some distance from the wagon. There upon a natural cushion of moss lay a silver coin with the head of an unfamiliar king upon it. I stooped to look at it.

"What found you there?" Morgana called, dashing the tears from her face.

"Someone dropped a bit of foreign money," said I, reaching down to pick it up.

"Touch it not!" Morgana cried, and thrust out her arms. A

wave of force thumped into me, and the nearest moths were sent a-tumble, with me after them. I flailed through the branches and alighted upon my head twenty paces from where I'd begun.

"'Tis a sigilantum," she said to her magical companions, who had fluttered over to see. Lily made her way to where I was to see if I was fatally injured, but as I'd landed on my pride, I wasn't badly hurt. I was, however, infuriated. It was one thing to fling caprizels about at her foes; quite another to loose them at me.

"What in heaven's name is a sigilantum? It looks more like a silver crown to me," I complained, getting to my feet. "Except for the king's prodigious periwig."

Morgana stood over the object, panting, her cheeks flushed. "That pirate witch the Duchess has marked it."

"You sense enchantment upon it?"

"No, and that's why I am certain it's a sigilantum. They bear no trace of magic. But there can be no other reason for this coin to be here. It's manling-size, so it's gobling silver, and there have been no goblings here. It was left in this place to be discovered by you."

"Pray tell, what harm would come of retrieving it?"

"Sigilanta allow someone in Faerie to observe the progress of something in the manling world without having to employ spies or do a ruckins. No enchantment is required; the object merely has to come from Faerie. With that in your pocket we'd always be found out. That cunning pirate! She knows a manling can never leave money lying upon the ground. But her minions must be some-where near, lying in wait; we must fly!"

"I just flew," I complained, and only then did she recall what she'd done.

"Forgive me, Kit," said she. "I know not—"

"You know not your own powers," I concluded for her. "I, on the other hand, am becoming well aware of them."

In less than a minute the whole company was piled into the wagon, and I got Midnight up to a good speed, despite the burden he pulled. In ten minutes we were well away from the wood, and by sundown we'd gone up every crooked lane and cart path in the countryside. I guided our craft through pig-yards to perfume it and brooks of swift water to render it scentless, and performed every dodge that came to mind like a large and lumbering fox endeavoring to escape the hounds. In the end, Theseus himself could not have found us afoot, though he raveled all the string in England.

The question uppermost in my mind was most disquieting: How had the Duchess known we would pass through that place? It was no good scattering thousands of coins across the countryside on the chance we'd pick one up, for *anybody* might do so, and then she'd be tracking all sorts of people she wasn't looking for. So it wasn't thus. That coin was meant to be found only by one of our party, which meant that somehow the Duchess knew where we were, or what our route was.

$ $ $

It was twilight when we heard the shrill scream of gryphons, at a height so great we could not see them. I halted the caravan against an immense haystack and scooped straw over the roof to conceal it from above; Midnight was so weary he could not take another step. We cowered in the hay and listened to the faraway wailing of the creatures circling in the sky.

They came near sometimes, and then drew far away, and eventually there was silence, except for the crickets. We spent the night without fire, and none but the horse slept a wink. Even poor mad Cornelius knew there was some fell pursuit behind us. He thought it was the Turks, come to take away the dancing-girls.

For the last couple days of our journey, we rolled along with a tarpaulin of rotten sail canvas over the roof of the wagon to disguise it from above, and only took it down to enter the towns where we would perform.

Chapter 29

THE COMPANY SOON TO PART

THE CLOSER we drew to the coast, the more bees went back and forth, until the wagon began to look like a rolling bee skep. These insects made superb messengers, because not only were they impervious to threats or bribery, they were also all but impossible to follow. For absolute security, they could even be instructed to pass messages by relay, so that an entirely different bee would appear before the recipient. But there came a time when the sheer volume of bees was suspicious. Willum, Gruntle, and Morgana held council on this, and concluded that their frail anonymity could not last much longer.

It was agreed that Puggle's Spectacular should do one final performance that evening, and then we would make for the coast as fast as we could, abandoning our subterfuge. We would travel just as swiftly as Midnight could bear, even leaving the caravan behind, if necessary, in the final stretch of the journey.

At the docks, the company would part ways. I would sign up as crew on a ship to the Americas, if I could get such a berth, and see Midnight joined a grand stable. Lily, for her part, had vowed to return her mad old uncle to the nursemaid Prudence Fingers—

consequences be d___d. At least she'd enjoyed some time with him again, even if he had not known he was enjoying time with her, and he had spoken fondly of her memory. She was resigned to the fact that he would never recognize her in person again.

It was not clear what Fred the baboon's plans were; when the topic arose he would scratch himself and blink. Lily volunteered to take him with her, but if she went to gaol for kidnapping, his fate would be grim. He might well end up as a stole or hearthrug.

Morgana's future, I could not guess, nor did I wish to think upon it. It filled me with fear. Though I stared at it for hours, the borigium map told me nothing. The sketch of the castle gate was next on our path, whatever it meant.

꙳　꙳　꙳

We arrived at our penultimate destination, a market town of unhealthy countenance in a marshy place that eventually drained into the River Mersey. The air was humid and the clouds low and weighted with lead. It matched the somber mood of our little company, except Uncle Cornelius, who was in good spirits because we were all going to Calais, in his mind, for a last tour of the Continent. We rolled up to a place of low, damp fields, beyond which was the city. There we studied the prospect, looking for a likely spot to stage our show outside the town; the market was within, but I didn't like the notion of putting gates and guards between ourselves and rapid escape.

"Look at those castle walls and turrets, Harry," said Cornelius, to the fellow he imagined me to be. "Look at the height of 'em! We'll not cower outside. Tonight we perform behind those walls, and if this were Troy, we could smuggle in a dozen warriors through the gates. Instead we'll play our best, and if we're lucky we can smuggle a dozen maidens out!" With that, he winked and jabbed me in the ribs with a ribald elbow.

"Oh, Uncle," said Lily, at once sad and fond, her head poking out between us through the front door of the wagon.

Morgana joined her there and remarked, "If you can smuggle but one maiden out, I shall be content." So saying, she didn't look very content. She could not meet my eyes.

For my part, I noted that the gate in the wall of the city was equipped with a portcullis—very like the entrance to a prison.

We decided to remain outside the walls until near the hour of our demonstration, and to depart shortly afterward, to travel through the night. So we had a few hours of time to spend waiting. Each of us was withdrawn and brooding. The feyín were so anxious, Gruntle worried his wings would fall out. Even Uncle Cornelius sensed the mood, and took to polishing the woodwork inside the wagon.

Morgana drifted past me while I was inspecting Midnight's hooves, and whispered, "I would speak with you alone."

"I'm at your Royal Highness's every beck," I said, sincerely. I had seen the great respect her people showed her, and it humbled me.

"Don't call me that," she snapped.

I was entirely bewildered, for this sort of forth-and-back had become routine: I'd say the wrong thing, and then, to correct my error, I would say nothing, which was the wrong thing to do; and round it went, back to the beginning, and I would say and do the wrong thing again.

"Morgana," I amended.

We walked out in a field of barleycorn, leaving our friends behind until they looked like puppets themselves, and the wagon their little theater.

"There are thousands of my people all over the countryside ready to rise against my father," she said. This wasn't what she had originally meant to talk about, I could tell. I had driven the original topic from her mind with my awkward obeisance.

But she continued, "I had not meant to start anything; I merely wanted to be free of an oppressive marriage. Have you ever done something for entirely selfish reasons, and then discovered there was a far better reason to do it?"

I thought about that. "I have never had the chance," I said.

"You've never been so selfish, you mean," she said, and managed to make it sound like a defect in my character. "I didn't expect to see you again after we collided outside that inn, and yet you have stuck by me: goblings, One-Eyed Duchess, and all. What profit can there be in it for you?"

"None," I said. "But not everything is a matter of gains and losses."

It seemed the conversation had come around to her original purpose—something to do with our tempestuous allegiance. I dared not call it friendship.

"Why not call it that?" said she, sharply.

"Don't read my mind!" I cried. "Or is it my fault again, for sending you mental bees with my inmost thoughts scribbled upon them? I simply do not know what is the right course of action with you from one minute to the next."

"As you know, I have never had friends before now, Mr. Bristol. Only subjects. My friends are precious to me, more precious than life. I would give up a thousand years so that Lily might enjoy ten minutes in the company of her uncle's right mind. If I would do that for a simple girl, what would I do for my people? I never thought of it before, yet now I find I would not merely defy my father for them, but fight back against him."

"That's why I called you 'Your Highness,'" said I. "When you cast off being a princess, you became a queen." The moment this sentiment left my lips, I must have turned purple; my face felt as if it were pressed against a frying pan. Where did these preposterous utterances come from? Had I swallowed a bad poet?

"It's not bad poetry, Kit," she said. "I merely wish to know if we are friends, you and I."

When she said this, she shyly took my hands in hers, and I saw a tear well up in her eye. Her dark brows quivered with some suppressed emotion. My heart was leaping in my breast like a spring hare. *Were* we friends? What should we call this troublesome bond, which seemed to have the power to heal or hurt with a single glance?

I must not have answered in time; truly I did not speak for far too long, my thoughts whirling like autumn leaves blown out to sea. For she tore her hands from mine, and pressed them over her eyes, and rushed away from me across the barley, trying not to let me hear her sobs.

Though I rose and took a few steps to follow her, I stopped. Whatever I thought of her, and she of me, it mattered very little. I was a wanted man, and she a princess, whether she liked it or not. Our destinies were unmatched: mine was small, and hers great, and our life spans equally mismatched. I'd be dead in a fortnight on the point of Captain Sterne's sword—or, if the map was correct, swinging my heels at the end of a rope. She might live for countless ages. I watched her figure disappear among the barley stalks, and sighed, and hung my head low.

꽃　꽃　꽃

You never saw a more gloomy band of entertainers in your life as Puggle's Spectacular was that evening. The colorful wagon rolled through the crowded streets and Uncle Cornelius barked our wares, outcrying the costermongers and fishwives, his wooden sword held proudly aloft. We set up our show-place at his direction, in a broad square aside a guildhall where we could stretch the tight-rope between the eaves of two timber houses, and there was room beneath for a riding-circus of the prescribed diameter.

As I was pulling on my boots for the performance, Uncle Cornelius sat down beside me with his pipe. "Have you a brimstone match?" he asked. I was certain I did, and felt in my weskit pockets. But instead of a match, I found something long and sharp.

I drew the object out: it was that accursed tooth of Magda's! With a gasp, I flung the bit of bone away from me.

"You can't light a pipe with that," Uncle Cornelius said. "Do you take snuff*, Li-Chang?"

I confessed that I did not. Uncle Cornelius told me I was mistaken, for he'd seen me take it only the previous day when we performed at Vienna. Then I recalled I did have my master's snuffbox still, in one of the saddlebags, and so was able to meet his request.

The old man thrust a generous pinch of the stuff up his nostril with an almighty snort. His rheumy old eyes rolled up into his head, his bristling white brows flew halfway over the top of his gleaming skull, and then he bent his mouth into a shape expressive of horror and delight at once. Thus composed, he hung in that position for several seconds as a ball, thrown straight up, seems to hang at the very apex of its flight before beginning its descent.

Then the suspense was shattered by a colossal explosion: He sneezed with such violence that his head shot down where his knees should have been, and his knees shot up to fill the void left by his head. Once all of his parts had returned to their customary positions by a process of subsidence, a matter of about half a minute, he wiped his eyes with his handkerchief, said, "Bless my Turkish slippers," and took another pinch.

Then rush torches and lanterns were lit around the square. It was time for the show to begin.

---

* Snuff, or tobacco powder, was believed to improve the eyesight, among other things. It is the only form of tobacco used by Faeries, although they don't consume it, but burn it to ash and compound it with walnut oil to create a polishing paste for silver.

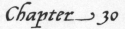

THE FINAL PERFORMANCE

CORNELIUS ANNOUNCED us as vigorously as ever, and Lily and Fred did their comic turn; for the discerning members of the gathered crowd, there was a hint of *tristesse* or sadness that loaned the comedy sweetness and made it all the more charming. Willum and Gruntle were across the square, where they could perform their puppet show and watch the city gate at the same time, and Morgana was fortunetelling at the stoop of the wagon, watching the other side of the square, where there were several outlets.

Midnight acquitted himself well; my own thoughts were in such a jumble I hardly knew what I was doing, but if my performance lacked precision, at least I didn't fall to the cobblestones. Then Uncle Cornelius delivered his monologue, and I discovered we had left one consideration entirely out of our plans: the possibility that the old gentleman might describe something accurately.

Until that moment, he had betrayed nothing of his unusual companions, nor spoken of the strange things he'd seen the last couple of weeks. We had ceased to guard against it. But this night, halfway through his rambling speech, he began to tell all.

"—As the Dauphin will attest, my merry company and I were

rolling along the road between Paris and Versailles in this selfsame little dogcart. We had paused for a pinch of snuff, when what should appear from out of the sky but ugly warlike creatures astride the backs of giant winged serpents—may Jupiter anoint my collar with mustard if I tell a single word untrue!"

The crowd thought it was all in good fun, and most folks laughed fit to burst their buttons. We fellow players were less amused. I motioned to Morgana to cease her reading of fortunes. She joined me beside Midnight for a whispered convocation while Lily made desperate throat-cutting gestures to her uncle from the foot of the bank upon which he stood.

Uncle Cornelius ignored her, and went on. "So these creatures— they might have been gryphons, or basilisks, I know not what— spake most haughtily to me, and demanded to know where my companions were. I told them not a word! Not a word, lest they trouble the ladies present. Well, my friends, off they went, and I didn't see them again. They think I travel alone, or rather, alone except for Fred the baboon. He's the one that drove them off, you see, with his stern countenance. Show them your countenance, Fred."

With impeccable comedic timing, Fred, who was seated at one end of the boards, happened to yawn. He showed his tremendous teeth and the laughter was tumultuous. Meanwhile, Lily was ascending to her tightrope prematurely, in hope of cutting her uncle's monologue short.

"I'm told there are pixies about, as well," Uncle Cornelius went on, "and that my fortune-teller is really a Faerie princess! Some people call me mad, but I'm the only sane person here."

He might have gone on in this vein, except that Lily began to sing from atop the rope, as loud as she was able, a popular local ditty. Uncle Cornelius was outraged—he'd been upstaged for the first time in three decades. But he had scarcely begun to complain when a flickering green glow lit up the rooftops and the low clouds. Then a dread horn rang out. There was a rumble of thunder, or the voices of giants; it was hard to tell which. A brief silence commanded the crowd. Then we heard the scream of a gryphon.

The scene that followed was pandemonium, and I can only claim to have witnessed it in glimpses, as a fellow falling through a glass window might catch glimpses of the scene around him reflected in the broken shards. But I will attempt to reconstruct what happened.

After that first supernatural wail, there was a hissing in the air, and a kind of smoke seemed to arch up over the rooftops, and then come down; by the time it reached the crowd, it was not a vapor at all, but a hail of pixie arrows. In a trice the spectators all about were screaming. The tiny darts were not capable of much injury to human beings, but they stung like wasp's tails, as I well knew, and enough of them would drive a victim 'round the bend.

Everyone was at once running for their lives and clawing at the places where they had been stuck with the missiles. People snatched up children, horses bolted, and Uncle Cornelius's stage was overturned, with him aboard. Torches were struck down and fires leapt up around the margins of the square. Giant shadows leapt over the walls. Then a strike of gryphons wheeled into view and descended upon the square.

These creatures were caparisoned in silver and green, with the Faerie King's crest upon their flanks. Their claws smote sparks from the cobblestones and their beaks snapped like meat-axes, menacing any who remained in the square. The goblings upon them wore bright armor, with helmets fashioned into grimacing faces even more fearsome than their own. The officer at their fore spied Morgana in a trice, and pointed his great spear at her. She pressed herself into my side.

"There's the royal whelp! Take her, and slay any manling gets between!"

Could I but get Morgana into the wagon, she might yet escape, for the goblings could not seize her. So the manling between would be me, if it came to that.

"Come with me, quick as you can," I said. But she held me back. "Something else approaches," she cried.

It was true: a cold fog came pouring in a tide through the city gates and over the rooftops. It extinguished the heat of the world and crawled across the ground like a living thing. I recognized it: The same fog had swallowed up the Duchess's gryphons.

But flying upon the tide of vapor came something worse than gryphons. Half man, half eagle, and neither half any credit to its origins, they stooped down upon the fleeing crowd with deep, roaring voices. Twice man-size, their heads were bald and red, with yellow eyes and hooked, beaklike noses so large that they possessed no upper lip. They had no legs, but powerful humanlike arms with long, scaly talons outstretched before them; vast shining wings feathered like a vulture's bore them up. Six of the apparitions there were. They snapped and shrieked as their wings beat the air, and whosoever had not panicked before was panicking now.

This new arrival had thrown the King's goblings into confusion. I caught up Morgana's hand and ran with her through a litter of abandoned hats and spilled market baskets; the crowd was pressed up all around the egresses from the square, struggling in the icy vapor, and we were caught out in the open.

"Mantigorns," Morgana cried. "Only the Duchess could command their like. We are caught between fearsome enemies, Kit."

The mantigorns came to ground opposite the king's gryphons, each upon one of their hands, the elbows tucked against their bodies, so that they could claw and snatch at terrified humans with the other. But they weren't interested in the masses. They were looking for someone.

"There!" the largest of the mantigorns bellowed, and pointed at us, who stood between the two dreadful forces. A moment later they had drawn weapons from quivers between their wings, and javelins rattled to the stones about our feet by way of a warning. We were but halfway to the wagon. I saw Lily in the background near the wagon, hanging from the tightrope, one leg and one hand hooked around it so she could pull the cruel pixie arrows from her exposed flesh.

In the next moment the swarm of pixies arrived, and there was no opportunity to look to the others. These creatures were in such a warlike frenzy they were manifested only as streaks of greenish light and shrill, fierce cries.

A mêlée broke out: The mantigorns were beset by the fearless pixies, which gave the gryphons courage to attack. The two grotesque forces came together with a crash and the roar of a hundred lions. Gryphons slashed with claw and beak. Mantigorns tore with their hook-nailed hands and stabbed at their foes with javelins. The goblings thrust with their lances. The entire scene was lit red with leaping flame and ringed about with terrified, screaming people.

I pulled Morgana along, skirting the combat. The stones beneath our feet shook with the violence of the struggling monsters. We reached the wagon—but too late.

One of the gryphon-riders had been unseated, and saw us in our flight across the square. Now he leapt between us and the caravan door, brandishing an ugly sword with teeth cut into the blade.

"You dies and she comes along," said the gobling.

I caught up a sword that stood against the wagon. "I'll distract him—you get within," I whispered to Morgana. Then I cried, "Have at you," and raised my blade.

Our blades met, and it might have been the shortest duel in the entire history of the world. For the weapon in my hand was not my own, but Uncle Cornelius's, which you will recall was made of wood. It broke off at the hilt and flew away. I'd have died at the very next sword stroke, except the gobling was so overcome with mirth that he couldn't swing again. I suppose that sort of thing is funny to goblings. In the brief delay, I plunged my hand into my pocket, scooping up a fistful of gold coins. I flung them directly into the braying gobling's mouth. The unfortunate creature's head exploded.

[*The Dread Mantigorn*]

I spun about to get Morgana safely inside the wagon, but she wasn't there. Instead, she stood upon one of the barrels that had recently supported the stage. I rushed to her side and reached up to hand her down; she took my fingers in hers, and shook her head. Then she turned to the enraged creatures tearing each other to pieces in the square.

"My people," said Morgana, to some other world. A strange wind was tossing her hair and skirts about; her eyes were like silver mirrors set with green jewels. I saw she was illuminated from within, as I'd first seen her. "We have forgotten our way. This is man's way."

She rose up to her full height, or more, as it seemed to me, and I released her hand. She thrust her arms out to her sides, and the light about her formed glowing serpents and phantoms; great iridescent wings of light appeared at her shoulders, and the entire square burned with the brightness of her. Long shadows were cast behind the mantigorns and gryphons. They cowered in the brilliant glow, but their blood was up; they turned on her again.

"That's but a parlor trick!" the leader of the goblings roared. "By order of King Elgeron of the Middle Kingdom, Liege of the Faerie Realm, you shall come away or *all* shall perish!"

Then a great dark shape obscured my sight, an enormous claw grasped my waist, and I was flung through the air. I crashed across the top of the wagon, knocked half senseless, but with wits enough to see there were three of the mantigorns advancing toward Morgana, striding upon their taloned hands.

"Curse your King," the largest mantigorn bellowed. "In the name of the Duchess, she is mine!"

Both sides rushed at Morgana now. She stood there like a burning beacon, her face fierce and proud, and then the creatures were upon her.

Her brilliant light went out, all at once. I was beset by pixies at the same moment, who now stabbed at me with tiny knives made of fox teeth so that I was struggling wildly; then I fell from the caravan roof and was briefly free of them. I cried Morgana's name, and despite all the chaos and noise, I think she heard me across the square; for she looked for me, and our eyes were joined again. *My love*, I thought. *Good-bye*. There would be no more buttered toast for us.

Then there was a deafening thunderclap, and a flash—not of light, but of darkness—and all the enchanted creatures, every pixie and mantigorn and gryphon, were gone in a spray of foul-smelling sparks. The cold fog crawled away like a devilfish. There was only the stampeding crowd at every gate and doorway, the wreckage, and the fire.

I whistled as loudly as I could for Midnight. When he came to me, shaking wee arrows off his flanks, I sprang none too spryly into the saddle, determined to give chase, no matter where the creatures had taken Morgana. Red-coated soldiers were pouring into the square now, in opposition to the jostling crowd. I cared nothing for them. They were but mortal men. I rode straight through them, shouting wildly. There came a great rattling and clanking ahead, and the gates of the town were sealed shut by the iron portcullis that descended from the stone ramparts. Midnight drew up only inches from the bars; redcoats seized his reins and I was dragged from the saddle.

Heavy hands fell upon my shoulders. Muskets surrounded me like a fence of pickets.

"Whistling Jack," said Captain Sterne. "It's been a merry chase."

CAPTIVITY

Y OU WOULD not call me an oversensitive man, I think. I have demonstrated well enough my immunity from subtle influences. But there was nothing subtle about the next month of my life, and had I been as nerveless as an anvil, yet would I have been miserable. The very tumbril that had borne those unfortunate highwaymen away in their cage some weeks past now bore me. Through every town and hamlet I rolled in that ignominious iron pen, attended by the man who regarded me as his worst enemy.

How many eyes fell upon me, filled with disgust and fear? How many mouths shaped vile calumnies and flung them in my ears? For that matter, how many spoiled eggs did the young boys throw? I think it was the boys I disliked the most, because if I'd been one among them, I'd have done the same thing. They were reminders of my own beginnings, and reminded me how low I had fallen since. At any rate, I had a good long tour of the countryside, and if it hadn't been for the frequent rains that slashed down upon ox-wain and cage alike, I dare say I'd have suffocated from my own smell.

Captain Sterne had refused to hear anything but that I was Whistling Jack. I told him those parts of my tale that didn't require mention of magical people, but there wasn't enough to it to exonerate me. I was guilty; I was his foe. When he wasn't riding along ahead behaving as if he would soon slay me with his own hand, he was riding beside my cage, conversing with me about the experience of death by hanging.

"The tow*, you see, is a coarse one; it prickles as it rides the neck," he said one afternoon, as we passed through some dull country of bogs and sheepfolds.

"Yes, I know," said I. "And when the nightcap goes over my head, I'll smell the last breath of the man hanged before me inside it."

"Yes! And then—"

"And then the knot of the rope is cinched tighter than a stirrup iron, so I can sample what the next few minutes will be like," I said.

"Will you stop finishing my sentences!" Captain Sterne barked. "It is a most irritating habit."

"But," I said, reasonably, "you've already finished them often enough."

"Anyway, I'll be glad to see you swing," he muttered. "I shall be bringing someone of particular interest to your execution. She was very taken with you before, but I think she'll soon see I'm the better man." With that, he spurred his mount to the front of the column of troops escorting me to London.

But none of these indignities meant anything to me at all, compared to the anguish of my heart. In all the time I'd spent with Morgana, I had not understood what my heart already knew: I loved the girl. All my confusion and irritation came from it. And the worst torment of this revelation was knowing that I would die without being able to confess my passion.

My mind revolved around this unhappy point in much the same way the string with which I measured out my riding-circuses revolved around the stake. It never got nearer or farther from the

---

* Rope.

locus, but circled it endlessly. I recalled a thousand little incidents that should have told me of my romantic affliction. Why else had I so often gazed upon her with delight? Why else did I find it charming when she smote me with a caprizel, or laughed, or gave me some trifling compliment?

I'd blamed her for bewitching me! I had thought it was magical influences distorting my mind. But all the while it was my own fault. I loved her more than all the things in the world. I loved her more than Midnight. But, being unfamiliar with the romantic illness, I had not known it for what it was.

She was captured now, in the hands of her father, or of that fearsome One-Eyed Duchess. Would her father shut her up in a dungeon and force her to marry? Would the Duchess tear out her soul? What would become of those who had assisted her flight, especially Willum and Gruntle? I could not rest for thinking of these things, and when they briefly left my mind, I saw only Morgana, with those shimmering wings of radiant light, in the moments before her apprehension. If only they had been real wings that could bear her away! But all was lost, except me. I had been found.

$$\text{\&} \quad \text{\&} \quad \text{\&}$$

When my foul cage reached the City, the prisons were full to overflowing, so I was assigned to one of the prison ships that wallowed in the River Medway. These hulks are floating hells; I shall describe the one in which I was shackled only as much as required to convey my tale, as a full account of such earthbound horrors would make the supernatural horrors to which I had recently been introduced, and the description of which is the purpose of this narration, seem paltry by comparison.

Hundreds of prisoners, scurf'd* for every imaginable crime,

---

* Scurfed: taken into custody (eighteenth-century slang). Not to be confused with *scurf*, flaking or scaly skin.

dwelled below those decks in almost perfect darkness. The hulks were decommissioned naval ships, demasted, so they were nothing more than immense wooden slop-buckets floating on the tide. Were it not for the gun-ports, we would all have suffocated within a few hours. As it was, the air was so putrid belowdecks that a candle would not stay lit: There was not enough good air to nourish the flame. Beside the reek of disease and filth, and the exhalation of a thousand rotting mouths, there were vermin. The hull was alive with lice, fleas, and rats.

Only a few days after I arrived in London, I enjoyed a brief respite from the prison ship in order to visit the court. There I was sentenced, alongside a number of less famous criminals, to death. This was no surprise, as in those days a man was generally found innocent, transported to America, or hanged, rather than fiddling about with intermediate sentences. And I was so obviously guilty that no evidence, testimony, or examination was required.

The judge, a crimson-faced man of immense girth, made a long and tedious speech aimed at my master, but addressed to me. I don't know why he bothered speaking of reforming my corrupted spirit when it was so shortly to depart. My sentence came just before lunch, and delayed the meal, which I think may have influenced the judge's remarks. I provide only the last of a long summation here, delivered from beneath a caxon of curled horsehair:

"Like a ripe pear, Mr. Whistling, you are soon to be plucked from the branch. But the branch from which you dangle shall be the leafless limb of the Tyburn Tree, which has been nourished at the root by the very blood of Cromwell.* Like a pear, I say, but your face will be the color of a plum, and your head swollen similarly, so that you will also resemble a roast of beef; as the pheasant hangs until its flesh has become fragrant, so shall you hang, and

---

* Oliver Cromwell was an immensely powerful and controversial seventeenth-century soldier, politician, and Puritan. After his death, his remains were dug up and hanged at Tyburn by way of posthumous execution.

the aroma of you, as of a good Stilton, shall waft across the road there, where there is an inn that does fish very well.

"Cruelly have you plied your trade upon the road, robbing many a fine coach that was stuffed with riches as a suckling pig is stuffed with apples, leaving nary a crust of bread behind. Why, you may not have heard, but the fine officer who apprehended you was deprived of his beloved's heart by your predations. How couldst you pluck such a succulent potato from his very dish? What pangs he has endured, what hunger gnaws at his soul! He is starved for love, and it is all because of you. I sentence you, sir, for your menu of crimes, to be hanged by the neck until dead, so help you God. Right, that's done. Lunchtime."

※ ※ ※

The court was pleased to execute me on a separate day from the others to facilitate public participation. Mass hangings always fall behind schedule. I had a fortnight to enjoy my thoughts until then. Two weeks of jolly captivity, then the rope.

So it was, with my nostrils filled with stench, my skin with bugs, and my ears with the wails of lost and dying souls, I whiled away thirteen days. During that time I drank as little of the vile water as I was able, and ate as little of the heaps of refuse with which they fed us as I could, and so languishing, began to drift in and out of consciousness, meeting old friends and enemies in waking dreams.

Captain Sterne visited me once, and I was escorted to the top deck for the purpose. There was a lady beside him, some years his senior, and by her costume provided with considerable wealth. She was blushing from her neck to the top of her head. Both of them kept scented linen pomanders under their noses to conceal the noxious stink rising from beneath the deck.

"You know her," said the captain.

"I confess I do not," said I.

"Then you know *him*," he said, addressing the lady.

"I never saw his eyes, but I do not recognize the lower parts of his face. His chin was not cleft before."

"Both of you conceal your feelings. I am not deceived."

"Oh, I see," said I. "Is this your fiancée?"

"She *was*," said the captain, scowling. "I have brought her here to reconsider her misplaced affection for a murderous dog."

"I do not recognize this young man," the lady said. "Were he Whistling Jack, I should say he may be a murderous dog indeed, but not to me. He was ever so kind and well-mannered, and handed me down from the carriage most courtly. He complimented my jewels as he took them off me, and looked upon me and said I needed not such bright baubles to ravish the eye. Can you imagine! What a charming thing to say. He took the contents of the cash-box at my feet and said I must be a lovely dancer, for my foot was so well-turned. Never raised his voice, unlike some. Never made a demand, but always a request. I know a gentleman when I meet one, and Whistling Jack was the gentlest."

"'That will *do*," said the captain, his face approaching the color of roast beef as mentioned by the judge. But the lady wasn't finished. Evidently this interview had unsealed some inner dam of emotions.

"It will *not* do, Captain. You cut a fine figure upon a horse and look very well on a lady's arm with your martial demeanor. But there's more to winning a woman's heart than that. In any case, this isn't him. Whistling Jack is as old as you, Captain. This lad is the age of my niece Fidelia—sixteen or seventeen, not a day more."

"Enough!" he spat, and rattled his sword to emphasize the point. "This is he. I pursued him all the way across England. I know him, and I know his horse!"

"Perhaps he borrowed the horse. Think what you will. You dragged me all the way here to this dreadful place. You insisted. This interview is nothing to do with me. Unfortunately, neither is this young fellow."

I bowed to her, grateful that one person, at least, knew me to be wrongly accused. And grateful, too, that she thought so well of Master Rattle—even at his very worst. The captain had not told me her name, probably to keep me from using it in some swooning speech to renew my grasp upon her affections, but whosoever she was, I hoped she would find a better match than Sterne.

Chapter 32

TIDINGS FROM AN OLD
ACQUAINTANCE

ON THE final day of my captivity, the gaoler's assistant, a Mr. Ratskalp, came down the companionway to the third deck where I lay, and addressed me thus:

"You, Whistlin' Jack! Stir thyself."

A couple of soldiers came down after him and unlocked my leg-irons, then retreated double-time, to be sick on the top-deck from the stench below. I could not stand, so the ship's surgeon took one side of me, and Mr. Ratskalp the other, and they hoisted me up to the outside world, which I had not seen since my interview with the captain. I was blinded by the sunlight, although it was an overcast day, and the cool, fresh air set me to shivering so that my teeth rattled like dice in a cup.

"Ye've got a visitor," said Ratskalp, drawing a dead fish out of his waistband. "Need a bathe." He proceeded to scrape the scales from the fish with his black thumbnails, while a couple of emaciated crewmen threw buckets of river water over me, then plied my bite-pocked flesh with gray mops until there were patches of skin visible through the grime.

Then they clad me in a canvas shirt and galligaskins*, none too clean and large enough for three of me, but better than the rotting clothes I wore below the deck. "For good appearances," Mr. Ratskalp explained. "Mustn't alert the public to the conditions on these 'ere barges. There mote be an outcry, and then humane prison policies follow, and me out of a job."

With that, he bit the head off his fish and directed me to the soldiers. They lowered me into a jolly boat, and I was rowed ashore in chains.

The visit was conducted in a fortified structure, once a customs-house, with bars on the windows and a fortified wall as tall as the eaves, only a few feet from the building; so the effect was of sitting at the bottom of a stone well. I was arranged behind a timber partition with bars set into it by way of a window, and shortly thereafter, my visitor was shown to a chair on the other side of the barrier.

"Narn," the visitor said, sitting down but getting no shorter. "Narn good came of 'ee."

It was Magda the witch. She was dressed now (beside her rags) in a flowered shawl of the type fashionable during the reign of James II. From beneath her skirts peeked out a familiar friend: Demon the French bulldog. When he saw me, he let out a catcall of delight and sprang against the barrier between us, hopping on his hind legs. I confess tears pricked my eyes when I saw that stout little fellow. Magda gathered him into her lap, whence Demon stared at me for the rest of the interview in the same manner he did when it was time to go for a walk in the countryside.

Magda's stone eye regarded me as intently as the living one. I confess I was happy to see her, although she was in some fashion the author of all my miseries. I imagined her to be what old aunts were like.

---

* Galligaskins: loose trousers.

"Magda," said I, and it being the first word I'd spoken in a week, it came out as a rasp, like filing a nutmeg.

"Nowt escapes yer keen eye, boyo," she muttered. "List! I ain't got time for the chatterin' nor idle talk—and nor does 'ee, for thou art hangin' soon. The darter of me heart, my Princess, she's near to be wed, and not a Faerie but 'as ther courage nor stop the nupterls, for the king is punishin' one and all for the uprisin'. With tharn dear girlie carptured, the rebellion's afeared ter act. Elgeron's bedoubled the punishments and set that narsty bit o' work the Arn-Eyed Duchess uparn the land. Nobbut the wind dast oppose 'er. So it's up ter 'ee to stop it."

"The Duchess?" I cried, and coughed like a consumptive. "She's working with King Elgeron? Last I saw, their monsters were at war with one another."

"Yar," said Magda. "'T'were the Duchess got to Princess first, and made a bargain wi' King to get 'er soul back in return for tharn poor girlie."

"A ransom. Do you know how we were found out?"

"Two ways, two ways. King's spies was everwhere. They o'erheard tha old madman of yourn tellin' the story of yer journey 'pon the stage. But Duchess, she *already* knowed. She reached through and snartched tharn toroise comb orff table, took it through yon lookin' glarss, and passed it back. Then it were a sigilantum, and ever nor then, she allus knew exactly where you was."

"So when we thought Lily had merely misplaced the comb, it was . . . on the other side for a few minutes? Pulled through by the Duchess?"

"If only tha had thourght a wee bit harder!"

I was eager to change the subject away from my ignorance. "And how fares Morgana? The Princess, that is?"

"Miserble," Magda said. "If ye 'ad any sense, ye'd stop of the weddin' and arsk her how she be yersel'."

I felt it was time to explain my circumstances.

"As perhaps you know, but cannot see, your sight being limited,

I am not at liberty, but barnacled with irons on legs and wrists and confined upon a prison barge, and have an appointment to be hanged tomorrow at Tyburn. So with such sorrow and regret as I cannot express, I am unable to be of help."

"But ain't you learned of nothing?" the witch protested. "Give you my tooth, did not I? You've all yer needs to be free of this place, but tha' carnventional human mind nor yourn thinks arnly on what you see, not on what be possible, nor what 'ee might *wish*."

I shook my head. "Even if I did escape, dear Magda, then what? I am a ragged pauper again; I have no means of anything, not even survival. How should I effect a rescue of the Princess? And all your little rebel feyín, I presume, have been captured and turned into moths for their troubles. Allow me to go to my fate, and Morgana to hers, and there's a sad end to the business."

The witch leaned close to me. Demon stretched his bull's neck to get close, too. We had already been whispering, as there was a guard standing at the door; in my condition I couldn't raise my voice if I tried. But now she pitched her voice so low it was more like a feeling than a sound. Which it may have been. She could have been projecting her voice into my very mind.

"Boyo," said she. "Narn. Ye knows not the upshot of the cap-turin' of the Princess. Knows ye the goblings came on their griffs, and with 'em the mantigarns and pixies alike, and fell right among your manling folk. Well, it's one thing for common Faerie ter break the Eldritch Laws. It's anarn for the King to do it, nor that's his priv-ilege. 'Is servants erased all the manling membries and replaced 'em with membries of a fire, norstead.

"But when King done this thing," she continued, "the Faeries what dwells here in your world, they stopped workin'. They ain't spilin' milk nor poxin' cows, they ain't turnin' leaves brown nor makin' flowern bloom. They refuses to work! The revorlution has begun."

"That's all very good, but I'm still hanging. Also, I threw away your tooth."

"Narn!" she fairly shouted. "It's in yer pocket. Stupid boyo. Guards!"

So saying, she demanded to be given release from that pestilent place. I didn't bother to remind her that my present costume was not furnished with a single pocket.

"Spare not the rope nor this one, lads," said Magda, on her way to the door. "He'll dance a pretty hornpipe on a sunbeam!" The guards escorted her away. Demon whimpered and struggled in her sticklike arms, endeavoring to get back to me. I heard him yowling all the way down the hall beyond my cell. Then the soldiers came for me.

"She your sweetheart?" one of the men asked me, and winked. I had no idea what he meant by that until I saw there was a delicate paper rose in my hand. How it came there I did not know. I'd seen one like it somewhere before.

🌸   🌸   🌸

As they left me to rot away my last hours in the prison ship, I was still trying to recall where I'd seen such a flower. Then I remembered: There had been one in my master's pocket the night he died.

All of a moment, I understood that the plan between Magda and my master had extended well beyond kidnapping Morgana from the enchanted coach. It included provisions for his capture. But what could a paper rose and an old hag's tooth do to spring me from this stinking oubliette, or loose my neck from the rope?

[*The Paper Rose*]

Chapter 33

BEING AN ACCOUNT OF MY
LAST HOURS

THE OTHER prisoners, those who still had some of their wits, thought I had lost mine. There was a gunport near my head, through which trickled a modicum of fresh air. A shutter was bolted over it at a slight angle to admit vapors, but not a human form, not even one of the emaciated creatures about me. I spent all of the afternoon of my final day with one arm squeezed through the gap in the shutter, holding the paper flower aloft. Every few minutes, I would retract my arm and inspect the flower, then thrust it back outside the hull again.

After several hours of this, my arm numb with squeezing it through the gap and raw where the splintered wood of the port chafed at it, I withdrew the flower and found upon it the object of my intentions: a single bee.

I knew not if it was the correct kind of bee, but I had no other, so I repeated my message to the little creature thrice, and apologized for the subterfuge of a paper flower, which could be of no profit to the insect. I released the bee through the port, and after it I dropped the paper flower, to drift away on the river. This accomplished, and ignoring my gaol-mates' catcalls, I settled myself to wait.

For a long while, my thoughts revolved around the absurdity of my situation. I'd been servant to a good-natured fellow who turned out to be, as well, a notorious criminal. I had impersonated him, and been mistaken for him, and been given his strange quest to complete. So doing, I became a criminal myself, in two worlds.

Was I, therefore, a criminal? I'd done much wrong upon my journey, but for the right reasons. The law didn't care about anything except the word of Captain Sterne. He thought me guilty and a peckish judge did not wish to waste time in cross-examinations. I was guilty. But I felt no guilt, only sorrow. These reflections went nowhere, but only around in circles. One conclusion I was able to draw: Whatever anyone thought, I was *not* a highwayman, unless by accident.

Then Mr. Ratskalp came with his guards, and I was unlocked and taken up onto the dark top-deck. There, by lantern light, I was mopped once more, and lowered into the boat.

An hour later, I had been transferred to a small, clean cell in a building, I know not where; it was so great an improvement over the prison hulk, which would have broken Jonah's faith, that my spirits lifted a little. Hope was extinguished in my bosom, yet there was something of peace to be had thereby. A man who thinks there is a future must, perforce, be concerned for the future. I had none, and so had nothing to concern me. I'd paid already for my foolishness, and tomorrow I would pay for another's, and there would be an end to me and my broken heart. I lay upon a bench and gazed into the shadows thrown by the sputtering tallow, and thought of little enough, unless it was a single dimple set beside a smiling mouth.

A knock sounded upon the door. "It's open," said I, and resumed my reverie.

There was a turning of locks and loosing of chains that went on for a good minute, and then Captain Sterne entered the little room, smiling indulgently. There was a large parcel wrapped in muslin and string tucked under his arm.

"Ah, Jack," said he, "well met. Soon you shall be dead, and my little list of names will all be crossed off, and I shall be promoted for my work to clear the roads. Then you'll be a footnote to my entry in the history books."

"I congratulate you on your success," said I. "Now, pray leave me. I'm preoccupied with other matters."

"Other matters?" said Sterne, looking about him in the bare, empty chamber. "If you don't wish to have one last civilized conversation before you meet your maker, whom I daresay is impatient to mark the occasion with a flaming trident, then so be it. But it occurred to me you might wish to know how you were apprehended."

"Not particularly," said I.

Captain Sterne looked well infuriated by this, and so, after he'd sputtered a while and adjusted his periwig to a more martial attitude, he said, "Perhaps you'll not be so flippant when you learn it was none other than your ex-sweetheart?"

Well, as I hadn't an ex-sweetheart, my curiosity was roused. "Who?" I inquired.

"The Duchess of Redsea. She sent me a letter detailing the precise time and location I should find you, correct in every detail. It's a miracle it found me, for I was bent upon your trail in the depths of the countryside. She expressed an interest in meeting me, in fact. I appear to be her sort of man."

That dreadful Duchess, thought I. It made perfect sense. She could have destroyed me at the time of Morgana's capture, but like the ogre who stole her soul and set her free, the Duchess knew there was no sweeter revenge than to have your vanquished foe survive long enough to drain the bitter cup of defeat down to the dregs.

For a moment I was all in a fury at the cruelty of her. Then it passed, for there was nothing to be done about it, and I was still a practical fellow by nature. Captain Sterne had been watching my face closely, but I think he saw none of the despair he'd hoped for, for his smile of anticipation melted into a frown.

"I see you are not contrite. Truly I have never seen a more hardened criminal than you. Be that as it may, you're in no condition to hang. Make yourself presentable, for I wish my *own* lady to see you at your best."

With this, he dropped the parcel upon the floor. "There will be washing-water brought up. Then you will, unless you've grown fond of your present stinking rags, change into the fresh attire I have brought. The public will be well pleased with the effect, and I know that the style is much to your taste. Anon."

With that, he smote his boot-heels together and left the room. A servant entered with a basin of hot water, a flannel, and a shilling's worth of good soap. It took me five basins and most of the soap to get passably clean and free of infestation by biting insects; if only old Fred had been there, he could have picked off every one of the little murderers in ten minutes. By the end of these ablutions my skin stung fiercely, but it felt delightful. Then, with my fetid rags carried away in the flannel by the servant, I was left alone, dressed as the Lord had made me.

I opened the parcel, and within discovered the extent of Captain Sterne's sense of humor. For he had provided me with an excellent replica of Whistling Jack's costume, from the tall red-trimmed boots to the black redingote and cocked hat. He had even provided the mask to go about my eyes, should I wish to meet my death incognito. But he did not furnish me with pistols or sword. Although the barb of his mockery struck home, yet I donned the clothes, for truly had I none other. The pockets were all empty, of course, but for a few copper pennies, and I hardly know why I searched them—until the discovery, in the tail-pocket of the black redingote, of a slender object with which I was now well familiar, for it somehow never left me: Magda's tooth.

This time, I kept it.

☞ ☞ ☞

You may read more detailed descriptions elsewhere of how those convicted to die are tormented in their last hours; it went much the same with me. Clergymen always come to offer rites, and are either sent away with abominable curses, or welcomed by the weeping penitent. For my own part, the visit was met with indifference. I think there was some reading from a book, either the Bible or Fielding's latest novel*. I do not recall, for I wasn't attending to the words.

After that, another hour was beguiled with visits by persons of wealth and station. They stepped into the cell, well guarded, to examine the convict as an object of curiosity. I received a dozen or more such visitors, mostly ladies who had been robbed by my namesake and master. They seemed universally to have found him charming. None suspected I was not he, though I was not charming.

It was also customary for a public reformer or two to come around for an interview, if they thought they could invent a conversation for the news-papers that would reinforce their position on capital punishment, pro or con. I disappointed the parties on both sides of the issue with my unresponsiveness.

In truth, I cared not jot nor fig for any of them. When the viewing ended, I was pleased to rest my head, and fell asleep until awakened by my gaolers at dawn—that is how resigned I was to my doom. "You're a cool one," the bailiff remarked, I think with some little admiration.

"I was practicing," said I, thinking of the long sleep ahead.

🜊   🜊   🜊

In the same accounts that describe the last night of the condemned, you may also find descriptions of the last morning. I'll expend little ink on that here, for I don't remember much of my own experience between cockcrow and arrival at the village of Tyburn. There were more clergymen about—I think they got a bonus for last-minute repentances—and spectators lined the route all the way from the cell to the horse-drawn tumbril that would bear me to the place of execution.

---

* *The History of Tom Jones, A Foundling*, by Henry Fielding (1749).

That road was a long one. I sat upon a bale of hay, shackled at the ankles and bound with cord at the wrists. The spectators along the way were not too abusive, but most interested; although the mask was in my pocket, there could be no mistaking the costume of Whistling Jack, even without it.

The tumbril took me to a crossroad, suitably enough, that being the sort of place one meets a highwayman. There stood the Tyburn Tree, the location of which had been the place of public executions for nearly a millennium. All around the intersection, old houses had been converted to viewing platforms, and there were stands erected for the purpose in every house-yard adjacent. The killing ground was a popular attraction for tourists, and a roaring trade was being done in beer, hot buns, and fainting salts.

As my cart arrived, traffic around the crossroad had become impassable due to the large crowd, and those whose business lay elsewhere were forced to take to the fields, or else find other lanes past the obstruction, miles out of the way. The better classes had brought lunch in hampers, and plenty to drink; in addition to the stands, viewing was done from carriage-top and horseback. It might as well have been a royal coronation.

The hangman accompanied me in the cart. He was seated beside the driver, who was muffled to the chin, his hat pulled low despite the warm weather—probably to escape identification for his conscience's sake, as his hand in the business was no less fatal than the executioner himself. The hangman wore no disguise, unlike his forebears in ancient times. He was a cheerful fellow with a cocked hat and ready smile, and described points of interest along the entire route, culminating with the "tree" itself.

"This 'ere is the himproved gallows, darlin'," said the hangman, with evident pride, as we arrived. "Had you been captured but a year past, we'd have hung you the same as Cromwell's rotten carcass and sprightly Duval, by the three-legged tree, and you strugglin' up a ladder with no 'ands, only ter be kicked off the top in a resoundin' failure of 'ospitality, like the carpenter in Chaucer's tale.

This 'ere up-to-date happaratus affords ye some dignity. A flight of sound steps, a fine firm floor to stand on, and then we drops a box beneath yer and ye hangs like a gentleman between them two posts. This is a time of hinnovations and marvels of hefficiency."

While I admired the handsome new fixtures, the rope was tied in a neat noose, and then a 'prentice hangman climbed a ladder to the top of the tree, which consisted (as the hangman said) not of the original three pillars with a triangle of hanging-bars at the top, but of a pair of posts with a beam between them for the same purpose. It was all erected upon a platform like a stage, surrounded by black baize fabric, swagged and pleated for a neat appearance. On the platform was the fatal step the condemned man would stand upon. The step itself was designed to drop down into a recess, leaving the guilty party suspended by the neck in precisely the manner advertised by my companion. The apprentice tested the mechanism as I waited, and so I was able to see how efficacious was the design.

There were various bits of official business: the reading of the judgment, then some prayers from a higher-ranking clergyman whose nose was the color of a hanged man's face, perhaps from grief, or perhaps from drink. What else went on, I did not mind, for I was dwelling upon other matters, chiefmost among them a pair of sparking green eyes. Then the hour was nigh, and between two rough bully-boys I was escorted forward, and my feet guided to the stairs. I was compelled to ascend, readily enough despite my quaking legs and bound hands, to the platform, where the hangman joined me, along with the clergyman and the two bully-boys, who waved at the crowd.

I was propelled toward the solitary step, and mounted it. The hemp was placed around my neck. It prickled and squeezed in just the way promised by Captain Sterne, whom I spied smiling in the crowd. He was in the company of the kind lady he so jealously guarded, yet so unpleasantly misused. She looked very unhappy. Both of them were on foot; perhaps the brown horse had no taste for hangings.

There I stood, and shivered, and looked upon the crowd for what seemed an eternity—perhaps because eternity was so near at hand. I might not have cared any longer for my life, but no man yearns to die, least of all with a knot at his ear.

Then I chanced to look down at the tumbril which had brought me there. I saw at last the driver's face, previously concealed: it was Mr. Scratch, the postilion of the enchanted coach. He touched his whip to his hat by way of greeting, and grinned. The scene lacked only Prudence Fingers and her henchman to be complete, but I did not see them. My attention returned to the eternal.

"Have you any last words to bestow upon us?" the purple-nosed clergyman asked.

"Say something bonny," said the hangman. "They likes a good last word."

"No obscene language, however," added the clergyman.

As it happens, I did have something I wished to say, so I said it. I had to start twice, however, because my voice was exceedingly faint upon the first attempt. On my next try, I imitated Uncle Cornelius's method of speaking, and this proved satisfactory.

"Fellow Englishmen," said I. "Ladies and gentlemen. You gather here to see a live man become a dead one, and for my part you shall have satisfaction. But I would offer you a moral lesson to commemorate my passing; otherwise it might as well be bullbaiting you witness here today. However: I shall not deliver a warning that crime does not pay, for it pays very well; nor that a life of drink and debauchery leads inevitably to destruction, for I haven't led such a life."

Well, that got the attention of the crowd, and ceased its cheers and taunts entirely. They lent me their ears.

I continued, "Here's what this little life of mine has taught me. There is only one reason to live, and there is only one reason to die, and that is love. If you have not known love, you have not lived. But if, when death comes to take your soul, you have loved someone dearly, then your soul is safe; for it lives in the bosom of your sweetheart, and death can make no claim upon it. That is all I know, and it is enough. Farewell."

The onlookers remained subdued after my words; some wept. Perhaps there were a few who knew the kind of love of which I spoke. I was not content, but had some peace, for I understood a great mystery. In any case, that was that. The clergyman was disappointed at my lack of contrition, but the hangman wrung my hand with as much sincerity as if it were my neck.

"A fine speech," said he. "They'll write songs about it."

I refused the nightcap he offered to put over my head, then squared my shoulders and awaited the rap of the latch beneath my feet that would signal the end.

There was little left to do but hang. The apprentice grasped the lever at his side, and upon the hangman's word, drew it back; I looked into the sky and saw only clouds. There was a thump as the latch was released, and for an instant I was falling into space, the noose leaping upward upon my throat.

But then I continued to fall. I plunged entirely beneath the floor, and out of view of the crowd, into the stuffy darkness beneath the hanging stage. With a painful crash I landed on my side in a heap of old ale jugs, my arms being still bound behind me. The air was knocked out of me. *This is the problem with Britain*, I thought. *Nobody cares about quality workmanship anymore.* But then exceedingly small hands were cutting my bonds with fox-tooth knives, and a faint green light sprang up. Willum and Gruntle were with me now, and with them were a dozen other feyín I hadn't met before.

"We got your bee," said one of the strangers. "Sorry to be so last minute."

"I told yer I'd return your kindness some day, sir," said Gruntle.

"The revolution has begun," Willum said. "Go get the Princess Morgana."

I tore the noose from around my neck and saw it had been severed a few inches above the knot. The rope end was burnt, so it must have been Willum's fire caprizel that parted the strands. The

Faeries were a cunning race, and knew how to shape their comprimaunts into both tools and weapons. My gratitude was beyond words, so I didn't use any.

"Now for them spectulators out there," Gruntle said.

The Faeries peeped beneath the baize skirt of the platform. Above us, visible through the trapdoor, the hangman and the minister were looking down to see what had befallen me, or rather, how be it I fell. Willum caused a great cloud of black smoke to issue up through the hole, which had the salutary effects of driving back the men atop the platform and of frightening the crowd. Half of them thought it was a fire, and they'd be burned alive, and the other half thought it was brimstone, and the devil was under the gallows.

Meanwhile, the other feyín were casting every manner of caprizel about—horses went mad, tree limbs fell, and spectator platforms collapsed; bottles of wine exploded into vinegar, cheeses ripened and burst like grenadoes, and a flock of sheep from a nearby field became as savage as wolves, charging into the panicked crowd and bleating ferociously.

A few moments into the frenzy, the curtains were flung aside and Willum cried, "Magda's by the mill! Get you to her!" and I was running like the rest of the crowd, pell-mell, with no idea where the mill was to be found.

I had been relieved of my hat by the hangman up above, but there was not much need of concealment in that mêlée. I saw Mr. Scratch tumble from the driver's bench of the wain, his features a rictus of fury. In all the struggling crowd, only Captain Sterne recognized my face, and drew his sword to cut me down. His lady was nowhere to be found. I had no avenue of escape, and no weapon to defend myself.

"Better than hanging," he cried. "I'll do you myself!"

As he rushed at me, a great wooly sheep propelled itself between his knees, so that he lost both his sword and his footing, and was seated upon the beast's back; the sheep ran onward, and the captain was lost beneath a writhing mass of humanity extricating itself from an overturned wagon. I took up his sword and ran for freedom.

On I raced, and not alone; spectators were running in all directions, many pursued by rampaging ducks and geese. But I saw the mill, fair enough, across a field of lettuces. There was a wheel at its side, turning over the water of a swift little stream. I dashed through the vegetables, made a circuit around the mill, and there found Magda.

"You never used me wishing tooth, boyo," she said.

"I know not what it's for," said I, using the sword as a crutch and panting for breath.

"Ye may yet sort it out," she said. "I brung 'ee this, little good as it's been."

She handed me a soiled and creased fold of paper—my master's will, the borigium.

"I shan't look at it," I insisted. "Not until I'm sure the hanged man isn't there any longer."

"Time a-wastin' be," Magda spat. "Whistle up that horse of yourn, for I brung him also. He's enchanted fair enough, but only nor three hours. Arter that, 'ee's but a fine horse again, and nothing more. The Princess is at Hampton Court Palace—in the Haunted Gallery. You can get there in a minute or two, but the weddin' is in five, so don't takes yer time."

"But that's miles from here," I protested—to the empty air. Magda had vanished.

So I whistled, which took about ten tries; my lips were not at my command, nor was my mouth possessed of even a single drop of the requisite moisture for such a feat. At last, I got a weak chirp out, and immediately heard my beloved Midnight's answering whinny—not from behind a hedge or wall, but from *above* me.

I looked up, and there he was, his great black wings shining like silk, the feathers outspread to slow his descent. His hooves pawed the air as if it was a field of grass.

"Midnight, bless your soul!" I cried, then sheathed the sword in

[*"I Looked Up, and There He Was"*]

my boot-top. I hurled myself onto Midnight's back as he trotted up to me. There was enough room between shoulder and wing that I could sit securely without a saddle. But without reins, I could only tell him where I wanted to go, and hope he understood. I named the destination, he kicked his hooves into the soil and sprang aloft, and the world fell away as we rose into the sky.

Birds must grow accustomed to it; I didn't have time. I'd never been up so high without something firm underfoot, and my head spun with the void all around. At a certain height, higher than the tallest building I had ever looked out from, or the tallest hill I'd ever ascended, the distance from the ground ceased to be frightening, for it no longer looked as though we were getting higher in the air; rather, it looked as though the world were getting smaller, and if I should wish to step off Midnight's back, my boot could flatten an entire village.

We flew at terrific speed, the wind beating our faces. Midnight clearly enjoyed it as much as possible, while I clung to his mane and tried not to fall off. Horses run so fast because their souls were born to fly, I think. The landscape beneath us slipped past with such swiftness that we covered the distance from the Tyburn Tree to Hampton Court Palace—a span of more than three leagues, about ten miles—in as little time as it takes to spend a farthing in a sweetshop.

There were the royal gardens, spread below us like an intricate Persian carpet, and there the roofs of lead and clay, bristling with twisted brick chimney pipes. I saw a stream of elegantly dressed people entering the palace. They resembled small, gaudy dolls from above, their toy carriages circling the drive. Then Midnight bore me among the rooftops and we were searching for a place to set down.

Chapter 34

THE ROYAL WEDDING

THE WEDDING was intended to be, as I was later to discover, a small affair, attended by only the few personages required to make the event legally binding. Apparently the alliance was a state secret. The nuptials would be followed directly by a great costumed ball—guests to which I had seen in the forecourt—which would allow the Faerie emissaries to mingle at court without detection. There was some other pretext for the ball, Midsummer Night's Eve or the like.

Midnight had landed us upon the roof of Hampton Court—or, to be precise about it, upon one of the many roofs. Never in my life had I seen such a vast construction, all to one purpose. But the great horse seemed to know what he was about, for he pawed the red clay tiles and ducked his head, as if to say, "Straight below."

I had less than a minute and a half to reach my destination, at best. So I did not question his wisdom, but flung myself over the nearest parapet and dropped to a balcony on the floor below. I entered by way of an unlocked window; there was no need to worry about intruders up here, after all.

Captain Sterne's sword in hand, I raced down a scuffed brown hallway in what must have been the servants' quarters beneath the roof, with apartments on each side for threescore people; before me was a stone stair spiraling through the floor. I leapt down it three steps at a time.

Everything I did there was at absolutely full tilt, never walking a step that could be run, and I spared not a moment for thought nor caution. Was I not already dead? Did not my throat still chafe from the embrace of the noose? Should any creature stand between me and Morgana in her peril, it would be to their peril. I hoped.

At the bottom of the stair, to my immeasurable relief, was the Haunted Gallery. It didn't appear haunted at that time, but rather, crowded with wigged and powdered servants in livery, King's Guards, and men-in-waiting. Nearly everyone carried swords at their belts, not to mention pikes and lances. I was at last inspired to adopt a little caution, and ducked out of sight. I bound the high-wayman's mask about my eyes. Perhaps they would mistake me for a costumed party guest, should I be discovered. It might also hide the terror on my face.

Captain Sterne's sword seemed familiar to me as I renewed my grip upon it. Then I recognized the weapon—'twas the very sword I had lost in my struggle with Mr. Scratch and Mr. Bufo! My master's own weapon. This gave me courage, for some nonsensical reason. Upon the blade, in freshly engraved floral script, was this message: *Captured from the Highwayman Whistling Jacques*, and the date of my apprehension, several weeks after I lost it. What I was most pleased to see was the golden hilt.

All of this happened in a twinkling—I had the damp mud from the mill yard yet on my boots, and between parting from Magda and the moment I hefted the sword in my fist, no more than three minutes had elapsed. If the royal wedding was taking place in the room around which the guards were gathered, I had all of two minutes to enact some plan of rescue, assuming the Chaplain of the Household spoke slowly.

The trouble was—and I find in life this is often the situation—I couldn't think of what to do. Between me and Morgana were three dozen armed men, besides whomever she was with inside that room, some of whom would surely be magical persons, and possibly goblings.

I must think of something! was all my mind could invent. A case-clock against the wall ridiculed me with its incessant ticking. Nearly another minute had passed.

A mad fugue of anxiety quite overtook me. It was time to act, and if I died, Morgana would surely know I tried my best, and perchance suspect what was in my heart, and forgive me for my incompetence and brusqueness where she was concerned.

I charged.

The effect must have been rather less impressive to the crowd of men at the door than it was to me. I shouted for all I was worth as I came around the corner, but my voice hadn't much volume since the hanging. And my muddy boots slipped terribly on the highly polished floor. Still, I gamely attacked, sword raised high. All eyes were upon me, and I think the only question hanging in the air was who should kill me.

This surprise mixed with indifference got me as far as the nearest footman, who drew his sword. I swung at him for form's sake, being useless at offensive fighting. He parried and sprang after me, and so my defensive training came into use. Then there were a dozen of them coming at me, all with swords, and a good deal of shouting, and I knocked over a suit of armor while escaping the many points flashing my way. Had there not been so many of them pressing the attack, I'd have been cut to laces in the first dozen seconds of the pursuit; as it was, they kept foiling one another's thrusts.

At the height of the fracas there was a tremendous *boom*, and the doors of the wedding-chamber burst open. A blast of green flame gusted out, like a diabolical bedsheet flapping in a high wind. A silver-gilt chair tumbled into the mass of guards, the tapestries blew off the walls, chandeliers fell and burst into sparkling fragments upon the floor, and every window in the gallery shattered at the same moment. Not a man was left on his feet.

A roiling pall of smoke issued through the broken doorway, flickering with green witchfire. The outline of a figure appeared within. For an instant I feared the One-Eyed Duchess had found some means to come to finish me off. But then Morgana emerged from the reek, her eyes flashing emerald as she surveyed the scene before her. In her white and silver gown, with flowers in her hair, she looked a paragon of beauty—but the bared teeth and blazing eyes gave her the aspect of a pagan queen, such as Boadicea, who led the ancient Britons against Rome.

"Morgana," I croaked, trying to extricate myself from a tapestry. My mask had turned around backwards and I could only see out the bottom.

"I'm getting better at magic," she said, and ran to my side while the guards all around us were still trying to get to their knees.

"Morgana," I said again, for there was nothing else in my head but her.

"Dear Kit," said she. "Are you badly hurt?"

"No. Are you married?"

"No."

"Good. There's something I'd like to tell you."

She looked about us; the guards were finding their swords. "Now?"

"Perhaps it can wait a minute or two," I conceded. Just then a new voice intruded into the scene.

"Grandpapa, are you injured?" I heard a fellow say, and a moment later, Georges II and soon-to-be III, king and prince, respectively, emerged from the wedding chamber, coughing and waving the smoke away. The old English king was unmistakable, the subject of innumerable portraits, and his pop-eyed grandson could scarcely be anyone else.

"Neffer better," King George said with his thick German accent, and irritably slapped the wig off his grandson's head.

Just then, the most extraordinary figure in this tale appeared out of the smoke from the wedding chamber, parting the two Georges.

He was as tall as my knee, as wide as my waist, and wore a wig of curls nearly twice his height, piled up in the fashion of the previous century—except his was on fire. There were silver hoops in his earlobes, which hung nearly to his waist, and he wore a tiny cavalier's uniform with silver breast- and backplate. A human-size sword dragged along behind him. His wizened face bore the exaggerated features of the feyín, but enlarged.

It was the Faerie King Elgeron.

"The poor child has got wedding nerves, that's all," he said. "Pray let us continue."

"*Nerffs?*" cried George II. "*Mein Gott*, sir, your daughter's a hellcat. Young George here couldn't handle her. We vill have to come up mit some less dangerous liaison." The senior George shot most unkind looks at his goggling grandson.

Elgeron tried wheedling next. "Daughter, come back here this moment and kiss your groom and all is forgiven."

Morgana had been at my side the while, clenching her fists and trembling with fury. The white streak in her hair had come loose of its pins, and hung in her eyes. We were properly surrounded by swordsmen again. Now she faced the brace of Georges.

"My father hath made a bargain with the Duchess of the Red Seas to bring me here. What was his price? Your kingdom laid to waste? Your navy sunk to the bottom that she might pillage the world? What else hath he to offer, that she could not as easily take?"

"Her soul, thou wretched child," Elgeron said. "Only her soul!"

This set Morgana back a bit, I think. I imagined the Faerie King must have it in a jar somewhere, or wrapped in paper and string— however one stores disembodied souls.

"I shall count to three," said Elgeron.

But Morgana wasn't having any of it. "Count the number of the stars. I shall never return, father. I denounce you."

"Wait a minute," said the tiny king, noticing me for the first time. "Who is that cretin with the mask?"

"A better man than you."

With eyes of fire to match his daughter's, Elgeron looked first at Morgana, and then at me, and cried, "Then by the Splinter of Time, I curse you both!"

There was a flash of light as he waved his hands, and the wall behind us burst apart. Morgana had raised her own defense, and the invisible shield diverted the impact around us, as a stone in the stream diverts the water.

The guards and attendants had been closing in, but this display of magic sent them to the floor again—or to the ceiling, in the case of those nearest us.

"This way," said I, and Morgana took my hand and we ran through the wreckage and up the stairs I'd taken down before.

Another blast of energy from King Elgeron shivered the stone steps behind us, nearly knocking off my boot-heels.

"Seize them," I heard the Faerie King bellow, and then there were footfalls on the half-ruined stairs at our backs. We raced up the spiral steps, and then down the servants' hall, which was filled with smoke and frightened servants. They screamed as we made our way to the far end. I chanced to look over my shoulder and saw the guards emerging into the hall, probably as eager to get away from the wee raging king downstairs as they were to come after us.

Moments later, we were upon the balcony from which I had entered, and I whistled fairly enough on the first try. Midnight soared around the parapets, swept his bright black wings out wide, and alighted beside us. I put Morgana between his wings; with my hands still about her slim waist, she bent down and turned my face up to hers.

"I would kiss you if I could," said she, and I sprang onto Midnight's back as the first of our pursuers made the balcony. We flew into the air and were a thousand yards above the palace before I had even settled in my seat.

I would kiss you if I could. Why couldn't she?

It was the best news I'd ever had in my life—except for that.

Chapter 35

MIDNIGHT'S FLIGHT

OUR ESCAPE was not assured. As we streaked through the sky, Midnight pumping his wings, a teeming green cloud whirled up at us. It was pixies. I wrapped my black coat around the princess to shield her from them. The pixies couldn't fly at a fraction of Midnight's speed, but bedeviled our way, firing arrows. Midnight ascended to a terrific height, even above the overcast, and we soon left them behind, the little creatures piping insults as we rose beyond their reach. The air was cold and thin.

"We have had adventures, haven't we," Morgana said, once we'd caught our breath.

"We have," said I. "Adventures enough for even a lifetime such as yours."

"They have only just begun," she said, with regret.

"So what I meant to tell you before—"

"There is so much to tell you, Kit. So much I was afraid to share with you. I didn't know how you felt, nor how *I* felt, and with all this turmoil in my own world—"

"It's much the same with me."

"I have never felt so close to anyone as you, but I don't know why. We've little in common."

"Scarcely anything."

"And I might live a hundred ages yet, and you not a hundred years."

"An obstacle I have dwelt upon."

"And yet nothing seems impossible with you beside me."

"We are astride a flying horse, with the clouds below us."

"But I am a princess, by birth if not by title any longer, and you—"

"You scarcely need to point out that my parents are unknown, and me an unemployed servant with a considerable criminal record."

"Have we lost our senses?"

"If I don't kiss you, I shall perish."

"Look there!" she cried, startling me so much I nearly toppled off Midnight.

She pointed below us. I spied a disturbance in the clouds, far beneath Midnight's hooves, the smooth upper surface in one place bubbling and steaming like a mud geyser a little distance ahead of us.

Then came the mantigorns.

They could fly at terrific speed. The six of them appeared below us and beat their foul wings until they were abreast of us, and above and below, always coming closer. They were no longer considerate of Morgana's safety, but hurled their javelins at us, and Midnight swooped and dipped his wings to avoid them. One of the lances passed through his feathers and left a smoking hole. Within a minute the mantigorns had come close enough to snatch at us with their long, hooked fingers. I had the sword, but I didn't see what good it could do us now.

How had they found us? "Morgana," I cried. "Are you still wearing Lily's comb?"

"It's right under your nose. I wear it to remember her by."

The mantigorns had retreated a little way, so I took the opportunity to run my fingers through her plaits of hair, and found the tortoise comb. It had been concealed beneath her tresses. I flung the thing away into the empty air.

"Kit! How could you!"

"It's a sigilantum. That's how that blasted Duchess keeps finding us!"

There wasn't time to explain. A keening cry pierced the air from somewhere above. The mantigorns slipped away, moving farther apart from us. I looked up and saw a solitary cloud that churned with some inward energy—it seemed to be streaking through the sky at the same speed we were. Then a white gryphon dropped out of it—an enormous creature, bigger than any of the others we had seen. As it plummeted toward us, I saw there was a rider upon its back.

And then I saw the flaming red hair that leapt up from the green face, and the patch across one eye. I'd seen that face before—in the looking glass.

"Morgana," said I. But she had already seen.

"The Duchess," she whispered. "She is here."

It seemed we had about thirty seconds left.

"That thing I meant to tell you—"

"Oh, Kit—"

"I'm not going to die without having said the words. Dash it, Morgana, I love you."

Morgana was silent a moment. Then she put her hand upon my cheek and said, "If I fall, they'll leave you be," and tried to slip from Midnight's back. I wasn't having that, and clung to her fiercely; as she struggled, the nearest of the mantigorns almost succeeded in catching me in its claws by dropping down from behind my right shoulder. I flung up my arm and the sword saved us—there was a bright concussion when the monster touched the golden hilt, and the creature's talons were flung back. It was hurled senseless down into the void with my sword spiraling after it. But I nearly lost my grip on Morgana. She hung across Midnight's ribs, her feet flailing in the empty air.

In the confusion, I had lost sight of the white gryphon. Now it appeared close to our port side, and there was the Duchess of the Red Seas, as near as two wing-spans. She wore a breastplate of shining black scales, a dark green cape that snapped and ruffled like a ship's pennant, thigh boots, and—to my eye, a shocking thing— trousers. She was at once regal, handsome, and menacing. I felt as a mouse must feel in the presence of a cat that knows its prey is cornered.

"Here it ends, hearties," said she, shouting to be heard over the roar of the wind. "Fight and die, or drop the girl and go where ye will."

"I'm of no value to you now," Morgana cried defiantly. "My father hath disowned me and curst us as well."

"Just so!" The pirate laughed. "I said drop the girl. I want nothing more from thee than a corpse!"

The remaining mantigorns drew back a little farther. This was parley, and they would wait for the Duchess's command.

"What about your blasted soul?" I shouted. "Don't tell me you found it behind the cushions!"

The Duchess was enjoying herself, I realized. If I could keep her talking, there might be some hope of . . . something. Not much, but hope endures.

"A wedding gift from that dwarf of a king," the Duchess said, and laughed again, a crowing, harsh sound.

At last, I had Morgana firmly on Midnight's back.

She spoke in my ear that our one-eyed foe should not hear: "It was never my father's to give. No Faerie can trade in souls. Whatever brought her here, it is false." Then she added, "I love you, too."

Of all the times to be flattered, this was the worst. I needed to concentrate my thoughts on the crisis at hand. But my bosom was filled with light and hope and joy, and at the same time a despair and fury that circumstance should conspire to sunder two creatures who might be so happy together as we. These emotions were perfectly matched and precisely opposed. It felt like madness.

"The King couldn't give you back your soul," I shouted. "He hasn't got it."

"Here I am, lubber! Alive and in thine wretched world!"

She snapped the white gryphon's reins and the beast dove straight at us. Midnight folded his wings and dropped below its claws, but in so doing, nearly collided with a mantigorn directly beneath us. It tore a couple of feathers from Midnight's wing before he had gained height enough to escape its reach. The Duchess howled with laughter again. She certainly seemed alive to me.

"Look at her," Morgana said. "She's wrong."

I saw it. As the wind battered the Duchess, fragments of her seemed to be flaking off and whirling away in the turbulent air behind her. Her cape was becoming ragged. She didn't seem to have noticed yet.

"Drop the girl and live, boy. I'll forgive thee for nearly cuttin' off me arm in that mirror. I want to hear her scream, all the way down."

"Can't you do a ruckins?" I whispered to Morgana.

"If I do, I'll only fall to my death in Faerie, instead of here."

The Duchess, meanwhile, had drawn a pistol from her belt. She trained it at me, her sleeve shuddering in the blast of wind that roared around her. Fragments of the sleeve flew away.

"You're coming to bits," I shouted.

I thought she must shoot and kill me. Or worse, slay Midnight. But a large scrap of her arm—not just her sleeve—flew away, and she saw it. She looked behind her and saw the particles swirling behind her like paper-ash up a chimney.

"Never trust a king," she snarled. "Never thee mind, shark-pups. If I can't have my soul, I'll have yours."

She guided the gryphon close. I could see every line in her fury-contorted face. Her ears came to points like Morgana's, I saw. One of these came off. Several scales of her armor flew away. An inspiration came to me—and my friend and foe, hope, sprang to new life.

"There is another way," said I. "Spare the Princess and I'll make it my quest to return what was taken from you!"

We were so close I could see a confusion pass over the Duchess. She swayed in the saddle and shook her head in a daze. The gryphon, without her will to guide it, dropped away, and the mantigorns, who had been flying in formation like ships of the line about us, also spread apart. But then the confusion passed, and was replaced by rage; when she regained her senses, she came swooping back with sharp teeth bared and her lone eye burning. There was a steady stream of matter flying away from her now, like sooty smoke. It left a trail in the sky behind her.

"On three," she shouted, and again the pistol came up.

"Does everyone in Faerie count when they're threatening people?" I said.

"Let me fall," Morgana begged me. "Her hatred is for me."

"One!"

"I suppose this is an opportune time to ask one last favor?" said I to Morgana.

"Two!"

"Say it!" my princess breathed.

"Kiss me?"

Morgana did not reply; she seemed paralyzed by indecision. I had a plan, now. There wasn't any more time for her to make up her mind. I drew my legs up so that I was crouching upon Midnight's back, using my trick-rider's balance to keep from pitching off.

"Duchess!" I cried, to forestall the final count. "I say again: Spare the Princess and I promise I'll see you reunited with what you have lost!"

The Duchess' face was a mask of ice. A slab of her scalp flew away, and part of her nose. She was coming to pieces. She spoke in low tones, but by some magic it was as if she whispered in my ear: "I've wasted a millennium on that quest, manling. You haven't got the time."

She twisted the reins and the white gryphon lunged at us. The Duchess couldn't have been ten feet away, the pistol-bore swaying in a narrow circuit somewhere around my heart. The mantigorns loosed their war cries and buffeted their wings to get within claw's strike. Midnight made a desperate evasion and we nearly fell off his back. Yet I got my feet under me again, and gathered for the spring.

"I wish," cried I, in frustration and despair, my eyes on the cruel Duchess, "you'd go to blazes."

And so saying, I leapt into the air, straight at her mount.

$ $ $

I only made it halfway.

As soon as I spoke the words, there was a great roar, the sky split open, and a bolt of lightning seared all around us. It forked and forked again like the branches of some burning tree, and smote each of the mantigorns at the same instant. They burst to pieces or plunged in flames from the sky, howling as they tumbled into the clouds below. A flotsam of huge, blazing feathers whirled down after them. The white gryphon lit up like a paper lantern and exploded, and the Duchess, unmounted, screamed an unearthly wail and shattered into a million dirty fragments. These particles themselves burned up, until there was nothing left.

I saw this very clearly, for the white gryphon ceased to exist when I was halfway through my leap, so even if I had reached it, there was nothing there to reach. Of consequence I was following an identical course to the mantigorns, landward, face down, with a superb view of the entire tableau.

A second after the lightning bolt, there was a detonation in my weskit pocket, and a puff of green smoke flew up behind me. As there was nothing else to do but fall to my death, I had the leisure to reach into the pocket to see what had exploded within. I withdrew none other than Magda's tooth! It was black from end to end. Then it turned to dust in my fingers and blew away.

There wasn't anything further to do, so I watched the clouds

grow closer. It was terribly cold and the wind
battered mercilessly; my downward speed was
increasing. By now the last of the mantigorns
had dropped through the clouds. I was next,
and beneath the clouds I'd see where my final resting place would be. A field would
suffice, thought I. Perhaps a field of radishes,
for remembrance.

Then there was a great roar of air and a mighty black shape
came up beneath me, stooping like a giant hawk. It was Midnight!
His wings spread out and I fell heavily across his shoulders, nearly
unhorsing Morgana, who reached out to secure me as I came down.
For several long, sickening moments I hung by Midnight's mane,
dangling over the abyss, and the fear that had left me when I was falling in the open air now returned tenfold, because there was hope.

Then I was astride him again, and clinging to horse and princess with legs and arms respectively and in equal measure.

"You made a wish!" Morgana cried. There was joy in her face.

"Are you unharmed?" I said, desperate for reassurances of any
kind.

"Very well," said she. "Never better, as I have you alive. Are
you hurt?"

"A bit chilly," I confessed. "But unmarked, except that Magda's
tooth exploded and singed my weskit."

"It's a wishing tooth!" Morgana exclaimed. "Why did you not
use it before?"

"I didn't know anything about it. I never make wishes."

"That's what they're for, you daft manling!"

We were in a new world: Above us, thin, elegant clouds ribbed
the great blue dome of the sky, and below us was an unbroken sea
of mist, the clouds here and there undulating in hills and valleys.
In the distance I saw great thunderhead clouds, iron-colored an-
vils that rose into the highest parts of the sky, and were there
tinged with lambent pink and yellow. It was cold, but the air was

deliciously fresh. I felt nothing of the chill, for I had one arm around Morgana, her hair flying in my face and her heart beating next to my own.

We flew in silence for a time, at what must have been incredible speed; I could not tell, for there were no landmarks below us by which to gauge our progress. Suffice it to say that it must have been some aspect of Midnight's enchantment that we were not frozen or deafened by the wind that swept all around us. We flew so fast that thunder pealed in our wake.

Then Morgana turned around so that she could look into my eyes. "Thank you," she said.

"For what?" said I. "You rescued yourself."

"For that lovely piece of buttered toast when we were parted."

"Whatever do you mean?" I said, and then remembered.

As the cruel mantigorns closed about her on that fateful night, I had thought, *My love. Good-bye.* Of course she had received the message, and my thought of toast beside.

If I had felt a little cold before, now I was quite warm, for I was blushing again. A thousand protests rose to my lips, along with apologies and explanations. I let them all clamor for my attention, but did not speak until the confusion had settled down. A little hard-learned wisdom: Never miss an opportunity *not* to speak.

"I've loved you since you came to my aid on that bridge, rad-ishes and all," she said. "That was rescue enough."

These words sent my heart flying on its own course; it must have circled the sun, for it returned to me glowing, and it seemed we must be soaring along in heaven itself. But there was an imper-fection in my great happiness that I did not understand.

"Why can't I kiss you?" I asked.

"Because," said Morgana, "in the Middle Kingdom, all it takes for a Faerie to be married is a single kiss."

"And what's the matter with that?"

"There's so much you don't know about Faerie." She sighed.

Chapter 36

THE IRISH SEA

A S THE miles went by, I told Morgana what had transpired since last she saw me, and explained the mystery of the tortoise comb. Then she told me of her own travails. She had been taken to her father in shackles, at which time he condemned her and threatened vile curses. When that didn't work, he threatened the common Faerie people with misery and pain instead, and, remembering the scene of the massacre we had encountered—the air thick with brails—she gave in. She was sent by the infernal silver coach to the palace. This time, a squad of King's men accompanied her.

It was only in the minute of the wedding, when young George was leaning over to place a kiss upon her lips, that Morgana had lost her temper entirely and performed the extraordinary caprizel I'd witnessed, all but blowing up both kings. It was the same one with which she'd knocked me off my feet some while back, but amplified a hundredfold. The rest, I had been present for.

"The look on King Elgeron's face will never leave my mind. I cannot decide if it was the most comical or the most terrible thing I ever saw. He was so twisted up with anger, you see, and puffed up like a bullfrog with his wig on fire. But still, my own father! The hatred on his features was unmistakable. I don't know what I think."

Midnight flew without tiring for a long time, and eventually I thought we must see where we were. I bade him drop down below the overcast, and as the floor of clouds became a roof again, we saw there was nothing below us but steel-colored water. Morgana fainted and might have fallen, but I caught her firmly around the waist and held her against me. It was darker here below the cloud, and it was clear we were above the ocean, for the air smelled of salt and there was no shore in any direction.

Not long after that, the ocean seemed to grow larger at a rapid pace. We were descending. Midnight was breathing hard, struggling to keep us aloft. The waves reached up greedily to snap at his hooves. I felt the spray on my cheeks. It revived Morgana, who clawed at my coat, wild with terror.

"Kit," said she, gasping, "soon we must part. Do not despair for me, but live your mad life well. Methinks I must undertake my next journey alone."

"I shan't leave your side," said I, as brave as I could manage.

Ahead of us was a thin white band along the horizon. It grew in size and revealed a coastline fringed with cliffs and rocks. Midnight was laboring, his head tossing with every stroke of his wings. Great black feathers flew from those wings, and turned to ash as they struck the lashing surface of the sea. Soon it didn't look as if their span could support us, so riven and ragged were they.

I saw a strip of beach, and directed the horse toward it. If we could but get close, we could swim there; Morgana might cling to Midnight, for horses swim almost as well as they run.

One hoof struck the water, and Midnight renewed his effort, but the largest of the waves now rose up higher than his back, and must soon overcome us. He twisted in and out between the foaming peaks. Before us the shore grew nearer, and seagulls wheeled overhead.

"You're the greatest horse that ever lived," I said to him, and meant it. "You are the mightiest and finest horse in the world. Just another stroke of your wings. And now, one more. And again!"

On brave Midnight labored. Half of a mile from the surf there was a great hissing sound, and his fine wings began to crumble into powder that whirled behind us, much as the substance of the Duchess had done. Morgana screamed in the most pitiable anguish, there was a stomach-twisting drop, and a moment later we plunged into the sea. Our three hours were up.

I sank immediately, and lost my grip on Morgana, for we had been flung violently from Midnight's back. I kicked to the surface, and spat seawater; Midnight emerged not far away, his great nostrils steaming. Morgana was nowhere about.

I cried her name, and swallowed half the ocean. I plunged deep beneath the water, but it was too dim and turbulent to see much more than a hint of the bottom rising up in front of me. Again and again I dived, until I could not make another attempt without drowning. Not finding any trace of my Princess, I thrashed the surface of the sea and called her name with desperation until there was so much water in my lungs I must swim or drown. At last, I kicked for the bank, and after a long and weary struggle, waded upon a pebble strand. The tide was out. Midnight swam up after me. We could walk the rest of the distance to dry land.

But Morgana was gone.

I waited there in the shallows for a long time, watching the water for some sign of her. If only I still had the wishing tooth! No one has ever wished for something so fervently as I did then, but the waves cared not at all.

Midnight stood beside me for a time, the water up to his belly. Then he nuzzled me, pushing me toward the beach with his nose. At length, with the sky beginning to show sunset through the clouds, I turned back to land, and sloshed my way ashore.

At the tide line there was a fisherman mending a net. He obviously hadn't seen us arrive, for he looked startled when Midnight and I emerged from the foam.

[*The Cruel Waves*]

"Fell you in?" he inquired, and I might have laughed aloud to hear his Irish voice, except laughter had died inside me.

"Did you see a beautiful young lady emerge from the sea?" I begged him, clutching at his sleeve. The man's merry face fell.

"None have come from that water, son, but you and that great pony," he replied, and solemnly plucked the cap from his head. "The last time a woman come ashore in this place it was a century past. Borne up by the water sprites, she was, as rule this part of the sea, and rose out o' the waves with her feet in a blue flame and a crown of white feathers upon her head, dry as sunshine. My great-grandfodder seen it with his very own eyes."

A few months before I would have chuckled to hear this silly, superstitious tale. No longer! Instead, I took his words entirely to heart, and spent another long watch with my eyes bent upon the ocean.

At one point, hugging myself for warmth, I found there was something in my breast pocket, waterlogged and lumpy; I drew out my master's will, about which I had entirely forgotten. With numb, blue fingers I unfolded the sheet, and there found the map had changed again. In fact it was gone, and all the little sketches beside; the hanged man was no longer there.

Instead there was only one drawing upon it, a fair portrait of Morgana. Even as I gazed upon the picture, the lines began to run, and the portrait was obliterated, and I held nothing but a very wet sheet of ink-blotted paper.

I remained at the shore until the daylight was all gone and I was chilled to the marrows. The fisherman had long departed up a path on the cliff to wherever he lived; but presently he returned with a tallow lamp and a sealskin cape, wrapped up my shivering frame, and led me away. Midnight followed, his head held low. He, too, felt our loss.

Chapter 37

THE ENCHANTED LAND

THE NEXT morning broke with a storm that churned up the sea and brought the stony clouds down low to meet it. Rain blackened the cliffs and pelted the fisherman's cottage where I had spent the night. It was a low, dark place, the walls barely as high as my shoulder and the thatch above rustling with wood lice, humid with the stink of peat smoke. I recalled I had ridden Midnight clean through such a dwelling, a lifetime ago. But it was snug, and I was exhausted almost beyond reason.

So I lay on a pallet of straw while the fisherman went out—his trade ignored all but the most violent weather—and stayed abed until his stout wife awoke me with a smoking porringer of oat gruel.

The remainder of the day I spent with Midnight, for the shed in which the fisherman had installed him had its back to the cliffs, and a shutter that could be opened to command a view of the coast for miles in either direction. I looked down upon the foaming surf that beat the rocks, and out upon the hammered iron skin of the water, and all the while hoped to see a maiden rise from the waves with her feet in a blue flame and her head wreathed in feathers.

All the day long, nothing rose from the water except the rotten hull of a years-old shipwreck, which rolled drunkenly ashore and came to pieces in the surf. The boom and rush of the storm was the only conversation I heard that day, Midnight my only companion.

My mind was fixed on Morgana's last words to me. She had begged me to live my life well. That had a ring of finality to it. But I also knew that the Faerie people didn't speak of "next journeys" as manlings did, referring to the afterlife—if Morgana said her next journey must be undertaken alone, there was a very good chance she meant it quite literally. So she might somehow have survived the plunge into the ocean. Perhaps she went back to the Realm Between, and there must remain.

Whatever the truth of it was, I was alone, and as the hours passed and the sea gave up nothing but wrack, I came to understand Morgana was not going to return.

That was why she had told me to live my mad life. Otherwise I might have waited there atop the cliff forever.

$$\text{※} \qquad \text{※} \qquad \text{※}$$

My troubles weren't over, of course. I was a wanted man across the sea, and I'd set down in British territory. I hadn't more than a few small coins that had happened to be in the coat I'd been given by Captain Sterne; even Midnight's saddle was borrowed from a nearby farmer. I needed to earn a living, but hadn't yet determined what that living should be. There wasn't much need of trick-riders or manservants without letters of recommendation in those parts.

I wasn't worried, though. After what I'd been through, it seemed to me I could do anything. The trouble was, without Morgana beside me, nothing seemed worth doing.

I didn't much fear discovery. Ireland was a wild place, and the people were isolated and kept to their own folk, so no word of me reached the ears of anyone who might have caused difficulty— although it seemed that everyone for miles around knew me to be that same fellow they had heard was washed ashore.

"Tales," as the fisherman's wife said, "travel swift and far, for they're light as a feather. It's truth goes slowly, heavy as 'tis." She didn't know that the tale, in this case, *was* the truth. So it was that I became the "fellow swum ashore with his horse," and wherever I rode, there was a different version of how it transpired. The Irish love a sad tale better than a happy one, so they dwelt mostly upon the loss of my fair lover to the waves.

So did I. Morgana had told me to get on with my life, but that was a thing easier said than done.

The Irish enjoy only one thing better than a sad story, and that's a sad song, so it wasn't long before I was sitting in a tavern in the company of a short brown ale and heard a lilting melody sung with the following words:

Farewell to thee, cried the maiden of springtime
Farewell to thee, then no more she spake
For the waves they rose up
And the sea overtook her
And over her head did the cold waters break.

Long did he seek with an eye to the ocean
Long did he seek on the stone of the shore
But the sea ne'er gave up
The maiden of springtime
And laughed for to tell him he'd see her no more.

I don't think the singer recognized me, but others must have done, for I hurried out and sorry eyes followed me.

But that very night, something occurred to remind me I hadn't died myself, and might have reason to hope after all. As I was returning to the cottage after a long aimless day, Midnight walking slowly in the gloaming, following his own path, I saw a single light dancing within the hedge beside me, like a spark that wouldn't burn up. There was a greenish cast to it, and a familiar look to the way it flitted about, and excitement was new-kindled in my bosom. I sprang from Midnight's back and bade him wait for me at the stile, then went through a gate. The wee light danced away, teasing me. I followed it, and crossed a dark field to the woods.

I'd hardly entered the deep darkness beneath the boughs when the glowing point of light winked out. It had been a Faerie. I was certain of it.

My heart leapt against my ribs—this was the first I'd seen of the magical people since coming ashore, and I hadn't dared to hope I might encounter them again in my lifetime. This was rather a change from when first I had met Willum and Gruntle and felt nothing but trepidation, for I had come to know the feyín for a fine, brave people, willing to risk everything if they thought it might help a just cause.

I stumbled through the darkness to the heart of the stand of trees, and heard a familiar snuffling sound, as of a hog seeking truffles in the loam. I stopped in my tracks, and ahead saw a shape I took at first to be a stone jutting out of the mossy ground.

"Don't stand there gaping nor a fool," came a rusty old voice. "Come to me yarms, boyo!"

It was Magda, the old witch, with Demon the bulldog grunting at her side. I embraced her as I would have embraced my own mother, had I ever the opportunity. It was like hugging a handful of sticks, but I was grateful. Demon leapt up and down and yowled with delight, then capered in circles.

"Magda," I gasped. I was overcome with emotion. "Everything you said—I was a fool not to trust you."

"And a fool if you did, manling."

As I clung to the ancient crone, she wept—wept until the scrying stone fell out of her eye socket. I was about to strike a lucifer match to find it when the very leaves seemed to light up around us, filling the trees with a glow like fireflies. But it wasn't fireflies, as those insects are unsuited to Ireland's climate. It was Faeries. A great shimmering song filled the air.

Through the shrubs and bushes wound a footpath, and along this walked a file of feyín, bearing lanterns on tall stalks. These were made from flowers, and gave off a most beautiful light. Behind them came a lean gray wolf, and on the shoulders of the wolf stood a tiny but proud figure, a red-haired feyín woman clad in silver, who reminded me in some way of Morgana.

"Bow to the turf, boyo," Magda whispered. "'Tis Étain, the Queen of these parts. Cousin to your poor Morgana."

Morgana! A thousand questions crowded my mind, but I spake none of them, for there was a deep solemnity to the moment.

After the queen upon the wolf there came a file of feyín warriors carrying spears about as long as goose quills, and after them a brace of small bearded gentlemen with goats' legs and sleeved weskits who must have been fawns.

There were some speeches made back and forth between Magda and the Queen, spoken in the Faerie language, which had a ceremonial sound to them; there was some bowing and saluting, which I imitated, to be polite. They had a different attitude toward the Eldritch Law here, and mingling with manlings was not entirely forbidden, so I was not regarded with any special concern. Then the Queen turned her face to me and spake at some length. She did not speak English, so Magda translated into her own manner of gibberish, which I could more or less understand.

The matter of it was this: The Free Faerie People thanked me for my assistance, which was of immense value in their defense of independence; I was to be celebrated this night.

"A shindig nor yer honor," was how Magda expressed it.

The Faeries would have come to me sooner, she translated, but had lost track of me once I came ashore—although every bee in Ireland had borne a description of me far and wide. But as I was too near the sea for the feyín, and too far for the sea sprites, I'd gone undetected.

"What tole 'em where you was to be found?" Magda said. "A

pixie o'erheard a terrible tragic song nor the local pub, she did. What sounded a deal like yer own sad tale. Thus they found 'ee."

I rushed through whatever words of thanks I could invent in my overexcited brains, then blurted to Magda: "Has anyone here heard what happened to Morgana—is she alive? Did she suffer and drown, or retreat to the Realm Between? I beg you, end my suffering ignorance!"

Magda shook her head.

"You manlings and your impatience! Ye lives so short a life, yet 'ee always be in a hurry ter get t' the end. Patience, young rake-hell."

I wasn't at all reassured by that, but in one way Magda had reminded me of something important: There was no hurry. If Morgana had slipped away to another realm, or perished in the sea, what difference if I knew of it today, tomorrow, or threescore years hence? With a sort of weary resignation, I bent my attention to the magical doings before me and tried to make myself a gracious guest.

Beneath the trees that night the feyín held a great feast, a hundred times the revel I'd participated in with Willum and his associates back in England. There was a bonfire of green and blue and white flame, these being the fire-colors of the respective bloodlines present (or so I was told). There was a great circle of flat stones around the fire; upon them the guests dined, or sat, or danced. The male feyín's hats were decorated charmingly with knotted flowers and leaves; the females had flowers plaited in their hair.

There were other species besides. I saw fauns, pixies green and blue, stout little people I took for dwarfs or leprechauns, and others I knew not: Foxes that walked upon their hind legs, toads with side-whiskers and jeweled brows, and ant-size folk who rode about on the backs of beetles, among others. Strange eyes winked green and yellow and blue beyond the circle of the firelight; who looked through them, I do not know. Perhaps they were things unfit for human sight.

I ate from tiny dishes that overflowed with food no matter how much was consumed, and knew hardly anything I ate. The dishes obviously made from insects I politely declined, although I'm fairly certain I consumed a cunningly garnished dragonfly. A delicious drink, served in the cups of bluebell flowers—far more delicate than glump—was served in tremendous quantities.* Bluebells are poisonous, but the poison in these had been somehow enchanted so that it had a merry effect on the feyín. I did not feel it; still, it quenched my thirst nicely, if only a very little at a time.

There were orations in several tongues by the feyín chieftains present. Then Magda screeched out an emphatic speech (in Gaelic, I believe) that was met with ferocious yells of approval, distinctly warlike. Then Queen Étain bade silence, and stood before the fire and addressed the entire company. The roaring blaze died down to a flicker while she spoke, as if a lid had been placed over it, so that she could be seen by everyone around the circle.

What she said, I cannot tell, for only a few words in English met my ear, but I heard my own name repeated several times, and Morgana's, and Midnight's, and others who had been a part of the adventure. I thought as well that I heard a phrase once spoken by my dying master, which I had taken at the time for delirious nonsense. As she spoke, more and more pairs of eyes were turned my way, until I was dreadfully self-conscious. At last her tale was done, and three rousing cheers rang into the boughs.

I was instructed to advance and kneel before the tiny queen, straight through the fire.

"Garn wi' ye, boyo!" Magda cackled. "It ain't a mantigorn!"

I passed through the flames. The fire didn't burn, but crackled and pricked upon me like a very dry blanket will do when rubbed

---

* This liqueur, called "fairy drops," came into brief vogue in 1919 when Faerie enthusiast Sir Arthur Conan Doyle was given the recipe by a well-meaning feyín. Without the necessary caprizel to render it nontoxic, it killed a number of people at séances and *planchette* readings—most notably the spiritualist Madam Edith Lafoon.

against itself. Upon the far side of the blaze, I bent on one knee. The Queen fluttered up higher than my head and delivered another speech, which sounded very formal. Thus was I awarded the Silver Bough and Acorns, apparently a mark of considerable distinction. It entitled feyín and other magical creatures to interact with me without restriction wherever I went, although I was but a manling. It also came with a sort of pension (paid all in silver on the full moon, naturally), and a pretty little pin of leaves and acorns to fix upon my lapel.

This last item was applied by a feyín girl, the first child I'd seen among them. She was the size of a chickadee and covered in downy fur. Her wings beat so fast I couldn't see them. I wondered if Morgana had been covered with fur when she was a child.

The ceremonial part of the evening had ended. I returned to my place, and the large, lean wolf sat down beside me; it seemed to be a friend of Demon, for they touched noses. Midnight was led into the circle of light by a couple of feyín who guided him by the ears; I have no idea what he made of the scene. His mane was braided through and through with wildflowers, and friendly pixies took turns alighting on his underlip to feed him bits of honeycomb.

There was much cheering and shouting and diving through the air. Then a command rang out and dozens of the flying sort took to the air at once. They commenced a Faerie dance that took place upon the wing, the dancers bowing and whirling in the air like cherry blossoms pinwheeling in a capricious breeze; the music was at once absurd and moving, played on strange instruments, tiny strings and woodwinds and silver horns.

The fire leapt up again, and daredevils took turns flying through the upper reaches of it, scorching their wings to uproarious applause. A flight of Faerie maidens draped garlands of flowers around my neck, and blew sparkling pink kisses at me from a modest distance (the acceptable form of kissing among their unmarried people). The revelry went on for hours, with Madga, the chieftains, and the Queen in long counsel together, and various dignitaries offering their regards to me. Songs were sung, including the sad song I'd heard in the tavern; it was rendered in English, and ran to many increasingly fantastical verses. It struck me with melancholy, which I did my best to conceal.

Demon had long since fallen asleep in my lap, snoring with tremendous force. Despite the wonders all around me, after countless rounds of bluebell liqueur, I joined him in slumber where I sat.

Chapter 38

WORD FROM ABROAD

MY LIFE settled into a small routine. I once offered to help the fisherman, as much for some thing to do as to be useful to my kind host. I was useless—besides the seasickness that overcame me in the tossing boat, my eyes were bent continuously upon the waves, as if I might spy my love paddling about with the fishes. We were not even in the same part of the water where I'd lost her, but in a bay several miles distant. I may have reduced his catch by 20 per cent that day.

I also assisted his wife, with better results, for all she required was sweeping and scrubbing, at which activities I was adept due to cleaning up the Manse once or twice a month.

About two weeks after my unusual arrival on Ireland's shores, I retuned from exercising Midnight to find a man in knee-garters arrived at the gate with a letter. It was exciting to receive news that wasn't borne on the wings of a bee. I eagerly tore open the envelope.

Sweet Morgana and dearest Kit [it began, unhappily],

It is me Lily. I trust this finds you well for I am told by Master Willum that you have arrived safely in Ireland as he learnt by long-distance bee. I am well and Willum and Gruntle are well also who are here staying with me until such time as it is safe for them to make passage there to you. I take up pen though not a good hand at writing because my message is too long for magick bee. [I have omitted the unique spellings, which would have proved Lily's critique, in the cause of legibility.]

It was a great sorrow to part from you unexpectedly the night of the fire in that silly town. You may not know what happ'ned afterward. I fell from the rope and cracked a bone in my foot and Uncle Cornelius was knocked senseless in the confusion and broke his dear old head. I did not see you again but heard of your capture some days later and lost heart altogether and a few days after that Uncle Cornelius was ailing sorely abed in an inn and begged me to deliver a message. He told me of a lawyer he kept in secret from that wretched nursemaid Prudence Fingers and that he had told the lawyer also the three questions to make sure Miss Fingers did not attempt to lie about the answers in order to keep herself in command of his fortunes. Which as you know is just what she done.

Uncle Cornelius never came to recognize me but told me how much I looked like his niece Lily and how he loved her and wished her happiness and if I met her would I tell her so and I said I was sure she already knew. He said he had never had such delight as traveling with us and it was the best tour he ever made of the world and hoped we might do it again the following year.

Well then that very night my poor blessed uncle died and how I wept you can only imagine. I went with heavy heart to the lawyer he named. A very handsome young fellow not like a lawyer at all to look at him. He is very clever and had an idea to test my claim right away.

He took me back to Uncle Cornelius's house with me in a veil so my features couldn't be seen and Prudence Fingers asked me the questions again and I answered them right and that wicked girl said I did not answer them right. But the lawyer whose name is Mr. Stoker, Esquire knew the answers already and seeing that I knew them also he knew then that Miss Fingers was a liar and a thief and I was truly Uncle Cornelius's Lily so now I am mistress of the estate and set handsome for life.

That Prudence Fingers and the man with the red hair have fled and hid somewhere but I have old Fred here to protect me once Willum and Gruntle have departed. And not only Fred but Mr. Stoker, Esquire for we was married but three days past and at last I am a honest woman. I miss Uncle Cornelius every day but I am used to that. I miss you every day and it pains me still. Be well.

With all my love,
Lily Stoker

P. Yes—Fred misses Midnight he said so.

I am not ashamed to admit my eyes were wet with happiness at the conclusion of this letter, for I had often wondered about what had become of Lily after that terrible night. I read the letter through several more times.

That same morning, I had awakened in my corner of the fisherman's cottage to discover a sack of small silver coins in the crook of my arm; I gave as many of these to the fisherman and his wife as they would accept, which was as few as need would permit them. They were honest folk.

Not wishing them to see my confusion of moods, I determined to go down the cliff to the shore and watch the sea awhile. I hadn't ventured back to the fateful beach since my arrival. It was a cold day with a good breeze tugging at my borrowed hat, autumn in the breath of the wind. It was a time to be philosophical, not to drown in misery. I had won the heart of a princess, after all. How many fellows in all the history of the world—this world, or another beside it—may make that claim? But I hadn't been able to keep her.

That was the Faerie way. There seemed always to be a trick at the back of their doings, no matter how long it took for the thing to reveal itself.

I was lost in thoughts of this nature when a tiny figure emerged from the water. It was a feyín, more or less, but different from any other I'd seen: She had long, stiff wings like the fins of a fish on her back, and she was entirely silver in color except for the black tiger stripes that wrapped all around her body. She had no hair on her head, nor garments on her person. I guessed this must be a water sprite.

She skipped out of the creamy surf between the going of one wave and the coming of another, and stood before me. "Art thou Master Kit?" she inquired.

"I am he," said I, doffing my hat.

She curtsied. "I am Ribbonfish. We have been waiting for you to come down to shore this past fortnight. We cannot venture far from the water's edge, and you seemed content to sit at yon window evermore." Here she indicated the shed, up at the top of the cliff.

"You could have sent me a bee," I suggested. I was in agonies of excitement and dread. Surely this creature would know what had happened to Morgana!

Ribbonfish bowed low. "So few bees beneath the water. I have a message for you, Master Kit," she continued, and my heart leapt almost out of my mouth. Her next words would either dash my hopes forever or set them aflame.

The sprite tipped her head to remember the exact wording, and then said, "The Princess Morgana ne Dé Danann Trolkvinde Arian yn Gadael ou Elgeron-Smith sends thee her affection."

I can tell you this without fear of seeming ridiculous, I think: I all but fainted, right there on the strand. It was as if the cold, blustery day had vanished, and the whole world was made of warm honey, new butter, and fresh bread for toasting. I sank to my knees and clasped my hands over my heart. Ribbonfish's tiny, black-eyed face was bent with concern.

"Art thou ill?"

"Merely overcome. That is very good news," said I, when I'd got my wits back. "Pray tell, is there more? Surely she said more. When may I see her?"

"Between now and never," the water sprite said. "She begs thy forgiveness, but the Princess would not risk thine life so freely there as thou wouldst do. The One-Eyed Duchess survived, and is most wroth; wouldst have your lungs for a bath sponge. And there are perils worse than she. Princess Morgana journeys through dread places in the Realm Between, seeking allies to our cause; the first is the Fortress of Teeth. Thither and there no manling may go, according to chapter nine, verse twelve of the Eldritch Law."

"May I trust you to deliver a reply?" I said.

"The Princess eagerly awaits your word, Master Kit."

"Tell Morgana no law shall keep us apart. I'll see her soon."

After all, what did the Eldritch Law mean to me?

I was a *highwayman*!

END

ACKNOWLEDGMENTS

No MATTER how solitary an author is at work, everyone he knows plays a role in shaping his stories. And not just friends and family—other authors may have the biggest influence of all. This story would not exist without J. R. R. Tolkien, Ursula K. Le Guin, C. S. Lewis, Susan Cooper, Lewis Carroll, Madeleine L'Engle, Harry Harrison, Mary Renault, Robert Louis Stevenson, Jane Austen, Henry Fielding, Charlotte Brontë, Antoine de Saint-Exupéry, Charles Dickens, and so many more. I encourage you to read them all and fill your head with worlds.

I also wish to thank Prathima Bengalooru, my London-based researcher of non-digitized archives; Roscoe the French Bulldog and Quincy Ryan for modeling; the Faerie Council of Leeds for information regarding the Book of Eldritch Law; Trinity College Library in Dublin; Netherfield Farm in West Tisbury, Massachusetts; and my lifemate, Corinne Marrinan Tripp.

The Accidental Giant

READ ON FOR A PREVIEW FROM
KIT AND MORGANA'S NEXT ADVENTURE

I T WAS a chilly morning. The grassy commons where my appointment with death would occur was a half-mile away. It seemed a thousand times that distance. As I approached the green through the pale, flabby mist, I saw my seconds and a couple of spectators had already gathered at the killing ground, despite the early hour. They had the advantage of horses, which I saw stamping and steaming beneath some trees nearby. It wouldn't do to have one struck by a stray pistol-ball. They were valuable animals.

My seconds were the local undertaker and Doctor Mend, still suffering from the drink he'd taken the night before. They beat their sides to stay warm and traded jokes about tuberculosis until they saw me coming through the gloom. Then they straightened up, and indulged in only one more laugh before cloaking themselves in solemnity. The spectators smiled nervously—what a thrill to see a man about to die! I'd seen that look on many a face before, when I went to Tyburn to be hanged.

I greeted them all in a voice pitched uncommonly high, more of a squeak; this spoiled the insouciance I was hoping to affect in saying hello to begin with. The seconds and I shook hands. Mine continued to shake afterwards. There was a space of a few minutes during which we all stood in a group, facing the same direction looking at nothing but the paling mist, and then there were foot-falls approaching, and three silhouettes came near.

There was my opponent in the middle; I recognized his shape. To either side of him were figures that seemed familiar to me. Their outlines filled in with every step. When they were twenty paces away, I knew them. It was Mr. Scratch and Mr. Bufo, King Elgeron's infernal coachmen. Scratch whipped the horses while Bufo played footman; both of them were cruel beings, and bewitched. The last time I'd met them it was nearly at the cost of my life, and as I had enabled Princess Morgana to escape their clutches, it seemed likely they would finish me perchance I survived the encounter with pistols.

"Gentlemen," said Captain Sterne. He was grinning like a skull. "A chill morning, but ere the blood has dried I think it will brighten into a fine day. Shall we to't? I've an appointment at eight o'clock."

He shook hands with my seconds, and lastly with me, and clasped my hand with great force, whether out of aggression or a desire to weaken my shooting grip, I do not know. If a man must die, I thought, better to die in the course of a brave business. I didn't much believe this, but that's what I told myself, and returned Sterne's grip with all the strength I could muster.

Now we observed the usual formalities. There is a very partic-ular set of steps to undertake in the course of a duel, whether with pistols or swords. Every boy knows them, for duels are famous occasions and it's a popular game lads play to reenact the latest fights. I'd done it myself, never dreaming I was practicing for my own demise.

"If I may intercede," Dr. Mend said, "the cause of this quarrel seems to me a small one. I witnessed the offense, and in truth can scarcely call it an offense at all. If apology can be made, and with grace accepted, all may be carried from this ground upon their own legs."

This speech was not a spontaneous outburst of concern from the doctor. It was part of the ritual, intended to establish the point of honor. Duels were supposed to settle only the most egregious insults, although in practice—especially in Ireland—they were often fought for the most trifling of reasons, or none at all. In order that the victor should escape a charge of murder, the cause of the duel must be firmly established.

"I disagree," said Captain Sterne, his eyes fixed upon me and smoldering like coals. "To the contrary, the insult was a grave one, for this road agent and blackguard tried to ruin me, and then laughed about it. All you witnessed was the laughter."

This speech, too, was obligatory. Now he had, in his reply, insulted me. He had called me names. That meant I should have to offer him a challenge, whether or not I apologized for the original offense. Now both of us had cause to strike flint.

"You will retract those words, sir," said I, and to my great surprise my voice was steady and reasonably manful. I think I had begun to grow angry at this vain, quarrelsome man.

"I will not," said the captain, and that was that.

Mr. Scratch handed the pistols to Mr. Bufo and the undertaker; each made a cursory glance at the weapon. Mr. Bufo was satisfied, having no reason to doubt its efficacy; the undertaker didn't know a pistol from a candlestick, and so was equally satisfied. The weapons were then passed to the seconds, Scratch and Dr. Mend. These men, using the furniture provided in the pistol-case, loaded their respective weapons with powder, wad, and ball. All eyes observed the process and no fault was found with the arming of the weapons. Then they were handed to Sterne and myself.

He took his almost negligently, holding it loosely in his hand as if considering the weight. For my part I wished to dismantle the pistol given me and inspect every part for tampering, then load it with fresh ball and powder—if only to delay the inevitable. But I could do nothing of the sort. Honor demanded I accept it without question. The only action I was permitted to perform upon it was to depress the trigger at the appointed time, and hope something like a pistol-shot occurred.

So burdened, Captain Sterne and I stood a few feet apart and bowed at the waist. A droplet of sweat fell from my brow and I hoped none of the others saw it. My legs felt like columns of cold air; they were so weak it's a wonder they held me up.

"Dost thou wish to measure the ground?" hissed Mr. Scratch.

"Not for myself," Sterne said.

"Nor I," I replied.

If he wasn't afraid to blaze away at close range, then neither was I. Or, to be more accurate, I was so frightened of being shot that it didn't matter to me if we stood an inch or a mile apart. Any distance was too small.

Dr. Mend completed the ritual observances. "Then you, Mr. Bristol, take your ground, and inform the Captain when you are ready to settle the matter."

"Here is as good a place as any," said I.

I know not if I spoke faintly, or if the rush of blood pulsing in my ears was so great I could not hear my own voice. Sterne's eyes were locked upon my own like cannon-bore: unfeeling, cruel, and certain. My own eyeballs felt as if they were mounted on clock springs, but I was able to master them sufficiently to maintain my stare against his.

The rules of dueling have changed over time; most people now believe the practice has always been to stand back-to-back and march some fixed number of paces apart, then turn and exchange fire at more or less the same time. It was not thus when I fought my duel.

This is how it went: now that my place was established, the seconds moved well back from the field of fire, so that none might be wounded. When they had found their ground, Sterne tore his eyes away from mine and nodded to them. Then—as if he was merely strolling a little distance to pick a flower, he walked away from me. When he stopped, he would turn and fire.

I tried my best to stand still and ready, my eyes upon Sterne's back. The pistol in my hand seemed to weigh as much as a mountain. How would I find the strength to raise it? In truth it took my entire will not to break into a run at full tilt across the field, pursued by the gibbering phantoms of unfired guns. Who would prosper because I fell to this ruthless man's bullet? What honor should I gain in death? My opponent regarded such encounters as trifles, because he so often had them; he no more expected to fall to my shot than I expected to fall from Midnight's back. Poor Midnight, thought I. He should never know what befell his best friend, and whomever became his master, he could never be the friend that I was.

Each pace Sterne took brought to me a new specter of doubt and sorrow. I would lose Morgana, as well, and fail her cause, and all the Faerie people, for an absurd human ritual of destruction. I was giving up a life that promised two worlds. But most of all, I was facing the end of love.

It's difficult to explain romantic love to a person who has not been so afflicted. Some know the love of a parent, or both parents; some love also brothers and sisters and relations. I had never enjoyed this kind of love, being an orphan. It wasn't unusual. There were many orphans, and many whose families did not love them at all, although they had them. Those were hard-hearted times, and it wasn't advisable to indulge in sentimentality. Even husbands and wives were mostly joined of necessity, having fallen in together to improve their odds of survival, rather than from some bond of selfless love.

Most times are hard, as I have learned over the years. So I expect romantic love is still scarce. If you've endured it, you can skip over this bit and get to the shooting a little farther down the page. But indulge me if you will. I speak of the species of love that causes all else to dwindle to nothing. It makes life seem trivial, and at the same time desperately important. In that moment, all my cares were but distractions compared to the consuming interest I had in

Morgana's well-being. The leaping fire in my heart drove out any chill, always spreading and never burning. The brighter it blazed, the more fuel there was.

That aspect of love is what makes it most formidable. It nourishes as it devours. The more I loved Morgana, the less of me it seemed there was; that is, the part of me that was my own had dwindled until it was but vapor, like the mist that lifted away from the grass as it ascended into the heavens (as I expected to do within a few seconds). Yet I was no less for my love. My being was fed by the love Morgana had for me, until we were mingled into one bright soul with two expressions in the world, both together something greater than the sum of two.

So Sterne's leaden ball would not merely strike me down; I cared little for myself. But it would pierce Morgana's heart as well. I was sure of it. Yet I was not. Had she not left me alone, without a note or word of farewell? Did I not feel some tremor of doubt, wondering if she might after all have forsaken me for the love of her people, a far more pressing and selfless cause? Had I any right to claim her, after all? I was a peasant, by any standards. She was a princess in two worlds.

Thus did I occupy my thoughts as Sterne paced away, torn between anguish at the loss of so great a love as ours, and the terrible question of whether that love persisted still in her bosom; I would go to my grave not knowing. This was the worst thing.

Even as I thought this, the captain ceased pacing, and the world slowed down until all around me might have been carved of marble. My fingers tightened upon the pistol-grip.

I wondered what made honor the trajectory of man. Of all the things I should never know, this was the one that taunted me the most. I had known Morgana's love once; I was certain she had truly loved me during our adventures together. To have earned such a love, even for a moment, was enough for my meager lifetime. But I would never know if she loved me still, or what became of her, or anything, because I had *honor* to satisfy. There may be some day when honor is not the central pillar of a man's existence, bearing the whole rickety edifice up; there may come a time when fortune or fame or a fine garden are the things a man will not hesitate to die for.

That is all conjecture. In my time, it is honor makes the man. So I stood there at the very end of my life, pistol at my side in a sweat-slicked hand, heart beating under my jaw. My opponent began to turn, twisting his heel in the grass as he came about, the pistol already rising in his hand. I doubted he was concerning himself with love or loss or the riddle of honor. He might be considering whether to have another breakfast kipper before resuming his day. He surely did not expect to die.

But even as I dragged my own weapon upward, I realized I had measured his courage wrong. For he had scarcely completed half his turn about before his pistol was raised, which wasn't good form. We ought to have faced each other and raised our guns eye-to-eye. He intended to shoot me like a pheasant, sweeping his barrel across me. It would make it harder for me to aim, as he would be moving when he fired. *He was also afraid.*

In that moment I understood that no man faces a duel without fear, not even a gentleman accustomed to such contests; he simply learns to master it better. When the guns came up, there was no further time for showmanship. Only marksmanship mattered then.

Even as I stiffened my arm to make it steady upon Sterne's top coat-button, exhaling the breath I'd been holding since he began to pace away, there as a flash of fire. The black eye of his pistol bloomed like a yellow rose, from bud to flower all at once, and I hadn't even time to hear the report.

He shot me dead between the eyes.

ABOUT THE AUTHOR

After attending the Rhode Island School of Design for illustration, BEN TRIPP worked as an experiential designer for over twenty years, creating theme parks, resorts, museums, and attractions worldwide. He is the author of the adult novels *Rise Again*, *Rise Again: Below Zero*, and the forthcoming *Fifth Chamber of the Heart*. *The Accidental Highwayman* is his first book for young adults.